PRAISE FOR STINA LINDENBLATT

"A feel good, sensual, intoxicating and sexy love story; if you love contemporary romance you do not want to miss *Decidedly Off Limits*." —Slick, Guilty Pleasures

"Sweet, sexy and invigorating, *Decidedly off Limits* is a friends to lovers story that is truly a breath of fresh air!"—Read & Share Book Reviews

"Oh my goodness this book was so much fun!!!"—For the Love of Books (*Decidedly With Baby*)

"There are steamy moments but you are just left with feel good melty moments more."—Books Are Love (*Decidedly With Baby*)

"Be warned dear reader, this book will have you giggling and blushing as you devour it."—The Subclub Books (*Decidedly With Love*)

"...a truly unique and utterly swoon-worthy romance." —Mary Dubé at Frolic/USA Today's HEA (*Decidedly by Chance*)

"This is a great read, fresh, funny, sweet and romantic, with amazing characters and lots of surprises." – Blog on the Run (*Decidedly by Chance*)

"Stina Lindenblatt writes an emotional, heartfelt story about single parenthood, friendship, and love. Add to that great chemistry and tons of feels and this is a great book for anyone who enjoys this trope." – Ari at Red Hatter Book Blog (*Decidedly by Chance*)

"…you'll laugh, you'll cry, you'll swoon and you'll fall in love"—Book Addict Reviews (*Decidedly with Luck*)

"This book needs more than 5 stars, heck, it needs all the stars." —Happy Ending Always (*Decidedly with Luck*)

"I can't wait for more Daniels brothers."—Mary at USA Today HEA (*Cowboy Most Wanted*)

"Are you in the mood for a fun, hot, sweet, romantic read that will have you blushing, laughing and glued to the pages then look no further than *Cowboy Most Wanted*."—The Subclub Books

"HOLY HOTNESS!! Not only this book was a fun read, but it was so sexy as well!"—Blog on the Run (*Cowboy Most Wanted*)

"I'm loving this series!"—Red Hot Blue Reads (*Once Upon a Cowboy*)

"Filled with emotion, intensity, a lot of sexual tension and the perfect amount of heat."—*About That Story* (*This One Moment*)

"Romantic angst powers this fast-paced novel, and readers will return to the series to learn more about the enigmatic side characters whose own stories are waiting to be told." —Publishers Weekly (*My Song for You*)

"A just-right balance of comedy, tragedy, heat, and ice."— Publishers Weekly (*Heat It Up*)

ALSO BY STINA LINDENBLATT

Contemporary Romances

Carson Brothers Series

One More Chance

One More Secret

One More Betrayal

One More Truth

Spicy Romantic Comedy Novels

By The Bay Series

Decidedly Off Limits

Decidedly with Baby

Decidedly with Love

Decidedly with Mistletoe

Decidedly by Chance

Decidedly with Luck

Decidedly with Wishes

Copper Creek Series

Cowboy Most Wanted

Once Upon a Cowboy

Fix Me Up Cowboy

Visit stinalindenblattauthor.com for more books

ONCE UPON A COWBOY

STINA LINDENBLATT

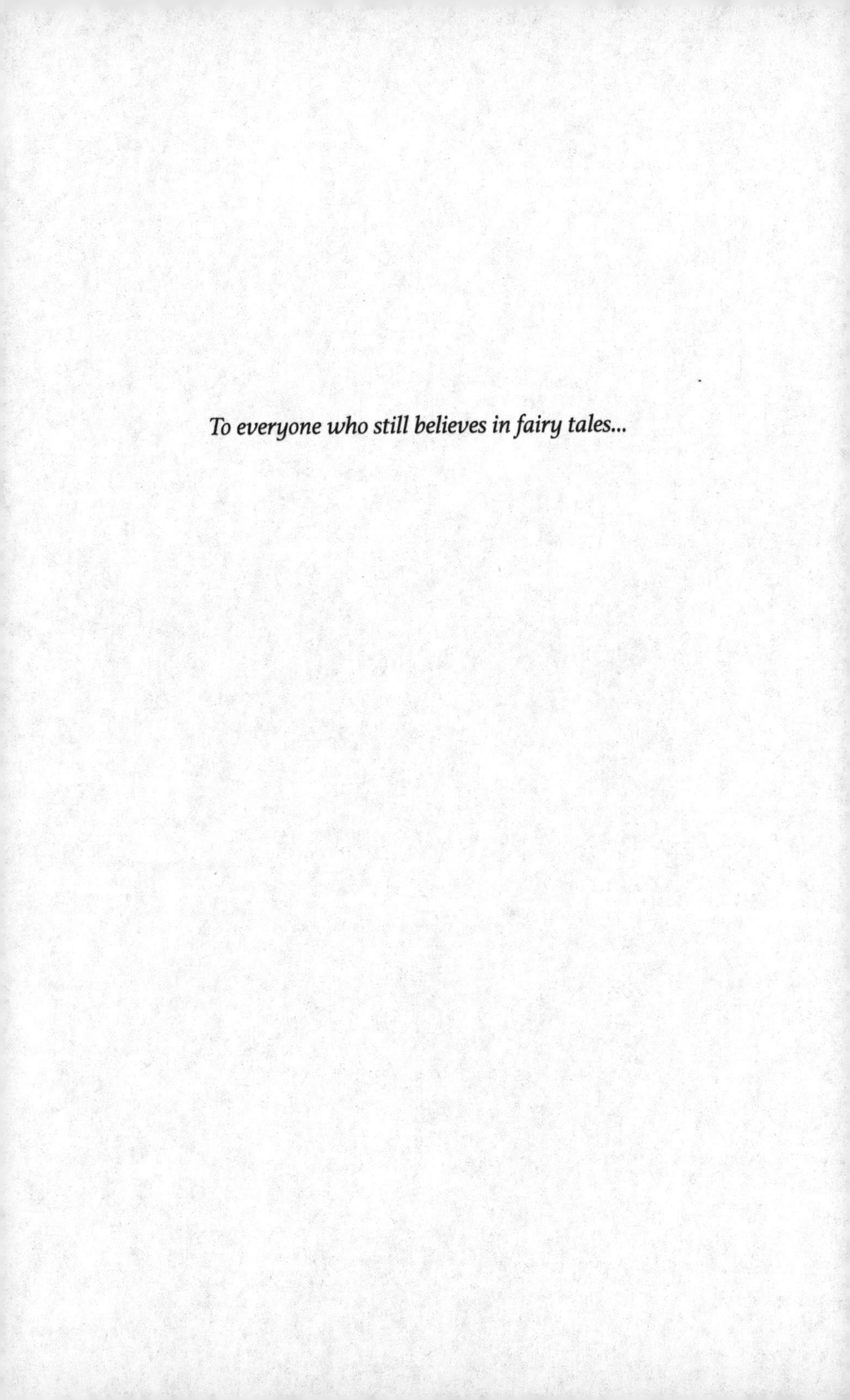

To everyone who still believes in fairy tales...

ONCE UPON A COWBOY

1

"**W**hat do you think?" Noah, my youngest brother, nods at Sophie—my best friend—and the brown mare in the outdoor training ring.

The sun is shining on her long, blonde ponytail. The Bitter-root Valley breeze, scented with the kick of manure, blows strands of loose hair about her face. Unlike my brother and me, Sophie doesn't have her cowboy hat on. Right now, it dangles in my hand.

She's holding the lunge line in her left hand, the training stick in her right, and slowly turning on the spot as the horse trots a large circle around her.

Instead of saying what I'm really thinking—how I'd like to shove her against the stable door and kiss her senseless—I simply answer with regard to the mare. "Looking good."

Noah laughs. "I was referring to the horse."

I scowl at him. "So was I."

He laughs harder. "If you say so."

I pretend not to understand what he's talking about.

Noah returns his attention to the training ring. "She definitely has a way with horses."

I

"Which is why I told you and TJ that we should hire her when you guys decided to switch from cattle to breeding hors-es," I say.

Our grandfather's life had revolved around cattle. There was a good reason for that. Cattle make money; breeding horses doesn't. But when he died and willed us the ranch, TJ and Noah itched to do something they were passionate about. And raising cattle wasn't it.

"I can't believe you weren't dating her in college," Noah says. "You should've dated Sophie instead of the thief you hooked up with."

No argument there.

This would be the same thief (aka ex-girlfriend) who was a business partner for the company I started with my roommate while we were in college. The same ex-girlfriend who did our accounting, who had all our company passwords, and who ended up stealing from us.

She was also the same ex-girlfriend who taught me that dating your co-workers is a bad idea.

Right, she wasn't the only one who taught me that. A friend of mine a year later dated one of the waitresses he worked with. It was all fun and games until he ended it. She got upset and... well, having a bull gouge your balls with his horns would've been less painful than what she put my friend through after that.

I shrug my shoulders in a *What-can-you-do?* move. "You know what they say about love being blind..."

"More like stupid."

The corner of my mouth twitches up. "That, too."

"So what's your excuse now? Why don't you just go out with her?"

Noah's idea of going out with a woman doesn't entail an actual date. It just means sex.

And until our older brother TJ fell in love with his best

friend's sister, he shared Noah's sentiment. Now he can't keep his eyes off his fiancée.

What about me? I'm no virgin when it comes to one-night stands. But my focus is more on running a business than on getting laid.

"You know why." I pretend not to be enthralled by the sight of Sophie's sexy ass in her slim-fitting jeans.

Noah snorts a laugh. "Because it's against a company policy you came up with. A policy TJ and I had no say in."

The infamous clause was written for Sophie's sake, not theirs. After I'd asked her if she was interested in working for us, she visited the ranch. And Noah had eyed her up in a way that told me exactly what he was thinking. Except Noah had no such policies when it came to women and was notorious for leaving behind trails of broken hearts.

Since I had no intention of watching him hurt Sophie, I added the "No dating and no sex with an employee" clause.

"First," I say, "Sophie and I are just friends. That's all. And even if I was interested in screwing around with her, I'd rather not risk our friendship over a short-term fling. Second, is this your way of saying you want to hook up with one of our employees? Which, when it comes down to it, is just me, TJ, and Sophie. And Violet—if you count the marketing she's doing to help the ranch's reputation after your dumbass plan with *Cowboy Most Wanted* backfired on us."

He lifts his hands, palms out. "Hey, I had no idea TJ would become the poster boy for sexy cowboys. And no, I'm not interested in hooking up with any of you."

"Smart answer, given that TJ won't take too kindly to you hitting on Violet."

Noah chuckles, the sound just short of devious. "So you don't have a problem with it if I hook up with Sophie? Or does the company policy still even exist, given that TJ ignored it with Violet?"

Maybe if I stopped eyeing Sophie's fine ass and the way she's handling the horse, I'd pay attention to the warning in my head. The warning telling me to say something...*anything*.

"That's what I thought." The low rumble of his voice gives away the barely suppressed laughter. "Don't worry. Sophie's more like a sister to me. I'm not interested in her that way."

The muted crunch of gravel approaches us from behind. "Which is a good thing," TJ says before I can turn around to see who it is.

Violet's two-year-old son is sitting on his shoulders, grinning. Deacon is wearing jeans, a cowboy shirt, and a toddler-sized black cowboy hat that matches the adult-sized one in TJ's hand. A small, floppy stuffed horse is gripped in Deacon's equally small hand and dangles in my brother's face.

TJ's Aussie shepherd, Asgard, walks alongside them.

"Hey, Deacon." I hold up my hand to fist-bump him, which he does like a pro.

"Hi, Uncle Jake." He reaches for me to help him down.

I haul him off TJ's shoulders and lower him to the dirt ground. He toddler-swaggers to the bottom wooden rung of the fence, folds his arms on it, and watches Sophie and the horse. Asgard sits next to him.

"Yes, the company policy is still in effect," I tell Noah. "TJ and Violet are exempt from the rule because they're getting married. They fall under the exception." Which I haven't added in yet, but I guess I should. "They were fooling around behind our backs before we hired her to help us."

Noah snorts another laugh.

"What's a good thing?" I ask TJ, happy to move away from discussing the company policy.

"I happen to know that Sophie's the kind of woman who's interested in having her own happily ever after."

"Happily ever after?" I sound out the words as if they're a foreign concept. "You've been watching those Disney Princess movies with Deacon and Violet again, haven't you? Has the Man Card Club demanded you surrender your membership yet?"

Noah laughs. Deacon points to the horse and says something to Asgard.

"Hey, at least I'm man enough to admit I've watched them. You both could learn a thing or two from them."

I roll my eyes. "What? How to say bibbity bobbity boo?"

"How the fu—fire truck do you even know that?" Noah asks, keeping his cussing Deacon-friendly.

"Oh, please. Who doesn't know that?"

Noah doesn't look so convinced. Guess he's forgotten how he once had a thing for Cinderella—back when we were kids and went to Disneyland one year.

Must be selective amnesia brought on by fucking too many blondes. In blue dresses.

"You two might mock me," TJ says, "but that still doesn't change anything. Sophie wants her happily ever after. Husband. Kids. White picket fence. And neither of you is the kind of man who can give her that."

He has a point there—about Noah and me.

"That's where you're wrong," I say. "She's not interested in any of those things."

"Sure, she is."

"Why? Because she's a female? Not all women are interested in settling down." Just a large percent seem to be. Or at least they seem to be around these parts.

"I overheard her talking to Violet and Aubrey. Hate to burst your delusional bubble, but that woman wants to fall in love, get married, and have kids. Lots of kids."

Oh. Shit.

"You didn't by any chance overhear when she plans to do that by?" Noah asks. "You know, some deadline due to her biological clock?"

I harrumph. "What difference does it make?"

Noah flashes me a Christ-you're-an-idiot look. "In case you haven't noticed, it's not like there's an abundance of single men in Copper Creek. And she's obviously not interested in the ones who do live in town and the surrounding area. She doesn't get tongue-tied around any of them."

Yes, as beautiful and as perfect as Sophie is, she has that one big issue when it comes to men she's interested in. That's how I know I've been friend-zoned. She's never had issues talking to me.

I mean, sure, back when we met in college, she was shy and didn't say much to me the first few times. But that all changed once she met my girlfriend.

How did Sophie and I meet? Through a mutual friend at a party. I was studying business. She was studying to be a horse trainer. Soon after, she started hanging out with my circle of friends.

She and I eventually became close—just not romantically close.

I shrug. "She's just super shy, other than when she's with friends and co-workers. So what's the problem?"

"If she doesn't fall in love with anyone around here, she might move away. Which means we would lose a great trainer."

Fuck. I didn't think of that.

I turn to TJ. "Okay, Mr. Estrogen Expert. How long do we have before we need to worry about her biological clock?"

How long do I have before I lose my best friend?

He tosses his hands up. "How the hell am I supposed to know?"

Noah and I exchange looks. "Because you're engaged," Noah says. "You're supposed to know these things."

"He's right," I point out. "Being engaged gives you an insight into the woman's psyche that single men don't have."

"How the fire truck do you figure that?"

"So what you're telling us is that you're no help?" I ask.

"Pretty much."

I glance at Sophie. She's smiling and talking to the horse, now standing next to her. The mare nods her head, fully engaged in the conversation. "She's twenty-eight now, so I reckon we have a few years before we have to worry about any ticking clocks."

"Maybe if she's *only* interested in having one kid," TJ says. "And she'll probably want to date the guy for at least a year before they get married. Then be married for a few years before getting pregnant."

"Didn't it take four years before Philip Mackenzie and his wife finally popped out their first kid?" Noah asks. He's right about that. They'd been trying for years before it eventually happened. "That doesn't give us much time. She'll probably want to fall in love sooner rather than later."

Great. "So what are you suggesting?"

"I'm not suggesting anything," TJ says. "I'm just pointing out what Sophie wants. Noah was the one pointing out the ramifications for us if she leaves Copper Creek in search of love."

"You two are overreacting. Sophie loves it here and she loves her job. She's not going to leave just because she'd like to fall in love, get married, and have a family."

"If you say so." TJ's tone is not that of a man who sounds convinced.

"And as you've pointed out, she can't talk to men she's interested in. Which means it doesn't matter if she's in Copper Creek or Missoula or Texas, the problem will be the same. So why give up a great job to move somewhere else?"

Sounds like logical reasoning to me.

Sophie walks toward the gate. Dust kicks up with each step. She opens the gate and the horse calmly follows her out of the training ring. Watching the mare now, you'd never guess she was once skittish. She's come a long way since Sophie first began working with her.

"Hey, Deacon. How's my favorite little man doing?" She leans down to give him a high five. He isn't as skilled with high fives as he is with fist bumps. His hand skims off the outside of her palm, causing him to fall forward before he catches himself.

But despite that, he beams at her. "Hi." Then waves at the horse. "Hi, horse."

The mare whinnies her reply.

Sophie's phone pings from her back pocket. She pulls it out, checks the screen, and replies to the text. "Can you give me a ride to Aubrey's clinic instead of Mike's Garage?" she asks me.

"Your car's at Aubrey's clinic? Since when does she fix cars?" I ask, unable to resist teasing her.

"I'll walk to Mike's afterward. Someone found some abandoned puppies and dropped them off at the clinic. Aubrey sent me a photo. They're just so adorable, I want to go see them first."

"I can take you to the clinic and then drive you to Mike's afterward. I'm almost done for the day."

What I haven't finished I can always bribe Noah to do.

And judging from the expression on his smug face, he knows that's exactly what I plan to do—even though the cost will be great.

2

ophie and I enter the vet clinic. Only two individuals remain in the waiting room: Old Man Jeffery and a sheep.

"*Baaa*," the animal says—as if to explain why his owner brought him to the clinic instead of waiting for Aubrey to visit the farm.

Sophie walks over to the pair, her hips swaying enticingly in a way no other woman can replicate. She takes the seat next to him. I join her, sandwiching her between Old Man Jeffery and myself.

"Hi, Mr. Jeffery. How are you doing?" She strokes the sheep's head. He bleats again.

Yes, I'm assuming it's a he. It could be a she for all I know.

Old Man Jeffery gives Sophie a toothy grin, his smile not particularly white. His crazy Einstein hair is whiter. "I'm doing well, young lady. I hear congratulations are in order." He pats her hand.

She returns his smile, but I know Sophie enough to recognize the confusion in her eyes. That, and because I also have no idea what he's talking about.

"Congratulations?" she asks, still smiling. "For what exactly?"

"Hear yeh getting married."

Welcome to Copper Creek. The home of Tilly Douglas's Facebook Page. It's supposed to report the daily goings-on around town and the county. The truth? It's mostly a gossip page.

But I can't imagine Tilly posting that Sophie is engaged without checking with her first.

Sophie cringes. Not a lot. But enough for me to notice. "Sorry to disappoint, but I'm not getting married. I don't even have a boyfriend."

He makes a strange sound—a cross between a disbelieving harrumph and a grunt. "A pretty girl like you not having a boyfriend? What's wrong with the boys in this town?" He grumbles the last part. Then he flashes her another toothy grin. "Well, if you would like a husband, I'm available."

"That's sweet of you," she says on a giggle, "but I think I'm good for now."

He pats her hand again with his gnarled fingers. "Well, if you change your mind, you know where to find me."

The sheep bleats once more.

Brianna, the vet assistant, calls out for Norman.

Yes, apparently that's the sheep's name.

"You still showing up for chess club tomorrow evening?" he asks me.

"Wouldn't miss it."

He gives me a nod and leads the animal toward the exam rooms like it's a dog—with a collar and a leash.

"Aubrey will be out in a few minutes," Brianna tells us. "Just wait until you see the puppies. They're sooo adorable." She follows Old Man Jeffery and his sheep through the doorway.

Sophie removes a magazine from the coffee table.

"This is a vet clinic," I say. "Why does Aubrey have wedding magazines?"

Yes, of all the magazines Sophie could've grabbed, she had to pick that one.

She flips it open. "People donate magazines once they've finished with them." She flashes me the front cover. "See, this one is from over a year ago."

"So why did you pick the wedding one?" I gesture to the assortment of magazines scattered on the table. The topics range from celebrity gossip to cattle breeding and everything in between.

Still studying the page, she shrugs. "It was the first one I happened to grab." She turns the page.

"Okay. I wasn't sure—especially after what Old Man Jeffery said. I thought maybe you were keeping something from both of us."

She holds up her left hand and pointedly examines it. "Nope, definitely not engaged." She goes back to flipping through the magazine.

"Do you want to be?" I'll swear to my dying day—I have no idea where that question came from. It just shouldered its way out of my mouth.

She glances up from her magazine, mouth tilted to one side. "Are you asking me to marry you?"

Good thing I wasn't drinking. I would've spewed the liquid all over the magazine. "God, could you see me getting married?"

"Good point." She places the magazine on the table, opened to the page she was reading, and starts typing on her phone. She looks back at the page and types some more.

"What are you doing?" I ask. The page doesn't have tips on being a bridesmaid. The article is about wedding nightmares and how to avoid them.

"I just got a possible idea for a book, and I'm writing it down before I forget it."

"You got an idea just from reading an article?"

Sophie's a romance author. Have I read any of her books? No. First, I'm a guy. Guys don't read romances. Second, she won't tell me her pen name. I've already searched for the ones I can think of, but nothing shows up.

"Hey, you two," Aubrey says, still in her scrubs, preventing Sophie from answering. Her long, dark hair is pulled back in a loose braid, and a black Labrador puppy sits cradled in her arms. A brilliant vet, Aubrey's a good friend of ours and I've pretty much known her forever. We were in the same classes for most of our childhood. "I wasn't expecting you, Jake."

I don't have a chance to respond. Sophie jumps up from her chair as if it's on fire. "Ohmigod! Is that one of the puppies?" She strides over to Aubrey and starts cooing at it like it's a baby.

"Yes. Do you want to see the rest of them?"

"Yes, please!"

The two women turn to leave.

"Do I get to see them too?" I ask.

Aubrey looks over her shoulder as if surprised I'm still standing here. I have no idea what to make of it.

"Of course you do." Sophie's face glows with excitement. She can barely stand still.

Aubrey directs us to an exam room and slowly opens the door. Her foot blocks the way for any puppies considering a jailbreak.

Excited yaps greet us. She nudges her way into the room, keeping the gap we're supposed to wiggle through from getting too wide.

We're barely inside when four energetic puppies tumble over each other to get to us. If you could attach a fan to their tails, you'd harness enough wind-generated energy to power Copper Creek for a week.

Sophie crouches and fusses over them. "Oh, you guys are sooo adorable. I could kiss you to pieces."

"Too bad their owner didn't feel the same way," Aubrey says. "They were found in the dumpster behind The Coffee Nut. Maddie discovered them when she went to throw out the trash."

Sophie gasps. "You mean someone just threw them away? Who would do something like that?"

Good question. I can't think of anyone in Copper Creek who would be capable of doing that.

Sophie sits on the floor and all four puppies attempt to clamber onto her lap. Aubrey lowers the one she's holding, and it too rushes to Sophie.

A muffled knock at the door doesn't even distract them from their goal. They yap at Sophie.

"Come in," Aubrey says.

"Is it safe?" a man's voice on the other side of the door asks.

"Absolutely. They're a little preoccupied right now."

The door slowly opens and a good-looking, dark-haired man I've never seen before, in jeans and a plain green T-shirt, steps into the room. Sophie's too busy fussing over the puppies to notice.

He closes the door and peers down at Sophie and her furry friends. "I see what you mean." His gaze slides over her—and a strange tightness grips my gut, but I have no idea what to make of it.

He crouches next to Sophie and scratches behind the puppy's ear. It's only then that she tears her attention away from them.

Her eyes widen at seeing the man next to her. Not the *Where-the-hell-did-you-come-from?* kind of widening. More like, *Shit, you're hot.*

"Sophie, Jake, this is Ryan—our new vet," Aubrey says.

Ryan holds out his hand to Sophie. "Nice to meet you, Sophie." He looks up at me. "You too, Jake."

I nod at him. "Likewise."

He returns his gaze to Sophie, who is still holding his hand.

"N...nice to me...meet you too. Have you long been in Copper Creek?" She lets out a soft yet frustrated sigh and releases his hand.

"I just moved here a few days ago," Ryan says.

"That's slave-driver Aubrey for you. Doesn't settle in give you a chance."

Ryan's gaze shifts to Aubrey as if she's Sophie's translator.

"Hey, don't blame me," Aubrey says, laughter sitting squarely in her tone. "He told me he wanted to start as soon as possible."

Sophie tries talking again. "You from where?"

Ryan doesn't need his trusty translator this time. "New York City."

Deciding to save my best friend from further misery, I jump into the conversation. "Moving from a big city to a small town is quite the change."

Especially since New York City isn't known for its sheep and cattle and horses. And I'm not referring to the horses that pull the carriages through Central Park.

One puppy gives up climbing onto Sophie's lap and sniffs Ryan's ankle instead. He scoops the dog up. The puppy, in turn, attempts to lick Ryan's face.

"It is, but it's a welcome change," he says.

"How so?"

"My sister was a huge fan of the reality show *Cowboy Most Wanted*. Have you heard of it?"

"I don't think there's a person in Copper Creek who isn't familiar with it," I say, bending down to stroke one of the puppies eager for Sophie's attention. "My brother, TJ, was one of the cowboys."

Chuckling, Ryan strokes the puppy squirming in his arm. It calms right down. "My sister was crushing on him big-time. She wasn't sure if she should be disappointed that he didn't last until the end of the season or be happy he didn't end up married to the show's star."

"She wasn't the only one. It's not often a ranch gets fan mail because women think one of the cowboys is hot."

We still get Facebook messages requesting we go back to posting shirtless photos of TJ. We ignore them.

Sophie doesn't say anything. She's studying Ryan, her head tilted to the side. She's also frowning slightly, but I can't figure out why. All I can tell is that she's confused.

How can I tell? She always gets the cutest expression whenever she's attempting to figure something out. Something within arm's reach, but too far away to get a firm grasp on.

"So you came to Copper Creek because of the TV show?" I ask.

"Bailey kept mentioning how beautiful and peaceful the place looked. I Googled the area, then contacted Aubrey."

"Which was perfect timing," she says. "Scott had been looking to sell his portion of the partnership, so he and his wife could return to the city."

"I figured it was fate." Fortunately, Ryan isn't looking at Sophie when he says it. That saves his words from being a cheesy pickup line best reserved for the bar.

Not that I've used pickup lines like that before. Cheesy isn't my style.

"You...you familiar look?" Her expression turns adorably flustered, and I fight back the urge—just barely—to kiss it off her face.

Ryan shifts on his feet, looking like he would rather be anywhere but here. Looking ready to make a break for the door.

Interesting.

Unless...unless it's interesting because he's on a wanted poster and that's where she's seen him.

All right, there are two problems with that theory. First, unless Ryan has been in hiding since moving to Copper Creek, Austin—our sheriff and a former Navy SEAL—would've already arrested him if the FBI is searching for him.

And the second problem? Since when did Sophie pay attention to wanted posters of dangerous felons? Crime shows—both fictional and reality-based—aren't her thing.

"I did some modeling while in vet school." Ryan shrugs in a way that hints he's embarrassed to admit it—which instantly makes him likable. He's not full of himself. "It was good money and helped with expenses."

The confused expression on Sophie's face transforms into a *Holy-shit* one. Her mouth drops open, and her gaze shoots to Aubrey. "He was a Calvin Klein underwear model. That's why he looks so familiar."

And now he's aware that she can form coherent sentences... as long as she's not talking directly to him.

Aubrey gives Ryan a once-over. "That would explain why Brianna keeps staring at you like she's seen you before." She turns back to Sophie. "He's great with the animals."

The man in question gently bounces a rubber ball against the floor, then lets it roll across the tiles. The puppies yelp and go chasing after it.

"Are you thinking of adopting a puppy?" Ryan asks Sophie.

"No house rented let me," is her very coherent reply.

The ball bounces against the wall and rolls back toward where she's sitting. The puppies bound after it.

"Aren't you guys just the cutest little bundles of energy?" Sophie says to them.

One of the puppies who was clambering to get onto her lap earlier parks his paws on her leg. It gives her a little puppy bark.

"If the owners of the house I'm renting would let me keep you. I'd definitely adopt you."

"You know, I've been thinking of getting a dog," I say, surprising myself because up till now, the thought hadn't even crossed my mind. But it's not like I don't like dogs. I do.

TJ's dog is great.

"I could adopt one of these puppies. You spend more time at the ranch than at home anyway, so me adopting him makes sense."

"Sophie works for Jake and his brothers," Audrey explains to Ryan. "She's a brilliant horse trainer."

Sophie ignores her. The level of hope in her eyes that I'm being honest with her almost brings me to my knees. "Are you sure about this?" she asks.

Am I?

There's nothing I wouldn't do for Sophie.

Even back in college, she'd always been there for me. Whenever I was stressed about something, her calming presence always eased the growing storm inside me.

So I repeat. There's *nothing* I wouldn't do for her.

"But what about Asgard and Loki?" she asks, a shadow of doubt marring the hope.

"I doubt Asgard will have a problem with another dog, especially a puppy," Aubrey says. "He's always great around the other dogs that come to the clinic."

Loki, on the other hand, will be a problem. I swear he's pure evil like the Norse god he's named after. TJ's cat is a chubby gray British shorthaired cat who thinks he runs the ranch.

We're just his minions.

"I'm sure it will be fine. It's a big house. They'll probably never even cross paths." Do I believe that? Not for a second.

Aubrey strokes the closest puppy to her. "Labradors enjoy having space, and they love exercise. Lots of it. The ranch would be a perfect place for one...I don't suppose you would like to adopt two of them?"

I laugh. "No, I'm sure one will be plenty." Even though it would be entertaining watching Loki deal with two energetic puppies.

"Do you know anything about puppies?" Ryan asks me.

"What's there to know? You feed them, give them lots of exercise, and train them to heel and play dead."

All right, I'll admit it. Asgard wasn't a puppy when my brothers and I took over the ranch after our grandfather's death. Before that, we'd been living in our own places.

But if TJ survived the puppy stage, surely I can, too.

How hard can it be?

"Oh, boy," Aubrey says under her breath.

"Do you know anything about puppies?" Ryan asks Sophie.

She nods—not bothering to attempt a coherent sentence and have it go bizarrely wrong again.

Her face turns up to me. "I can go back to the ranch with you and help you set things up in case TJ isn't there."

"That sounds like a good idea," Aubrey says, "but I thought we could go to Joe's and have a beer first. Give Ryan a chance to meet more people." She gives Sophie a meaningful look that is lost on me.

"Right," Sophie says. "That sounds like a good idea. Is that okay with you, Jake? Or did you need to get back to the ranch?"

I can't tell if she wants me to join them or not. But since I'm now the new owner of a puppy and she's going to help me get him settled at the ranch, I guess she's okay with me joining them.

"No, I'm good to get a beer. So, do you have a name in mind for the little guy?" I nod at the puppy, who is giving her his best puppy-dog eyes.

"How about Maui?"

"Why Maui?"

She beams up at me, and my heart squeezes at her breath-taking smile. "Because I would love to go there one day. And it seems like a great name for a dog."

I catch Ryan studying her again. He's probably wondering why someone as gorgeous as Sophie gets tongue-tied around men she's attracted to.

Not that he knows she's attracted to him. He might believe she's normally this way around strangers.

But it does bring up a good point. Why does her ability to speak English take a hike whenever she talks to a guy she's interested in?

Until now, it wasn't a question I'd thought to ask. As long as she had no problems talking to me, what did I care?

But now inquiring minds want to know. *I* want to know.

3

———

Forty minutes later, Sophie and I enter Joe's Bar after retrieving her vehicle from the mechanic. Her car is back at her house; Maui is still at the clinic. We'll collect him and his stuff when we head back to the ranch.

"What's with your inability to speak English whenever you see a good-looking guy?" I ask her as we walk to the table, where everyone is waiting for us on the other side of the dimly lit bar.

And when I say everyone, I mean Aubrey, Ryan, TJ, and Violet.

Discarded peanut shells crunch underfoot. You can't hear the sound over the country music playing in the background, but you can definitely feel them meet their fate when you step on them.

The smell of beer, burgers, and fries from the dinner crowd wafts through the air. All right, not so much a crowd. More like Joe's Monday night regulars.

"That's not true." She says it at the same time as the men playing pool at a nearby table groan out loud.

I stop walking and gently grab her arm. She turns to me.

20

"What do you mean, that's not true?" I ask. "In case you didn't notice back at the clinic, your use of the English language bordered on nonexistent."

"*You're* good-looking and I don't have problems talking to you." She starts walking again.

I stop her once more. "News flash, sweetheart. I'm the only good-looking guy you *don't* have issues talking to."

"TJ and Noah are good-looking, and I don't have problems talking to them either." She smiles sweetly, as if she has just scored a point.

"Okay, you don't have issues talking to certain good-looking guys. But what about guys you're interested in? What about Ryan back at the clinic?"

"It's no big deal." She says it a little too brightly. "For some reason, I tend to be interested in men who aren't interested in me. Maybe that causes my brain to short-circuit."

"Oh, hi Jake." The velvety voice purrs close to my ear, preventing me from continuing my conversation with Sophie. Kennedy runs her hand down my arm.

Sophie rolls her eyes and keeps walking.

I'm unable to do the same.

Kennedy steps in front of me. Her long auburn waves hang loose about her shoulders, and her dark-green dress clings to her lean dancer's body.

Yes, I've had sex with her.

It was a one-time thing.

"Hey, Kennedy."

"I've missed you."

Make that two times.

"How's New York City?"

"Loud and crazy and fun." She drags her fingers across my chest, reminding me of a farmer plowing a field. Probably not the image she was going for. "How long has it been?"

I know exactly what she's thinking. I sidestep it. "At least a year." A few months after Sophie started working at the ranch. "So, Broadway didn't pan out?"

A seductive grin slides onto her face. It's her standard-issue smile—the smile she uses on everyone. It's the Kennedy version of puppy-dog eyes. "I wouldn't say that. I'm just taking a short break before rehearsals begin for the new musical I'm in. I came to visit Granny in the meantime. I missed her and her stories and her trying-to-relive-her-twenties-again craziness."

The same craziness that describes Gertrude's close friends, too.

"She did mention something about you doing well in New York City." The last I heard, the eighty-year-old is hoping her granddaughter will one day get a signed shirtless photo for her from Ryan Reynolds.

"And Granny mentioned you're still single," Kennedy says.

"Like the day I was born." I glance at the table where everyone is sitting. Ryan says something to the group and they all laugh.

"Look, it was great catching up with you, Kennedy. But I'm meeting up with some friends. I'll see you around." I say the last part half-heartedly and walk away.

I claim the empty chair next to Sophie.

She smiles at me. "I ordered you a beer."

"Thanks."

"What's this about you getting a puppy?" TJ asks, laughter taking up residence in his tone.

"What can I say? I was jealous of you, bro. Man and his beast and all that crap."

You know that expression people get when they don't believe you but they're humoring you? That's the one on his face. "If you say so."

"What's he like?" Violet asks Sophie.

Sophie taps on her phone and shows Violet the screen.

"Oh, he's adorable."

"Do you have any pets?" Violet asks Ryan.

"Not yet. I love big dogs, but small New York City apartments and large dogs aren't a good mix."

"Well, you know where to go if you want a Labrador," Aubrey says. "The little golden girl seems to have fallen for you." Smiling, she flashes Sophie a quick glance.

"Ryan Kessler? Is that really you?" Kennedy says from behind me.

At his name, he looks over my head to the woman who clearly recognizes him. Maybe it's my imagination, but I swear he flinches.

Kennedy parks herself between my chair and Sophie's, her body blocking my view of Sophie. "You're the last person I expected to find in Copper Creek," she says to him.

"I take it you know each other?" I also take it Ryan wishes they didn't. Or at the very least, he wishes he didn't know her at this particular moment.

Kennedy rests her hand on my shoulder and strokes her thumb against the fabric of my T-shirt. Turning to her, I subtly shift away from her hand and it falls to her side.

"Ryan's fiancée, well, more like ex-fiancée now, starred in the last Broadway production I was in. I was shocked when I found out she'd been screwing around with our director. You're so much better off without her." The last part is said directly to him, sympathy in her tone.

What do you know? Ryan and I have something in common.

Minus the engaged part.

"How long are you here for?" Kennedy asks.

Sophie fidgets with her beer, picking away at the corner of the label. Everyone else stares at Kennedy, wondering what other dark secrets of Ryan's she's about to spill.

Or maybe that's just me.

Hey, as long as she's not talking about the two times we fucked, all is good.

"I didn't know you live here," Ryan says, avoiding Kennedy's question like it's a pothole you'll never climb out of once you fall in.

"I don't. I'm just visiting my grandmother for a few days before it's back to work." She grins her peacock-proud smile. "I'm in a new production. You'll have to see it once it's live. And don't worry, Shakira isn't in it."

"Shakira?" Violet says, her eyes wide. "As in Shakira Johnson?"

"You know who she is?" TJ asks, mirroring my own thoughts.

"You don't know who Shakira Johnson is?" Violet is even more shocked about that than she was about Ryan possibly being engaged to the woman at one time.

TJ shakes his head. "Should I?"

Violet smiles adoringly at him. "Sometimes I forget how oblivious you are when it comes to the entertainment business. She used to be a model and then moved on to making movies. Mostly romantic comedies. She recently starred on Broadway, where she became a bigger name than she was onscreen."

"Was she a client with the company you worked for?" TJ asks her. Violet used to work for a marketing and publicity firm in LA that specialized in the entertainment industry.

She nods. "But that's all I can say."

"It's all set then," Kennedy says to Ryan. "Once I get back to town, I'll send you a ticket to the show."

"That will be a little tough—given I no longer live in the state of New York."

Now it's her turn to look surprised. "You don't? Where do you live?"

"The same town you once referred to as 'God's forsaken hellhole,' I believe." I feel the wicked grin stretch on my face, and I spread my arms wide, gesturing to the town outside of Joe's four walls.

"You live in Copper Creek now?" Kennedy's eyes might not be wide with disbelief, but the emotion is definitely there in her tone. "You gave up all those great parties and the excitement the city brings and came *here*?" Her normally smooth and smoky voice screeches slightly at the last part.

Yep, she still believes Copper Creek is a hellhole.

The most boring place on the planet. Population: 3017.

"Looks like it." The corners of Ryan's mouth twitch up.

"But why?"

He shrugs. "Why not? The mountain range and the valley are gorgeous. The town is small and friendly. And just this morning, I saw a fox enter the woods near my home." His smile widens. "By home, I'm not referring to a small apartment. I mean a house with a yard that's perfect for kids to play in."

Aubrey perks up at the last part. "So you're hoping to have kids one day?"

"It wasn't something I considered back when I was engaged. Shakira felt her lifestyle wasn't ideal for having kids. She opted not to have any, and I was fine with that. But sure, why not? I like kids. I could see myself being a father one day."

Aubrey flashes Sophie another meaningful glance.

A group of people at the table next to us gets up and walk away. For a second, I figure Kennedy's going to grab an empty chair and join us. Instead, she gives an excuse as to why she has to go and leaves.

Ryan takes a long gulp of beer before she's more than two strides from us. Yep, I'd say he got off easy. The Kennedy I grew up with didn't handle boredom well, or even the idea of being bored. Just ask Miss M, our fifth-grade teacher.

Kennedy was always getting into mischief. Let's just say that when she was around, leaving your purse unattended was like dunking a finger with a paper cut into shark-infested waters.

No, she didn't steal from Miss M that one day. But the toad Kennedy put in Miss M's purse was the last thing our teacher had expected to find when she reached inside.

And that's only a small taste of the trouble the girl got into growing up.

Like I said, boredom doesn't suit Kennedy well—which is why it's a good thing she lives in a place like New York City.

"Hey, Jake," TJ says. "The dart board's free. You wanna play one round?"

"Sure. Do you play?" I ask Ryan.

He shakes his head. TJ and I wander to the back room alone. There's another pool table here, which some guy and his girlfriend are currently using. By using, I mean they're busy making out.

I remove the darts from the board.

"So, what's really the deal with the puppy?" my brother asks without missing a beat.

"He and his siblings were found in a dumpster, and I figured I'd give one of them a home. I didn't think Asgard would have a problem sharing the ranch with another dog."

I walk back to the throw line.

"You've never mentioned before that you want a dog."

"I never mention I want sex, but that doesn't mean I don't want it."

TJ grunts a laugh. "Thanks for sharing that. What I meant is did you get the puppy because *you* want a dog...or because Sophie wants one?" He gives me that look—the look warning me not to waste my time bullshitting him.

"I guess a little of both." I align the dart with the target and throw it at the board. It hits just inside the triple ring. "Another dog would be helpful, especially since Asgard is your dog. And Sophie would love to have one but can't because the owners of the house she's renting won't allow pets." I throw the second dart.

TJ doesn't say anything. I line up the final dart with the bull's-eye.

"And you have no issues with Aubrey setting Sophie up with Ryan?"

He says it a millisecond before I release the dart. It assaults the wall behind the board. "Why would I? But you've got it all wrong. Aubrey isn't setting Sophie up with Ryan. He's new to town, and she figured we could all go out for a beer so he has a chance to get to know us."

I walk over and yank the darts from the wall and the board.

"It was Violet who told me about Aubrey's plan," TJ says.

"That might be what Aubrey's *hoping* to do, but it'll never work."

"Why not?"

I hand him the darts. "How many coherent sentences have you heard Sophie say to him since we arrived?"

He considers it for a second. "I haven't actually heard her say anything to him."

"Exactly. That's because she can't. It's like with those other guys she's been attracted to in the past."

He aims the dart at the board and throws it. "And that's why you think Aubrey's plan will never work?"

"Yup."

"That's too bad. It might've been the solution we're looking for." He throws his second dart.

"Solution? To what problem?"

"Sophie's ticking biological clock. Just think, if she and Ryan end up together, it would solve our potential problem of her one day moving away to find love."

"True. But that's assuming he's good enough for her." The last thing I want is for my best friend to end up with some asshole.

"I guess we'll never know, given she can't talk to him."

Also true.

TJ tosses the final dart and lands a bull's-eye.

We rejoin everyone at the table. It takes only a few seconds before Violet is on his lap, and they're caught up in one of their no-one-else-exists moments. A moment that now feels like an unexpected punch to the gut. Unexpected because this is the first time it's happened when they've shared that look—and I have no idea why.

The rest of us finish our drinks and leave the bar. TJ and Violet end their moment long enough to walk out of Joe's with us. They head back to pick Deacon up from Grandma Meg's house.

Aubrey's car is parked next to my truck. "It was nice meeting you guys," Ryan says to Sophie and me.

"Nice meeting you," she replies, which is probably the most coherent thing she has said to him during the past two hours.

Aubrey shakes her head, the movement barely perceptible and unnoticed by Ryan. "I'll meet you two at the clinic."

Sophie is silent as we drive down Main Street with the rush hour traffic. By rush hour, I mean only a dozen or so vehicles are currently on the road. Another dozen or so pedestrians stroll along the sidewalk, enjoying the early evening sunshine.

"Are you okay?" I ask her.

"I'm fine."

Right. The one thing I've learned in my past twenty-eight years on this planet is that when a woman says she's fine, it usually means she isn't.

I've also learned that unless you're a fool, you never call her on it.

A few minutes later, I park the truck in front of the clinic. We then join Aubrey inside. I load the puppy supplies into the back of my vehicle while she and Sophie talk.

Aubrey explains how to gently introduce Maui to Asgard and Loki, and gives me pointers on puppy care. "Call me if you have any questions." She hands Sophie a book on raising a puppy. "Consider this your puppy-warming gift."

She escorts us to the truck. Sophie carries Maui. Around his neck is a blue collar with a little bone-shaped tag. He sits calmly in her arms, watching the world.

"Good luck," Aubrey says to us. She turns toward her car, but not fast enough to keep me from catching the smirk on her face.

Somehow, that's hardly reassuring.

Sophie peers up at the sky. "It's going to be a cloudless night. Perfect for stargazing."

"It is. You wanna go out once it's dark and check out my telescope?"

No, that isn't a euphemism.

I really do mean my telescope.

"You've got yourself a deal."

As we drive back to the ranch, Sophie holds Maui up so he can see out the window. "Don't worry. Once you're a bit older, you'll be able to see where you're going."

He squirms in her arms and licks her face.

She giggles the sweetest sound. "Is it sad that this is the most action I've seen in a while?"

"Action? As in dogs kissing you?"

"I was thinking more like men. I don't remember the last time a man kissed me."

"Sweetheart, if you think a kiss involves a man licking your face like a dog, you've obviously been with the wrong men."

"You might be right about that."

I strain to remember the last time Sophie dated anyone. I draw a blank. But just because we're close friends, it doesn't mean she tells me everything.

"When was the last time a man kissed you?"

She doesn't answer right away. I glance at her. She's looking at the ceiling as if the answer is written there. In hieroglyphics.

"That long, huh?" I might be dealing with a dry spell, but even mine hasn't been that long.

Maybe a couple of months.

Or five.

"I can't even remember the last guy. It's been that long."

"He couldn't have been a very good kisser if you can't even remember him." Because I can guarantee if I kissed her, she wouldn't forget it anytime soon.

My body chimes in...agreeing with the idea of me showing her how a real man kisses.

I ignore it. It has nothing to do with Sophie. It has to do with me going monk for the past few months.

Maui gives a small bark.

"See, even he agrees with me."

"It's easy for you to judge," Sophie says to Maui. "You're only a six-week-old puppy. What do you know? It's not as easy as you think. You have to find the right man, and he has to like you enough to want to kiss you."

"Trust me, most men aren't that fussy when it comes to kissing." Or fucking.

"Says you. You go into a bar and women throw themselves at you."

I chuckle. "That's definitely an exaggeration."

"What about Kennedy? She was trying to hook up with you again, right?"

"Kennedy's an exception."

"But she wouldn't be if you lived in a larger town. I'm not saying all women are ready to throw themselves at you, Jake. But I do know a good number who are interested in you."

"Even though I'm not looking to have a girlfriend?"

"Yes, I'll admit that does cut down the numbers. But there are a few who have said they, and I quote, 'Would be happy to bang him from sunup to sundown and beyond.'"

Most normal single guys would be ready to yell "Sign me

up" at an offer like that. Me? Right now I'm wondering what it would be like to be inside Sophie...from sunup to sundown and beyond.

To feel her legs wrapped around my hips.

To bury myself as deep as I can go.

To experience her heat clench down on me as she comes.

Which is exactly what I shouldn't be thinking about.

Pay attention to the road, dumbass.

4

When TJ was a kid, he wanted to grow up to be a superhero or a Norse god...or any combination of the two.

What did I want to be? I was *that* kid who spent his days dreaming of one day traveling through space. Only my bedroom walls weren't covered in posters about the solar system. They were covered with those glow-in-the-dark stars you stick on the ceiling. But I didn't randomly place them. I had my father arrange them to replicate the real constellations.

They say Rome wasn't built in a day. It also didn't take only a day to put up the thousands of stars needed to complete the project. That was how I knew my father loved me.

Yes, I'm an astronomy geek—and proud of it.

"I would love to check out your telescope," Sophie says as I steer my truck onto the long, curved driveway leading to the ranch.

Good—because while she's doing that, my mission will be to find out what prevents her from being herself around men like Ryan.

I park in the three-vehicle garage at the back of the house.

We step into the laundry room. Sophie carries Maui; I transport his crate, which is filled with some of his supplies.

Having heard the garage door open, Asgard plods into the hallway as we enter.

"Sorry to disappoint. It's just us." I scratch Asgard behind the ears.

He looks at me...then at Maui in Sophie's arms. He tilts his head as if to examine the eager puppy that he's not too sure what to make of yet. Maui gives him a friendly yap, not at all shy of the big dog.

That, or he's thinking Asgard's long fur will create a cozy puppy bed.

Asgard looks back to me, confusion in his eyes.

"I got you a new friend," I tell him. A new friend or someone to torment him like Loki enjoys doing.

Sophie kneels and lets the two dogs sniff each other. She then places Maui on the floor. The curious puppy tries making a break for it and scampers down the hallway.

Asgard looks back at me with what could be a good-luck-with-that smirk, and trails after Maui.

"At least that went well," I say. One down. The more problematic one still to go.

Sophie removes the blue rubber ball from the supplies in the crate and follows the duo, who are now headed for the main foyer. I set Maui's crate in the laundry room and make sure there's nothing he can get into trouble with while he's in there.

I find Sophie, Maui, and Asgard in the living room. The huge room was my grandmother's favorite due to the rustic antique furniture she had collected over the years. Sophie's ass is in the air as she searches for something under the modern, leather sectional couch.

She reaches under it as I mentally list the constellations to keep from focusing on her backside.

"Got it." She sits back up on her heels. Maui barks and parks his paws on her lap. She rolls the ball along the hardwood floor. "Okay, Maui, go get it."

He tumbles after the ball.

"Hey, what's going on here?" Noah asks.

I peer over my shoulder. "What does it look like?"

"It looks like Sophie's playing ball with some overly eager little critter. But the question really should be, 'Why is there a puppy in the house, and who does he belong to?' "

"That's two questions."

Ignoring my smartass comment, he walks to Maui and crouches. "Hey, little guy." He lets the puppy sniff his hand and scruffs him behind the ear.

He looks up at me and his mouth tugs to one side. "Mommy, can we keep him?"

I roll my eyes. "Yes, I adopted a dog."

"He and his siblings were found in the dumpster behind The Coffee Nut," Sophie tells him.

Noah frowns. "Who the fuck would do that?"

I fold my arms across my chest. "Your guess is as good as mine. As for why I adopted him, I just figured it wouldn't hurt to have another dog around the ranch."

Sophie picks Maui up and holds his face against her cheek. "And how could he turn down this adorable face?" She kisses him on his head, then places him back on the floor. "If my landlords allowed dogs, I would have gotten him."

Noah's smirk widens. "I'll let you two get back to your dog." Chuckling, he turns to leave.

"Maui's siblings are available," I say. "In case you're looking for a dog."

The plus side? Sophie will be so busy taking care of the puppies, she won't have time to worry about boyfriends—or the lack thereof.

Maui yaps. Enough talking, according to him. It's playtime.

Sophie and I eventually wear him out and get him settled in his crate. I grab my telescope from my room, and she and I go outside.

Sophie's quiet. It's not that she's usually super chatty. We can easily hang out together without needing to fill in the silence. But this time is different. This time there's a new kind of energy buzzing around her.

We walk along the gravel path leading to the pasture. The chirping of crickets escorts us through the darkness. But even though it's dark, I'm as familiar with the route now as I am in the daylight. I recognize each shadowy figure, recognize where each sound comes from. I've walked this path so many times since I was a kid.

Eventually, we approach my favorite spot for studying the stars. I climb the wooden fence, drop to the ground on the other side, and help Sophie over.

"If I ask you something, you promise you won't laugh?" she asks once she's joined me on the grass.

"I can promise I'll *try* not to laugh. How about that?"

"It will have to do." She turns her face to the stars. Because my brothers and I live far enough away from major light pollution, you can clearly see the stars and the Milky Way. "I need your help with something."

"Sure. What do you need help with?"

She doesn't answer. The distant howl of a coyote does instead.

"You know you can ask me whatever you want," I say. "I'm your friend. You know I'll do anything for you." As Maui proves.

"You're gonna think it's ridiculous."

"Trust me, nothing is more ridiculous than Noah signing TJ up to be a contestant in *Cowboy Most Wanted* because he thought it would be great publicity for the ranch."

"This might even top that."

"Now you have me even more curious."

"I'll never grow tired of seeing all of this." She points to the sky. "It's one of my favorite parts about living in Copper Creek."

"Not quite the bright lights of Broadway Ryan's used to." I couldn't imagine giving this up to live in New York City.

"That's right. This is a million times better."

All right, enough of the change in topic. Time to pick up the train and put it back on the track. "So what's the ridiculous favor you want to ask me?" When she doesn't answer, I go with, "You know I won't drop it until you tell me. Or should I guess?"

I pretend to be deep in thought, tapping my index finger against my lips. "Hmm. You're thinking of having a baby and you need me to donate my sperm?"

Never mind that it would violate a million parts of the company policy on dating employees.

She laughs softly. "I do want kids. One day. Maybe one day soon. But I'm not at the part where I'm desperate enough to visit a sperm bank. At least not yet."

And now she's pacing.

"I mean, unless I can't get past this stupid problem of being unable to talk to guys I'm interested in. You saw how I was back at the clinic. I couldn't even talk to Ryan. I can talk to you—no problem. But the guy who I might have a chance with? Nothing. And if I can't get past that, how will I ever fall in love and get married and have kids?" A runaway train racing down a steep mountain couldn't keep up with the words from her mouth.

What's the first step when recovering from a drug addiction?

Admitting you have a problem.

At least now we're finally getting somewhere. She's no longer in denial.

I rest my elbows on the top beam of the fence behind us and watch her. There's enough light from the moon to distinguish her features. "Okay, so we've established you aren't hoping for any of my super sperm. Then what is it you do need from me?"

"I need you to help me sound like less of an idiot when I'm talking to men I'm interested in." She lets out a hard breath. "I'm twenty-eight years old, Jake, and I've never been in love. Hell, I'm pretty much still a virgin. I'm tired of being single. I want to fall in love with a nice man, get married, and have a family. And not just kids. If I'm dreaming big, I would like the husband, the kids, a dog, a cat, and horses."

While her words continue barreling down the mountain, my brain is stuck on one major part like it's whipped cream on a sundae...complete with the cherry.

"Pretty much?" I repeat. "How are you still '*pretty much*' a virgin? Either you are or you aren't one."

She doesn't answer right away. Even though it's dark out, I can tell she's blushing. "Well, technically I'm not a virgin. I've had sex. It was a one-time thing back in college."

From the way she says it, I get the impression it wasn't a memorable occasion.

"You've seriously only had sex once, and you're still alive to talk about it?"

She snickers and leans back against the beam where my elbows are resting. All I have to do is shift my hand slightly, and I can stroke the soft skin on the back of her exposed neck.

"Pretty amazing, huh? What can I say? I'm not comfortable with the whole one-night-stand thing...which is pretty much what my first time was, ironically enough. Fortunately, I'm the queen of self-service—because like every twenty-eight-year-old woman, I have needs."

Now that's an image I don't need.

Not because it's TMI.

But because it will now be playing in my head the next time I take a shower.

When my hand is fisted around my cock.

While I'm thinking about her as I make myself come.

Yes, while it's against company policy to date her or fuck her, nowhere does it state I can't imagine how amazing it would feel to be inside her.

And yep, my cock is now hard.

Thank God for the darkness.

"So will you do it?" she asks.

I'm about to say "Hell, yes." Of course I'd be more than happy to give her all the orgasms she can handle...and then some. But a voice in my head points out that I'm a dumbass. That's not what she's talking about.

"Will you be like my fairy godmother? You know, the one who turns Cinderella's rags into a ball gown and a pumpkin into a sparkly coach?"

Here's the thing about men. Half the time we have no idea what women are talking about. What might seem highly logical to the woman is miles from there for the man.

This is one of those times.

"I have no idea what you're talking about, Soph. For one, I'm a man. Two—while I might not know anything about the movie, I'm pretty sure the fairy godmother performs some sort of magical spell. Unfortunately, my business degree didn't include any courses along those lines."

Chuckling, she pats my arm. "That doesn't matter. It's like the Cinderella trope in romances. A friend—sometimes a female and sometimes a gay guy—turns the dull, kind of ugly heroine into a beautiful swan. Then the prince—or whoever the guy might be—falls in love with her."

"One—you're already beautiful. You don't need help with

that. And two—are you telling me you think I'm gay?" I slap my hand against my chest, the move as genuine as veneer is to wood.

She laughs. "I'm aware that you're one hundred percent heterosexual man, which is why I need your help. Who better to teach me to be more comfortable around guys I'm interested in than you?"

Even though the words are coated with syrup to sweeten the blow, they're a sucker punch to the gut.

One.

Two.

Three...you're out.

I must have misheard her. That has to be it. There's no way she just asked me to help her land a boyfriend.

"Please, Jake. You're my only hope." The pleading in her voice is like going for another round with a heavyweight champ. You're already weakened from the first blow and now more likely to go down for the final count.

"Except I have no idea how to teach you something like that. It's not a skill I've ever had to think about."

She reaches up and kisses my cheek. "I'm sure you'll figure something out."

An electrical hum vibrates from the spot where her lips touched me, and I resist the urge to cover it with my fingers.

Remember how I said I would do anything for her?

Now I'm wishing that wasn't true.

But Ryan is a nice guy. Is he damaged after finding out his fiancée cheated on him? Possibly.

Sophie deserves to be with someone who makes her happy. She deserves for all her dreams to come true.

Ryan could be that guy...if he gives her a chance.

You really are *an idiot*, my heart says.

I ignore it.

"All right," I say. "I'll help you. I don't know how I'm going to do it, because I'm guessing this isn't something I can Google to find the answer. But somehow I'll help you win your man."

The bright side?

Once she and Ryan are headed toward their own happily ever after, I can finally move on.

I can finally stop lusting after my best friend.

She flings her arms around my shoulders. Her sweet scent of strawberries and cream teases me. *Not helping me, Soph.* "Thank you so much, Jake. I owe you big-time."

My arms automatically go around her and I hold her close. Closer than I should, given we're just friends and I promised to help her with her love life.

Even with our jackets on, I can feel her heat sinking into my body. It fuels my heart rate, causing it to kick up a notch.

This isn't the first time I've hugged her.

But it is the first time it's felt this way. This amazing.

Shit.

5

"You made it," Andrew says as I pull the chair away from the round table in the senior center rec room. The eighty-five-year-old doesn't sound too surprised. In front of him is the chess board, which he has set up already.

I grin. "As if I'd miss the chance to beat your cranky old ass."

He chortles. Cranky isn't a word you'd use to describe the man who's been like a grandfather to me. He was the one who introduced me to chess when I was a teen.

"You're just lucky the girls aren't around to hear you use that language."

I scan the other tables in the bright, cheerful room, knowing exactly whom he's referring to. "Where are Grandma Meg, Tilly, and Gertrude?"

"Knitting club."

"That should keep them out of trouble for a bit," I mutter under my breath.

Andrew barks a laugh, surprising me. Didn't think he could hear that well.

41

He moves his white pawn forward two squares. "You must admit, this town would be dull as volcano rock if it weren't for those three."

"You might have a point there."

"If you want, after I've beaten your cocky ass, we can join them and see if they need our help."

"You're kidding, right?"

He raises a white eyebrow. "Have an issue with knitting, do you, boy?"

"I was referring to the part about you beating me." I jump my knight over my pawn. "But can't say knitting's my scene either."

He studies the board for a minute, then moves his rook. "So what *is* your scene? TJ makes wooden rocking horses, and Noah's working on that old car he's restoring. What's your superpower?"

"I whip your cranky ass at chess and I love astronomy. What more do I need?" I grin at him.

"Well, as much as I love beating *you* at chess, Jake, and as fine as the stars are to watch at night...how come you've never picked up any hobbies that require the use of your hands?"

"That's right—because I've been using telekinesis to move the pieces around the board." I slide one of my pawns forward a square.

"Now that's a superpower I'd love to have. But that's not what I'm talking about"—he points a weathered finger at me—"and you know it."

"It's because I've never had time to learn a skill that involves my hands. I went to college to study business. TJ was the one who stuck around and ended up learning woodwork from Fred Jenkins." Well, mostly stuck around. Until TJ injured his knee three years ago, he was active on the rodeo circuit. "And Noah decided he wasn't interested in spending his life as a ranch hand and left to find himself. He got lucky and found a job working for a man who restored old cars."

"Until your grandfather died and willed the ranch to all three of you," Andrew finishes for me.

That's right, Granddad figured out a way to drag Noah back home. In order for TJ and me to gain possession of the ranch we'd practically grown up on—our future—all three of us had to run it. The will was very specific about that.

No one could ever claim Granddad wasn't a crafty old fox. Like some women I know, he enjoyed playing games to get what he wanted.

"It's never too late to start a new hobby," Andrew says, eyeing the chess board for his next move. "You're still a young whippersnapper."

I chuckle. "You do realize no one actually says that anymore, right?"

"Sure they do. And don't even think about changing the topic. We're not through with it yet. You're what? Thirty-two years old?"

"Twenty-nine."

"Even better. You need to learn a skill that will impress the young ladies. That's how you land yourself a wife."

Somehow, I hold back a smirk—but just barely. "Then I don't have to worry about it. I'm not looking to get married. I'm happy being single and pouring all my energy into the ranch. That's what Granddad would've wanted."

Andrew lets out a big guffaw and continues playing. "Is that what you're telling yourself, boy? Your granddad was happily married until your grandmother died. She was his world. And you know how he landed the catch of the century?"

"Are you now comparing my grandmother to a trout?"

He ignores my smartass comment. "He landed her because of his fine leather carving skills. She fell in love with the design on the belt he was wearing. They started talking, and that was all it took for her to fall in love with him, too. Of course back then, his skill was nothing like it was later on. He was just learning the craft when they met."

"What the heck are you talking about? My grandfather never had time for hobbies. Said so himself."

Andrew tuts. "That's what he claimed after your grandmother died. Then he threw himself into his work, so he was too busy to think about her." He moves his knight. "Word around town is you're a workaholic, Jake. The question is, what are you trying to escape from?"

I relocate a pawn to the square in front of it. "You haven't heard? I'm on the FBI's list for America's Most Boring People because I don't have a hobby. Heaven forbid they ever catch me."

Andrew rolls his eyes but there's no mistaking the amusement crinkled at the corners of them.

We play for a few minutes before I finally ask my burning question. "How come I didn't know about the leather carving?" The ranch house has all kinds of leather items with various flower, horse, or leaf designs on them, but I thought my grandmother had bought them over the years.

"My guess is because you didn't ask your grandfather the right questions. But I reckon a lot of his projects are still around the ranch house." He folds his arms on the table, leaning forward, as if he's about to share a secret. "Look, I'm not saying you need to do leather carving. But just think how great it would be to create something with your own hands. Something you're proud to display or share with other people."

I open my mouth to say I already work with my hands.

"And I'm not referring to working around the ranch," Andrew says, apparently able to read my mind. "I'm talking about fine craftsmanship. It could be anything. Knitting. Pottery. Weaving scarves. God knows the winters are cold enough around here for you to appreciate two of those skills.

But if you're interested in learning your grandfather's craft, I'd be happy to teach you."

He examines his pieces on the board and moves his queen. "Checkmate."

And I groan. "Was that discussion just a way to distract me so you could win?"

"I don't need to create a diversion to win. I'm naturally a gifted chess player." The man, who loses to me half the time, winks. "But I meant what I said about learning a new hobby. An activity to put hair on your chest and give you something else to enjoy beyond the comforts of a good woman's arms."

"I haven't exactly had time for the latter part lately either," I say.

It's Andrew who groans this time. "You really are a lost cause, boy. You need to live a little before you're too old to enjoy what God gave you."

The corners of my mouth dance with a barely suppressed laugh. "I'll be sure to keep that in mind."

6

For the next three days, Sophie and I are too busy to discuss Mission Fairy Godmother. Or rather, Mission Fairy Godfather—which sounds more kickass, if you ask me.

Between the usual craziness of running a ranch and helping Maui settle in, there hasn't been time.

And maybe there's a bit of stalling on my part.

Because what happens if I am successful in helping her?

What happens if she and Ryan fall in love?

Where will that leave me...as her best friend?

After checking on Maui, who is currently snoozing in his crate, I head for the training paddock. Sophie is finishing up with the horse she's been working with.

She leads him to the gate and smiles at me. I love that smile. It's the smile that makes you feel like you're the only person in her universe who matters.

My stomach hardens like a lump of cooled meteorite. One day soon, that smile will be redirected at Ryan. I'll no longer be the sole recipient of it.

I shove the jealousy aside. I'm being ridiculous—or at least that's what I try telling myself.

For a second I allow an image to flicker in my mind of Sophie in my arms as we watch our kids chase Maui around the backyard. But then I remind myself that I'm not cut out for marriage and fatherhood. I'm too cynical and distrustful and independent for that.

I swing the gate open for her. "I thought we could go for a ride and start your lessons."

What's the first lesson?

Fuck if I know. I'm winging things. And just so you know, winging things isn't my style. Whereas some people get hives at the thought of planning, I live for it. I have my lists, my goals, my business plans.

Which is why when Noah sprung on TJ and me last summer how he had submitted TJ's name for *Cowboy Most Wanted*—and TJ had been selected to be a contestant—I went into a tailspin. A mayday-mayday-mayday tailspin.

Why? Because it hadn't been part of my plan.

"Sounds good to me," she says. "Let me check on Maui first."

"He's snoozing in his crate." I grin like a proud father. The little dude has definitely grown on me. I'm looking forward to when he can follow me around the ranch like Asgard does with TJ.

Thirty minutes later, our horses are saddled and we're ready to go. Sophie is riding Carina—as in Carina Nebula. I'm riding my horse, Orion.

The late afternoon sun shines down on us as the horses walk along the dirt trail parallel to the River. Cottonwood trees, bushes, and the meadow—with splashes of color from the blossoming flowers—sandwich us on the other side. With the exception of the birds singing and the occasional horse's nicker, the world around us is peaceful and soothing to the soul.

Just how I like it.

I couldn't imagine living anywhere else.

Copper Creek has always been my home, with the exception of when I went away to college. And even then, there had never been any doubt that I would return after I got my business degree to help my grandfather run the ranch.

"Are you ever sorry you didn't study astrophysics like you wanted to?" Sophie asks out of the blue, as if she's just read my mind. Sometimes I think she can.

Which is freaking scary, given half the time I'm thinking about her naked. In my arms.

"Yes and no."

She laughs. "How is that an answer?"

"Being an astrophysicist wouldn't have been too helpful when it comes to running the ranch." According to my grandfather.

He had a point.

"But don't you ever dream of what it would be like if you were working for NASA?"

"Sometimes. But since it wasn't an option, I try not to dwell on it."

"It's okay to have dreams, Jake."

"Dreams or goals? Dreams are great if there's a chance they might come true, but most of the time they don't. And dreams aren't the same as goals. Besides, running the ranch is in my blood. It's what I was born to do."

She snorts. "You were born to be an astrophysicist. You just chose the more practical route and listened to your grandfather instead of your heart."

I burst out laughing even though she does have a point. "Why don't you tell me what you really think?"

"You know I'm right. I mean, look at me. My parents expected me to go to law school, become a prosecutor, and one day run for senate."

"But you didn't listen to them," I fill in because I know this is where she's headed. "Instead, you went against their wishes and pursued a degree as a horse trainer."

"That's right. I love my job. I would never have been happy stuck inside the office or in court. It would have sucked the life out of me."

I grin at her. "That sounds pretty painful. And I now have this image of a vampire sucking blood from your neck. Draining all the life out of you."

"That's pretty much what it would've been like." She makes a silly face and I laugh. Christ, she's fucking adorable. "Fortunately, my parents were okay with my decision in the end."

"Is this your way of saying I'm lifeless?" I tease. "It's not like I've completely given up astronomy. Or were you not paying attention to the stars I was showing you the other night?" We ended up spending at least an hour checking out the night sky while she asked me all kinds of astronomy-related questions. Our regular routine. A routine she never seems to grow bored of. "And if I had studied astrophysics, we would never have met. You wouldn't be here." I gestured at the land and the river. "You wouldn't be our horse trainer."

"True. And I'm really grateful for that. But that's the thing. I'm living *my* dream. Or at least part of it."

The other part being the husband and the kids and the barnload of animals. I mention that.

"Yes, but that's not all of it," she says.

"What other dreams do you have?" Beyond being able to use coherent sentences around Ryan.

"To train horses with behavioral problems. So they can go back to their owners—after I train the owners—or so the horses can be adopted out to a new home." She gives a barely there shrug.

At her words, a welcome sensation spreads through my

chest, and I sit up straighter in the saddle. "You'd be great at it. But how come this is the first I'm hearing about it?"

"Because it's a dream, and I'm not sure it's something I can do. At least not until I have my own place, with a stable and area for training the horses. I guess it's more like your dream. There...but still out of reach."

"Does Scottsdale Ranch have a similar program?" It doesn't sound familiar.

She leans forward and strokes Carina's neck. "Their trainer is talented with young horses, but he doesn't have the skill or patience to deal with problem horses."

That doesn't surprise me. There's a reason TJ, Noah, and I refer to Sophie as The Horse Whisperer.

And the reason we don't want her to move away to find her happily ever after.

"I'll have to talk to my brothers about it," I say, "but maybe we can figure out something to help your dream become a reality." It might also be the very thing the ranch needs to improve our bottom line—or at least grow our reputation in the industry.

Her head jerks in my direction, her eyes wide with shock and hope and another raw emotion. "Are you serious?"

"I'm not promising anything yet, but it's something we should definitely look into." God knows we have to do something after the disastrous run with *Cowboy Most Wanted*. "Maybe if you're not doing anything tonight, we could start working on the business model to see how feasible the idea is. I mean, unless you have a date with Ryan."

"You don't have to worry about that. I haven't seen him since Monday."

"You haven't? Wasn't he there when you went to the clinic yesterday?" I'd forgotten to ask how it went, and she hadn't volunteered any info.

Sophie's face flushes and she squirms in the saddle. "I didn't quite make it to the clinic. I chickened out."

"You chickened out? Why?"

"I was afraid I'd run into Ryan and have no idea what to say. And then I'd just say something idiotic, further confirming his belief that I've had a lobotomy and that's why I can't speak English."

My mouth twitches as I fight back the hovering smile. "He won't think that. You just need some questions you can ask him to get him talking, then you won't have to say much. Once you're more comfortable around him, it won't be a problem anymore." Perfect. We have our first lesson. "Give it a try. Ask me a question."

She glances around, possibly searching for that magical question. Growing on a tree. "What's your favorite season?"

"Spring."

She nods as if to encourage me to keep talking.

"The idea is to get him talking. So no 'yes' and 'no' questions. And no questions that can be answered in a single word."

"I was hoping you would at least *tell* me why you like spring."

"Never said I'd make it easy on you." I wink at her.

She lets out a hard breath. "All right, I'll try again. What is your favorite position?"

Screw holding back a smile. A laugh deep in my belly erupts like a once-dormant volcano. "Even though I'm one hundred percent in favor of that question—" *especially if it's directed at me* "—you might want to pick something that doesn't show how eager you are to have sex. At least wait until your second date."

Hey, look at me attempting to dissuade her from screwing Ryan's brains out on the first date.

I glance at her in time to see her roll her eyes.

"I was talking about his favorite position from when he used to play baseball in high school," she says.

"He told you that he played baseball in high school?" He didn't mention it when we were at Joe's the other night.

"Aubrey told me."

"Fair enough. But I suggest that in the future, you should be clearer with your questions. Now hit me with another one."

"Why don't you have a girlfriend?"

"Wow. Not only do you lack the ability to talk to good-looking guys you're lusting over, you can't even ask the right questions. You go right for his balls."

"The question wasn't for Ryan. It's for you, Jake. Why don't *you* have a girlfriend?"

If Sophie hadn't friend-zoned me (and forgetting company policy for the moment), the correct answer would be: There's only one girl I'm interested in who lives in Copper Creek, who has me fantasizing about her twenty-four seven. Only one woman I trust. That's you, Sophie.

"Because there's no one in Copper Creek I'm interested in."

Good answer. Maybe not very original or completely truthful, but still good.

"I'm not buying that for a second. There are a number of pretty girls who are single and have a thing for you. Why not date them and see if something develops between you and one of them?"

Orion nods his head in agreement with her and neighs.

Traitor.

"I don't have time for a girlfriend." Another good answer. Again, not original, but what the hey.

"You were busier in college, yet you had time for a girlfriend. According to your brothers and Aubrey, other than the one girlfriend after college, you've been living the bachelor's life since you moved back to Copper Creek. So what gives?"

I shrug—this time for real. "I did the girlfriend thing.

Twice. It didn't work out so well. So I haven't bothered going that route again."

"You had *two* girlfriends who it didn't work out with, but you don't throw the baby out with the bathwater just because you've finished giving it a bath. They were obviously wrong for you, so you try someone else."

"Yes, but in their cases, it was more than them being wrong for me. Lisa was stealing from me. Or more specifically, she was stealing from the company I was running with my roommate."

I turn Orion down the dirt path leading to the river. The path is too narrow for two horses to walk side by side. Sophie has to follow behind Orion, which makes it impossible for her to ask more questions.

At the water's edge, I dismount and let Orion drink from the river. Sophie does the same with Carina, releasing her hold on the reins to join me, confident her horse won't bail on her.

She places her hand on my arm. An electrical current hums throughout my body from where she touches me.

Nothing new there.

What *is* new is that the electrical charge seems stronger than before.

"What happened?" Her tone is sympathetic, not pitying. Maybe that's why I feel compelled to tell her the truth.

A truth that only my brothers know.

I nod and focus on the slow-moving water. "Connor and I set up a small business to bring in some extra cash. It started out as a class project that morphed into a real business. I began dating Lisa a few months later." She and I had already been dating for a year by the time I met Sophie. "She was also a business major. Connor never liked her. He didn't trust her. So you can imagine how he felt when I suggested that she become our business partner. She had contacts that I thought would help move our company to the next level.

"Plus we were still busy with our course work, and we

couldn't let our grades slip. We needed the extra help. Connor accused me of confusing good business with a good lay. We had a fight over that. I called him an asshole. He told me I had my head stuck too far up her cunt to see the truth."

If Sophie cringes at my crassness, I wouldn't know. I'm too busy selecting a flat stone from the ground.

"Did you love her?" Sophie's words fall from her lips like a soft breeze, warm and judgment-free.

"Yes. Or at least I thought I did. Who knows?" I straighten, the perfect skipping stone in hand. I adjust my hold on it, then fling it across the water. The stone bounces ten times before sinking.

"What happened after that?"

"Things were okay at first. They learned to get past their differences. But then Connor got suspicious, figuring something wasn't quite right with our books. Only, he couldn't put his finger on what exactly the problem was.

"He eventually discovered that Lisa had slowly been stealing from us. A small amount here. A small amount there. Before he had a chance to confront her, she went missing. She had quit the program and disappeared, along with a sizable amount of our money. She'd had me fooled the entire time. Turns out she had another boyfriend. She had been stringing me along to steal from the company."

Sophie rests her hand on my arm again. And the electric current returns for an encore. "I'm so sorry, Jake. I had no idea. But you can't condemn all women because of what she did. We're not all like her."

Why is this the first that Sophie has heard about what happened? Especially since it occurred while we were friends in college? No one from college knew. Connor and I had kept quiet about it—other than filing a complaint with the cops.

Pride can be a painful thing.

"I know," I respond, "but I swear my brothers and I are

cursed." I chuckle. "Or certain members of my family—especially me—are cursed when it comes to love and relationships. After college, I dated a woman for several months. She was looking to get married. I was still young and wasn't interested in going there yet. So she pretended I had knocked her up, knowing full well that I would do the decent thing and marry her for the baby's sake."

Sophie gapes at me like an owl who sat on a live wire. "How did you find out she was pretending?"

"A friend of mine overheard her discuss her plans to entrap me with *her* friend while they were at a bar in Golden Falls. And then there's my cousin. Bethany discovered her husband was cheating on her. With two women."

Sophie opens her mouth, possibly to argue that this still doesn't mean I should throw out the baby with the bathwater.

I don't give her a chance. "And let's not forget my uncle. He dumped my aunt because she was the wrong gender. Turns out he'd been living a different life than the one we'd known about. She got the car. He left with her grandmother's homemade antique linen."

"Like I said, cursed with a capital C." I cross my arms.

Sophie rolls her eyes. "That's not true. TJ has Violet now. That proves your family isn't cursed. And from what you've told me, your grandparents and parents all had happy marriages."

"So the curse doesn't strike everyone, but that doesn't mean it doesn't exist." All right, I don't actually believe in curses, but the argument about why I don't want to have another girlfriend still stands. I don't have time for one.

Sophie releases a *What-am-I-going-to-do-with-you?* sigh. "All this means is that you had two bad experiences and that your cousin and aunt fell for the wrong guys. The three of you had terrible luck with those people, that's all. It doesn't mean the right person isn't out there waiting for you. You just have to pick yourselves up and try again. You wouldn't give up riding just because Orion tosses you, would you?"

"That's hardly the same thing, Soph."

"Maybe not, but the idea *is* the same....Is Lisa the reason you have the company policy about employees not being allowed to date or be involved?"

I nod. "I screwed up once before, letting my heart and my dick run the business. No point taking that risk again." And no point telling her the truth about Noah's less-than-innocent thoughts when it came to her prior to her joining the ranch. The original reason for the policy.

She picks up a flat rock near her boot. "So you're never going to let a woman into your heart again because you made two mistakes and trusted the wrong women?" She flings it at the water, but her technique is all fucked up.

The rock doesn't skip across the surface.

It sinks on impact.

Which is odd, given her record is nine bounces.

"Yep, that pretty much sums it up." I select another rock. This one bounces thirteen times before sinking. "This ranch means everything to my brothers and me. We practically grew up here. It's our grandfather's legacy." If you ignore the part about how we switched from cattle to horses...which I'm sure he's rolling over in his grave at. "And one day it could be Deacon's and his siblings' legacy. I can't risk losing it because I lost focus on what's really important. The ranch."

Sophie nudges a stone with her foot. "Right. You have a good point."

She then smiles at me and rubs her hands together. "So, about you helping me land the man of my dreams. What's the next lesson?"

7

"**I** can't remember the last time I wore a suit," Noah grumbles to no one in particular as he searches through the rack in the men's clothing store. "Tell me again why we're doing this?"

It's been two days since Sophie and I went riding together. Two days since I gave her the first lesson on how to speak to guys she's crushing on. I still haven't come up with a lesson number two. So instead, I gave her a homework assignment.

What is it? Nothing too drastic. She has to ask a few random men in Copper Creek a question that can't be answered with a "yes" or a "no" or a single-word reply.

I continue leafing through the selection of suits. "Because we love Violet like a sister, and we want her to have the wedding she deserves."

"Good answer," TJ says. "Just be happy I'm not making you wear a tux."

Noah grunts, the sound half-hearted at best. "A tux, I could handle. Then I could pretend to be like 007 and pick up a hot babe at the wedding."

TJ, Austin, and I burst out laughing. Austin is one of

57

Copper Creek's finest—or more specifically, the town's sheriff. He's also Violet's brother and TJ's best man.

"Are you telling us the only way you can get laid these days is to have a fake English accent and pretend you're an international spy?" I ask Noah.

He scowls at me. "And when was the last time *you* got laid?"

"Language, guys." TJ nods at Deacon. The two-year-old isn't paying attention to us. He's busy playing on the floor with his toy cop car.

I shrug. "It's not like there are a lot of options in town."

"Ain't that the truth?" Austin says. Noah nods in agreement.

TJ's mouth quirks up on one side. "And you guys wonder why I'm settling down. While you're contemplating who your next lay will be, I'll be enjoying my wife."

"Hey, remember, I know how to dispose of a body so it's never found." Austin glares at his future brother-in-law. "I don't need to know that you and my sister are having sex."

This time it's Noah and I who are laughing.

"I take it you aren't interested in having any more nephews or nieces," I joke, "because that would involve your sister and TJ having sex." I remove a hanger with a black suit on it.

"Sure I am," Austin says. "But I'm also pretending a stork will drop them off."

Chuckling, I slap him on the back. "Good plan."

"If it makes you guys feel any better," TJ says, not sounding quite as smug as before, "Violet and I aren't allowed to have sex until after the wedding."

Noah flashes him a sympathetic look. "Shit, man. We really feel bad for you." He rolls his eyes.

"How come?" I ask TJ.

Austin groans and walks to the other side of the store.

I would apologize to him, but I really am curious about the no-sex-before-the-wedding rule.

"It was Violet's idea. Something about being a born-again virgin or some crap like that."

"And how long has this crazy policy been in effect?" I'm working at looking sympathetic but I'm sure that's an epic fail.

"Since the day I proposed to her."

So a month. And given the wedding isn't for another month...

"Hey, look on the bright side," Noah says, grinning. "At least you opted for a short engagement. Could you imagine if you had been engaged for over a year?"

"That's what I keep telling myself." TJ then smiles. It's a goofy smile—the same goofy smile he gets whenever he's thinking about his fiancée. "But if given the choice between having sex now with a woman who isn't Violet and spending the rest of my life with the woman I love, it's no contest."

Neither of us has to state the obvious. We both know which one TJ would choose.

Austin returns with a gray suit. "What about this one?"

"That could work. Let me ask Violet." TJ snaps a photo of the suit with his phone and sends it.

"Isn't it bad luck for the bride to see the suit before the wedding?" Noah asks.

"That's just the bride's dress," I tell him. But then I realize I have no idea either. I look to Austin for confirmation. He shrugs.

Well, there's one person who might have the answer.

I text Sophie.

> Me: Is it bad luck for the bride to see the groom's suit before the wedding?

She responds the same moment as TJ's phone pings.

> Sophie: No, just bad luck for the groom to see the bride's dress.

Another text comes through a few seconds later.

Sophie: Nice suit. Is that the one you're getting?

Me: Possibly. Depends on what Violet says.

Sophie: Judging from the dreamy look on her face, I'll go with that's a yes.

I laugh.

Me: How's the dress search going?

Because Copper Creek doesn't have any stores that sell wedding attire, Violet and TJ decided we would all spend the afternoon in Golden Falls. Sophie and Aubrey are supposedly searching for bridesmaid dresses while we're here.

Sophie: Good. Violet's gown is gorgeous. She looks like a princess.

Me: Did you find anything?

Sophie: Yes.

Me: Do I get to see a picture?

Preferably of her in it.

Sophie: Nope. You'll have to wait until the wedding.

Me: Why? Is it bad luck for the groomsmen to see the bridesmaids' dresses before the wedding?

Sophie: LOL Let's hope not.

Me: See you at lunch soon?

Sophie: Yes, see you soon.

TJ confirms that Violet loves the suit. We hunt for similar ones in our sizes...and then endure being measured so they can be altered. TJ even manages to find something for Deacon.

Once the salesman has finished measuring the restless toddler, Deacon reaches up to TJ with both hands. "Daddy, up!"

"Daddy?" I ask. "When did this happen?"

"Violet and I decided that since I'm legally adopting him, he might as well start calling me Daddy instead of Uncle TJ." He kisses Deacon on the cheek.

In return, Deacon parks his hands on either side of TJ's face and squishes them together, giving TJ a fish face.

And damned if something doesn't stir deep in my gut at seeing them this way.

For a second, Deacon's dark hair—the same color as TJ's and Violet's—changes into Sophie's and my golden hue.

I shake the thought from my head. Sophie dreams of getting married and having kids. I want to focus on the ranch and make it the success it once was when Granddad was alive.

Which won't be possible if Sophie moves away.

"Sophie and I were talking the other day about an idea that could benefit the ranch," I tell my brothers. This is the first chance I've had to mention it to them.

"What kind of idea?" TJ's tone doesn't hold the skepticism mine usually does whenever they approach me with an idea.

But what do you expect when the last big ideas involving the ranch were to switch from cattle to horses and for TJ to be on a reality show to help promote the ranch? You can't really blame me for being leery after that, can you?

While we wait for the salesclerk to write up our order, I fill my brothers in on the idea. Austin entertains Deacon with the toy cop car.

"That doesn't sound like a bad idea," TJ says.

Noah rubs his jaw. "Sophie definitely has a magical touch with horses. But what happens if she moves away?"

"She won't."

"How can you be so sure?" TJ asks. "Are you forgetting her ticking biological clock? You adopting Maui didn't put it on snooze."

"Don't worry, I've got it all figured out."

"How so?"

"I can't tell you. But I am handling the situation. By the time I'm finished, Sophie won't want to leave Copper Creek."

"Why? Are you planning to marry her?" Noah asks.

"Of course not. She wants to marry for love. Don't worry, I've got it figured out."

Both brothers nod, willing to trust me without reservation. Guilt squeezes my intestines tighter than a boa with constipation. I still have to figure out how to help Sophie with Ryan.

Who knew being a fairy godfather could be so tough?

After we finish at the store, we head to the restaurant where we're meeting the girls. Noah rides with me in my truck. TJ, Austin, and Deacon drive in TJ's vehicle.

"Okay, lover boy," Noah says as I follow them. Country music pumps through the speakers, but low enough so I can easily hear him. "How are you planning to fix it so Sophie doesn't move away from Copper Creek?"

"You're not letting this go, are you?" I quickly glance at him. His expression tells me everything I need to know.

"Nope. So you might as well spill it now and get it over with."

I let out a rough breath. "All right. Sophie has a thing for the new vet in town. I'm helping her so that she can talk to him.

Hopefully then, he'll eventually ask her out. They fall in love and problem solved. Sophie stays in Copper Creek."

And I spend the next few months ignoring the tightness in my gut every time I see them together.

How hard can it be?

There's a moment of silence....Then Noah busts out laughing. "Are you fucking kidding me?"

"About which part?"

"All of it. But let's start with how you're helping Sophie land a boyfriend. The same Sophie you get a boner over every time you're near her. I'm sorry, but don't you see how twisted that is?"

"First, I don't get a boner every time I'm near her," I say, somewhat truthfully.

I don't get them all the time.

Only a majority of the time.

"What's the second thing?" Noah asks.

"Sophie's my friend, and you help friends whenever they need it. It's part of being a good friend."

"All right, you got me there. But how do you even know she's interested in the guy?"

I give him a meaningful look before returning my eyes to the road.

"Oh. She can't talk around him, can she?"

"Stumbles over her words like a foal taking its first steps. But once I've helped her, she'll be able to talk to him in coherent sentences, and he'll realize how amazing she is and fall in love with her. I mean, how could he not?"

"Right—how could he not?" There's something off about Noah's tone. I ignore it.

Noah is silent for a few minutes. Possibly deep in thought.

Or thinking about his next lay.

On the radio, Brett Young is singing the lyrics to "In Case You Didn't Know."

But the moment of peace can't last forever. "How exactly are you planning to help her?" he eventually asks.

"I'm working on that part."

"Which means you have no idea."

"Sure, I have an idea." Good thing the sky is clear. The chance of lightning striking me is zero.

"Right. We *are* talking about you, Jake. You never do anything without a fully formed plan."

True. "Maybe I've decided to live a little and wing it." I inwardly cringe at the "wing it" part.

He throws his head back in laughter. "Yeah, have fun with that."

I grunt. That only makes him laugh harder.

"Since you're so smart, any suggestions for how I can help her?"

That sobers him a little. "Hell if I know. Women don't usually have issues talking to me."

"That you're aware of." I steer the truck into the restaurant's parking lot. "Do me a favor and keep this to yourself. You can't even mention it to TJ." No one else needs to know about it.

"Gotcha. Your secret's safe with me." Luckily for me, it's the truth. As much as he loves kidding around, he's like Fort Knox when it comes to secrets.

Sophie's car is already here, but there's no sign of the three women. We wait for TJ to get Deacon down from his car seat; then the five of us enter the busy Italian restaurant. We're directed to the table where the girls are waiting next to the window.

Deacon sees his mother and races over to her. A waitress steps into his path, not realizing he's there. Fortunately, he zags at the last moment, avoiding a collision with her legs.

Violet sweeps him up into her arms and hugs him. Then she lowers him to the floor and embraces TJ as if they haven't seen each other for a year.

While they're busy getting reacquainted—in a family-friendly manner—Austin helps his nephew into his booster chair. I sit next to Sophie.

She's looking as gorgeous as ever. Her hair is pulled up in a ponytail, and she's wearing a bright-yellow floral sundress, held up by two narrow straps.

"So you're really not going to give me a sneak peek at your bridesmaid dress?" I say it low enough so only she can hear me.

"Not even a tiny sneak peek."

"Are you at least going to give me a hint? 'Cuz as your fairy godfather, I need to know ahead of time if I'll be required to turn it into a pumpkin."

Grinning, she shakes her head. "I believe the pumpkin turns into a carriage. Cinderella's rags transform into a gown."

"You see, that's where her fairy godmother got it all wrong. She should have turned the pumpkin into a Lamborghini. Now that would've been more impressive. Carriages are for mere commoners."

"I'm pretty sure they didn't have Lamborghinis back in those days."

The waitress approaches our table and takes our drink orders. This is followed by the girls discussing the wedding plans. The guys and I pretend to listen. Every so often, we nod as if we know what the heck they're talking about.

All the guys except for TJ, that is. He's hanging on to his bride-to-be's every word.

And maybe the whole not-listening thing is why I missed Violet's question. How do I know she asked me one? Everyone is staring at me expectantly.

"Are you bringing a date, Jake?" she asks.

"We need to bring a date?" I've been to a few weddings in the past, but I always fly solo.

There's a reason for that.

Weddings are a great place to find your next lay. Or at least they are most of the time, especially when it comes to the single bridesmaids. They're usually eager for some fun between the sheets. Or up against a wall.

But for the last couple of weddings I've been invited to, Sophie was my date. Or rather, my fake girlfriend.

Why?

Because a few mothers got it in their heads that their daughter's wedding was the perfect location to find a future husband for their daughter who was still single.

"You don't need to bring a date," Violet says. "I just thought if there's someone you'd like to invite…"

"You're going to ask Ryan, right?" Aubrey asks Sophie.

Sophie shrugs, her face reddening. "I was thinking about it. But I don't know if he'll be interested."

"How can he not be?"

"Right, how could he not be?" I somehow manage to squeeze the words past the unexpected tightening of my chest. I grab my beer and drink down a long draw. It does nothing to loosen the vise-like sensation.

Sophie throws me a panicked look, unnoticed by the others as they go back to discussing the guest list.

I reach under the table and thread my fingers with hers.

8

I lightly squeeze Sophie's hand. The smell of spicy tomato sauces, the waitress taking orders at the next table over, and the clinking of cutlery reminds me that we're still in the restaurant, where everyone can overhear us.

"How about after lunch," I say, "you and I go somewhere so you can practice talking to good-looking guys? Noah can drive Aubrey home in my truck." It's a given Violet will be returning to Copper Creek with TJ and Deacon.

It takes Sophie a second before she nods. "All right."

Only she doesn't sound too okay.

"Don't worry, you'll be fine. I'll be right there with you. And afterward, I'll do a post-game analysis."

Cute grooves form between her eyebrows. "Post-game analysis?"

"You know, like how sports teams do it? Discuss what you did wrong and what you did well, and then I can give you pointers on how you can do better next time."

"Do you really believe it will work?"

No, but I'm hardly admitting that to her.

"Absolutely," I say instead.

After lunch, we send everyone off on their merry way. No one questions why the two of us stay behind in Golden Falls.

I hold out my hand to Sophie. "Keys, please."

"What for?"

"I'm driving."

She laughs. "I'm more than capable of driving, Jake. Or are you forgetting that I was drinking diet soda in the restaurant, not wine?"

"I know but...I big caveman. I drive."

She snorts. "Sorry, Mr. Neanderthal, but I'm driving."

She unlocks the doors with her key fob and climbs into the driver's side. With a sigh, I slide onto the passenger seat.

"All right, where are we going?"

I give her directions to a park where I'm sure we'll find some victims.

Great, now I'm thinking like a serial killer.

Since it's Saturday afternoon, the place is busy with joggers, people walking their dogs, parents pushing strollers along the path. A group of men not far from us are playing touch football on the grass. Young kids giggle and shriek as they roll down the shallow incline.

"What now?" Sophie scans the area.

"Too bad we don't have Maui with us. He would be a guaranteed conversation-starter." But since he hasn't had all his vaccinations yet, he has to stay away from other dogs...other than Asgard.

"I don't think this is going to work, Jake."

"Sure, it will. You aren't planning to date or marry the guy. You're just practicing so you can talk to Ryan."

Doubt still lingers on her face.

"Hey, you'll do great, Soph. No one here knows you. So it's not like you have to worry about anyone from Copper Creek finding out."

It's the main reason Golden Falls is the perfect location for her to practice. Plus, it wouldn't look good if she was caught flirting with guys when Ryan is the only man she's interested in.

"Right. So what's the game plan? What am I supposed to say to the guys?"

I consider it for a moment. "How about we begin with something super easy? Like asking for directions."

"Okay." She takes a step, then stops. A gust of wind plays with the hem of her dress, which falls above her knees, revealing slightly more of her mouth-watering legs. "Directions for what?"

"Hmm." More contemplating on my part. More admiring her legs, too. "What about you ask the subject where the fountain is?"

"Subject? You make him sound like a lab rat."

"In a way, he is. But just don't let him know that. Guys don't take it well when being referred to as any type of rodent."

She grins with the same mischievous gleam in her eyes that always causes my heart rate to kick up a few notches. "Not even a cute little bunny?"

"Especially not a cute little bunny. Let's not destroy his manhood, please. That won't score you any points."

She chuckles. "Got it. No thinking of the 'subject' as any type of lab rodent, cute or otherwise."

"You ready?" She's stalling—which wouldn't be so bad if I didn't need her to start dating Ryan. Only then can I move on from my unprofessional feelings for her.

"I think I can handle it." She makes a goofy face, chomping her lower lip like some sort of weird beaver.

I roll my eyes and go back to surveying the area for our first target.

A guy is strolling toward us. Good-looking. *Check*. Not a douchebag. *Hopefully*.

I nod in his direction. "How about him?"

I don't give her a chance to answer. I walk to the side of the path and pretend to examine the freshly cut grass.

Right—not the best way to look inconspicuous, but it's the best I can do under the circumstances.

Maybe I *should* be videotaping her, so we can review the game tape afterward.

"Hi," I hear Sophie say. "Can you tell me where the fountain is?"

My gaze shoots up to where she's standing. *Holy shit*. I'm a freaking miracle worker.

I didn't expect it to be *that* easy.

Maybe I can go into business helping women land the man of their dreams. With Sophie's glowing recommendation, I'll be a hit.

I listen while the man explains where to find the fountain. She thanks him and walks back to where I'm crouched.

I push to stand. "That was great, Soph. You didn't stumble once."

She shrugs. "That's because I wasn't interested in him. He was nothing more than a stranger to me."

"But he was good-looking."

"Yes, so? That doesn't mean I was interested in him. It's not like I'll ever see him again."

"Are you saying we didn't make even the tiniest bit of progress?"

I should probably feel somewhat disappointed—but I'm not.

She laughs and tucks a loose strand of hair behind her ear. "Well, we've established practicing with men I'm not interested in may not be useful. I tried to warn you it wouldn't work. But I really do appreciate you at least trying."

I gesture for us to start walking in the direction the man told her to go. Since we're in the park, we might as well make the most of it. "Does it mean you've given up on Ryan?"

She studies my face for a moment, gaze dropping to my lips. She then turns and starts walking. "Not at all."

I join her. "Good—because I'm sure we can figure this out. Have you ever *had* a boyfriend?" She'd mentioned that she'd only had sex the one time, and the guy had pretty much been a one-night stand. But this doesn't mean she's never had a boyfriend.

"I dated one guy after college."

"What happened with him?"

"There wasn't any chemistry between us. So I ended things with him."

"But at least you could date him. You're not completely a lost cause." I pat her on the back in congratulations.

"I wouldn't go that far. I only dated him because he didn't make me nervous. But he also didn't make my heart rate pick up every time he walked into the room. Every time I looked at him, I didn't have an overwhelming desire to kiss him. And when he wasn't around, I didn't give him a second thought."

So the opposite of what happens to me when it comes to Sophie. But since I can't admit that to her, I go with a different response. "For the record, I've never had any of that either."

"Not even with whatshername from college?"

"Not really. If anything, I was more of a horny bastard back then." Like most twenty-year-old males. "I just didn't realize the difference until it was too late. But this isn't about me, Soph. It's about you. So other than the one guy, you've seriously never had any boyfriends?" I still have a hard time wrapping my head around that. Sophie is gorgeous and funny, smart and sweet.

Any fool can see that.

A man and woman approach us. The man has one of those baby-carrying devices strapped to his chest with a baby inside. The couple is holding hands and smiling.

I might be wrong, but I swear I heard a dreamy sigh pass

between Sophie's lips. Is she imagining the couple as Ryan and her?

The thought is a karate kick to the gut—even though there's no logical reason for it.

I glance at her as we pass the couple. The dreamy sigh is accompanied by an equally dreamy smile. More than anything, I want to keep that expression permanently on her face.

Only I have no clue how.

The happy expression fades, replaced not by sadness—it's more like defeat. "That's right, just the one boyfriend."

"Since Ryan moved to town, how many times have you talked to him?" I ask.

"You mean *talk* talk, or sounded like an idiot when I talked?"

"You don't sound like that big of an idiot. And either option works for me."

She pauses at the edge of a flower bed, and her gaze sweeps over the colorful display of spring blossoms. "Just the one time when we met him and went out to Joe's afterward."

"That's it?" I would've thought that given how eager Aubrey was to hook Sophie up with Ryan, she would've found an excuse to have Soph visit the clinic on a daily basis.

Clearly she's an amateur.

It's not like you're much better, Mr. Fairy Godfather.

She nods and keeps walking. "That's it."

"All right—so the first step is getting you in the same room with him again. Otherwise, he'll never have a chance to see how amazing you are."

"Well, aren't you just the nicest man on this side of the Mississippi?" She uses her fake southern accent that never fails to make me smile.

"As if you ever doubted it."

She giggles.

"My brothers and I could have a barbecue and invite Ryan

and our friends. It'll give him a chance to get to know everyone. Guys tend to feel more at ease about dating a girl when he already likes her friends. Then he won't have to worry about them giving him the third degree."

Most of the time.

Because you can guarantee Ryan will experience one hell of an interrogation from me once he asks Sophie out. As her boss, I owe it to her to ensure he's the right man for her.

Maybe I could add the interrogation part to the company policy—under employee safety.

"That sounds like a great idea," Sophie says. "You would really do that for me?"

I stop walking and rest my palm against her face. "I'd do anything for you, Soph. You know that."

She smiles, the tug on her mouth small. "I know." She looks away. "So when's this magical barbecue happening?"

"I'll have to check with my brothers first and find out if Ryan's available, but how about Friday?"

Her gaze finds mine again. "Friday sounds great."

"Friday it is, then. And by the end of the evening, I can guarantee Ryan will be eager to ask you out on a date."

Now, if only it didn't feel like my stomach just head-butted my heart.

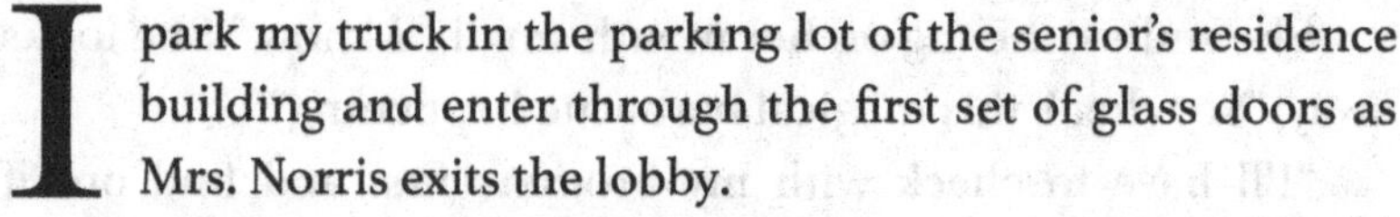

I park my truck in the parking lot of the senior's residence building and enter through the first set of glass doors as Mrs. Norris exits the lobby.

She grins at me, revealing her dentures. Curlers wrapped in strands of white hair peek out from under her bright pink scarf. The scarf that goes perfectly with her granny-style dress and the large orange tulips on it. "Here to see Andrew, are you?"

"Maybe I'm here to see you." I wink at her.

She giggles. "You're a little young for me, Jake. But I do have a granddaughter you'd be perfect for." This would be the same granddaughter who's married to a surgeon and living in Texas. "I hear Andrew's teaching you leather carving. The man is mighty talented."

She releases a dreamy sigh which I suspect has more to do with Andrew than his talent. He seems to have that effect on women over the age of seventy.

"I don't know yet if it's something I want to do. That's what I'm here to find out."

What I do know is, for the past week I've watched TJ work on the latest rocking horse he's donating to a kid with cancer.

I've also been watching Noah tinker around with the 1955 Ford Thunderbird he's been restoring for the past year. And I've been studying the pieces of leather around the ranch house that Granddad must have carved.

I even stumbled across his old tools we'd stored in the barn after his death. None of us had known what to do with them—or even what they were for.

I won't say this all led to a burning desire to follow in his footsteps. Because it didn't.

It was more like curiosity, along with a dash of jealousy swimming through my veins at what my brothers have accomplished with their hobbies. As much as I love astronomy and playing chess at the senior center once a month, it feels like something is missing.

But it wasn't until I saw Andrew yesterday in town, and he brought up the leather carving again, that I figured I'd at least give it a try.

"Well, I for one can't wait to see what you make," Mrs. Norris says. "Your grandfather was extremely talented, too. You're a lot like him, Jake. You never know—maybe this is another similarity you two share."

I chuckle. "Don't get your hopes up too high. But could you do me a favor?"

"What kind of favor?"

"Could you not mention this to anyone? I might decide it's not for me. And I'd rather not have everyone asking me about it." Welcome to small-town life—where your business is everybody else's.

"I can do that." An impish grin stretches on her face. "But it'll cost you."

"What exactly is it going to cost me?"

"One of Roxy's croissants. I have a sudden craving for them. The chocolate-filled ones."

"All right. As soon as I'm done here, I'll go to her bakery and pick one up for you. Is that everything?"

Her grin widens. "Are you certain you don't want to marry my granddaughter?"

I laugh. "Yes, I'm certain. And I'm sure her husband would agree with me."

I open the outside door for Mrs. Norris. She walks past me with a thanks and a good-bye. The inside door hasn't fully shut, and I catch it before it has a chance to close.

Five minutes later, I'm sitting at Andrew's small kitchen table, beer in hand, listening to him explain the different tools laid out in front of him.

"Unless you and your brothers got rid of your grandfather's old tools, you should have the same ones I do. For your first project, I thought you could make a leather bookmark. It's simple enough and will give you a taste of leather carving. If you enjoy it and want to continue with your lessons, we can come up with something bigger for you to practice on. Does that sound good to you?"

I nod, and he teaches me how to dampen the leather and how to trace the leaf pattern on it with a stylus. I mirror what he does with my own piece of leather.

He then shows me, step-by-step, how to use each tool to create the desired look.

"How's the ranch doing?" he asks at one point, after he demonstrates again how to move the beveler while hitting it with the hammer so the leather doesn't look like someone used their teeth on it.

"It's doing fine." I avoid his gaze when I say it.

"Even though you switched from cattle to horses?" His tone is warm and judgment-free.

I shrug. "It's not doing as quite well as it was for Granddad —given that cattle generates more income than horses—but give it time. I'm sure it'll do well. It'll just reach a different level of success."

For the first time since switching to horses, I actually believe we can make a success of it. We won't reach Granddad's level of income, but my brothers were right. I enjoy working with horses more than I did cattle.

But how about we don't tell them I said that?

"Your grandfather would be proud of you boys."

"Why? Because we destroyed his dream by switching our focus?"

"No, because you're following your own dreams. Okay, not so much your dream to one day work for NASA. Your grandfather could never understand why you'd want to do something so impractical. But you're making the ranch something you can be proud of. That's all he wanted. That, and for his family—you boys—to all return where you belong...Copper Creek."

My mouth jerks to one side. "I'm not sure Noah would agree with him there."

Andrew picks up the strap and begins polishing the swivel knife's blade. "Ah, that young whippersnapper will come around eventually."

He nods at the piece of leather I'm working on. "So how are you enjoying it so far?"

I glance down at it. Satisfaction dances across my skin—and for the first time, I understand why Noah and TJ have their hobbies.

Sure, my design isn't perfect. It's kind of a disaster, actually. But it's *my* disaster. The disaster created by my own hands.

With practice, it might one day be something else.

It's my turn to grin, my answer to his question.

"You think you'd be interested in dropping by the same time next week and continuing with our lessons?" he asks.

"I can definitely be persuaded."

10

"Are you ready, Maui?" I ask the black bundle of energy. "Today's your big day."

That's right—it's Maui's first day of leash training outside.

"*Aww*. Aren't you just the sweetest?" Sophie says.

"Of course Maui's the sweetest. He takes after me." I feel the corner of my mouth mockingly curl up. "Sweet" is the last word I'd use to describe me.

She grins. "I was talking about *you*—not the dog."

"I'm hardly sweet. More like a hard-ass."

Maui releases a little yap.

"See, he agrees with me."

"You're both wrong. You're the sweetest guy I know, Jake. You took one look at him and knew you had to adopt him. That's incredibly sweet." The way she smiles at me heats up my insides to a gentle boil.

I decide not to point out that I only volunteered to adopt him when she mentioned her landlords wouldn't allow her to have a dog.

I'd hardly call that sweet. I just want to make Sophie happy.

78

I pick up Maui's leash and his favorite treats from the kitchen table.

Sophie grabs his ball and we head out the front door. For now, Maui doesn't have his leash on. First lesson? Negotiating the steps. We haven't worked with him yet on the staircase inside the house. We figured he could learn on these to begin with.

Sophie and I crouch in front of them. Maui peers down at the first step, then gives a little puppy bark and backs away.

Sophie taps the next step. "C'mon Maui. You can do it."

He moves forward, leans over the edge, and reverses again. He walks along the top step, puzzling out a way down but not quite getting the pieces to fit.

"Let me show you." I return to his step and get down on all fours. "Okay, buddy, we'll do this together."

I move my hands to the next step. Maui whimpers and leans against me; then he cautiously maneuvers his front paws to the same step my hands are on. His back legs follow suit so he's parallel to the edge.

"You can't begin to understand how adorable you two look right now," Sophie says.

I glance up. The phone in her hand is aimed at us. "You aren't videotaping this, are you?"

"There might be a slight possibility that I am. Then I can give Maui the post-game analysis once you're done." She attempts to wink at me and I chuckle.

"Just as long as it doesn't end up on social media..." I leave the rest of my words hanging.

"Nope, this is only for me. To remind me of our son's first steps...down the porch stairs."

An unexpected warmth fills me at her words. More specifically from her saying "our son." I douse it. She didn't mean it the way it sounded.

What does it matter how it sounded? a voice inside my head points out. *You aren't interested in settling down with her. You aren't looking to start a family.*

I repeat the process to the next step. Maui does the same. By the third step, he's a little more confident.

My legs drag behind me on the stairs as I keep demonstrating what to do.

Maui keeps going, carefully climbing from one step to the next, until he's safely on the path.

"Good boy," Sophie says, fussing over him. "Who's a clever boy?"

Maui answers with a small, proud bark.

I grin and straighten to my feet. He's not the only adorable member of the duo.

Sophie stands up and throws her arms around my neck. Her body presses against mine, and I breathe in her familiar scent.

And because we're currently off the clock when it comes to me being her employer, I allow myself to envelop her in my arms.

It's a moment of weakness.

"You were amazing, Jake. Whether you believe it or not, you'll make a great father one day."

Before I can respond, she pulls away. "Okay, Maui. Time for you to go bathroom."

We escort him to the designated spot in the front yard where he's supposed to do his business. It takes us some effort, but Sophie and I finally get him to go where we want him.

"Playtime," Sophie announces once he's finished. She carries him over to the grass near the driveway and gently tosses the ball for him to chase after. "How many are coming to the barbecue on Friday?"

"Including the staff at Aubrey's clinic, I'd say about eighteen."

"Eighteen?"

"Yes, but that's also including Grandma Meg and her cohorts." Her cohorts being Tilly and Gertrude. Andrew couldn't make it.

Grandma Meg isn't really my grandmother, but she might as well be. She and my grandmother on my mom's side were best friends long before my brothers and I were born. She's really Violet and Austin's grandmother.

And Deacon's great-grandmother.

A grin breaks out on Sophie's face. "Well, if anything, the barbecue will be entertaining with those three there."

Don't I know it?

"Just remember, if Tilly brings her infamous deviled eggs, avoid them at all cost."

Imagine for a second what happens when someone adds jalapeños to deviled eggs but forgets how many she's already mixed in...and accidentally triples the amount.

Fortunately, no buildings were harmed from the flames shooting from people's mouths at the last picnic she attended.

Hmm. Maybe I should alert the fire department that she's coming.

"Good advice," Sophie says, laughing. She walks to where Maui dropped his ball and tosses it again.

He barks and goes tumbling after it.

"What's your plan when it comes to Ryan at the barbecue?" I ask.

"Plan?"

"Yes, plan. You've been avoiding Aubrey's clinic since we got Maui. How do I know you won't avoid Ryan when he comes over on Friday?"

She cringes.

"That's what I thought. Maybe we should come up with rules for Friday."

She blinks. Twice. "Rules?"

"Yes, rules." I fold my arms. "Rule number one. You are not allowed to avoid him."

"Okay."

"Rule number two. You must say at least five sentences to him."

Maui crouches in front of the ball and yaps at it, his tail wagging at supersonic speed. We head over to join him.

"Do they have to be coherent or is that optional?" she asks.

I pick up his ball. "It can be either one, but you'll get bonus points if they're coherent."

She laughs. "So you're going to reward me like I'm a puppy learning a new trick?"

Damn, why didn't I think of that?

"Great idea! How about we come up with a point system? And at the end of the evening, you'll get a big reward if you earn enough points. I mean, unless you want a puppy treat like Maui gets."

She snorts a laugh. "I'll pass on the puppy treat, thanks. What kind of reward are we talking about?"

"What kind of reward would you like?"

She deliberates.

And deliberates.

And deliberates.

While she does that, I throw Maui's ball.

Sophie's face shifts to an ooh-that's-a-good-one expression, and her head bobs side-to-side. But just as I think she's going to tell me what she wants, she surprises me with a "Can I get back to you on that?"

"Sure." I don't even hazard a guess as to what it is. But given that she loves chocolate, my money's on that. "So the way this will work is, break a rule and you lose a point. For every coherent sentence you say to Ryan, you get a point. Make it to fifty points and you get your reward. How does that sound?"

She smiles, her eyes gleaming with excitement. "You've got yourself a deal." She holds out her hand and we shake on it.

Maui yaps again as if to further seal the deal. And to remind us he's still here and wishes to play some more.

"Sorry." Sophie picks up the ball and tosses it slightly farther from us than last time.

"Do you think he's ready to try the leash yet?"

Let's hope it's easier to train him to walk on a leash than it is to train Sophie to talk to Ryan without tripping over her words.

"The book says to give him plenty of exercise first," she says. "Maybe I should throw the ball a few more times. Then we can try."

Christ, is having a kid this confusing? Always questioning the right thing to do? Fortunately, kids don't chew on your shoes.

Or at least I don't think they do.

That's right—there've been a few incidents in the past three days involving one of Noah's boots.

Noah gave it a decent burial. RIP.

But that's not all. A houseplant also befell a similar fate. Although if you ask me, it wasn't Maui's fault. My money is on Loki.

We play with Maui for a few more minutes before getting to work on his leash training.

"What are you wearing on Friday for the barbecue?" I ask. Wasn't part of Cinderella's fairy godmother's job description to ensure Cinderella was properly dressed for the ball?

While I doubt Ryan is expecting to see Sophie in a ball gown at the barbecue, it doesn't mean I can let that important detail slide.

I mentally groan. The Man Card Board of Directors will be revoking my membership for sure after this.

"I was thinking my lacy white sundress, my short denim jacket in case it's chilly, and my favorite cowboy boots."

"Good choice." Other than the part where I always get a hard-on whenever she wears the outfit. She's sexy as all fuck in it.

If Ryan doesn't have the same reaction to seeing her in it as I do, it means only one thing…he's a eunuch.

"What about your hair?" I ask. "How are you planning to style it?"

And wave good-bye to my man card. *Going. Going. Gone…*

"I was going to pull it up in a ponytail." Like she usually does. Like she's wearing her hair now.

I shake my head. "Leave it down. You're gorgeous and sexy when it's loose."

Yes, there might be a chance I've imagined tugging on her hair hard while pounding into her from behind.

Yeah, yeah, I'm aware that I shouldn't be thinking of her that way. God knows I'm traveling straight to hell.

"You think I'm gorgeous and sexy?" she asks, almost in a whisper.

"Of course. What guy doesn't?"

She releases a soft, sharp breath. "Right."

"You don't believe me?" Because she certainly sounds like she doesn't. "I see guys give you a double take whenever we're in town."

I've also seen some leering expressions, but I keep that to myself. Those are the ones I always have the urge to knock off the guys' faces. With my fists.

"All right, so my hair down." She retrieves the leash from the ground. "Hey, Maui. Let's go for a *walk*." She holds up the leash when she says the last word.

Maui cocks his head to the side, staring at the leash dangling from her hand. Like he's preparing to be hypnotized.

She crouches and lets him sniff it. So far so good. She attaches it to his collar and stands. "Okay, let's do this."

Maui looks at her expectantly. Sophie steps forward, the

leash held loosely in her hand, and encourages him to move up next to her.

I grin at how adorable she looks as I watch the pair in action. It's easy to see how much Sophie already loves him. And for a second longer than I should, I imagine what it would feel like if that love was directed at *me*.

Not that she would need to tell me to heel. I would follow her to the ends of the earth...even though I'm fully aware that I shouldn't.

Ten minutes later, Maui decides he's had enough walking for the day. He plonks himself on the grass and gives Sophie the puppy eyes that always melt her heart.

And Maui knows it.

"You can take a break now." She unclips the leash from his collar and fusses over him, again.

"He really has you wrapped around his paw several times, doesn't he?"

"You'd better believe it." She bites her lower lip and looks away.

I can't resist the pull she has on me—the pull she has no idea exists. I step closer to her, take hold of her chin, and gently force her to look at me. "Hey, what's wrong?"

"Nothing."

I raise my eyebrow. "Sorry, but I'm not buying that. You know you can tell me anything." My voice is low and husky. I'll blame it on how close we're standing. On how tempting her lips look.

Without meaning to, I run the pad of my thumb across her lower lip, unhooking it from her teeth. The flesh feels as soft as I imagined it would, and my own lips plead for a chance to see if they agree with me.

My gaze moves to hers. Her light-brown eyes are slightly wide as they study me, and for a moment I get lost in them.

I swallow hard, willing myself to look away from her, to step back, to say something—anything—to break the hold she has on me.

The hold she neither wants nor needs.

"What if I'm a terrible kisser?" she finally asks, surprising me.

"I doubt you're a terrible kisser." In fact, I would stake my life on it.

"You don't know that, though. What if Ryan wants to kiss me and then decides I'm awful at it?"

"He won't think that."

"Maybe you can kiss me. Then we'll know for sure. And if I'm a bad kisser, you can give me pointers."

Employee plus boss plus kissing never equals a great idea. You don't have to be a mathematical genius to understand that.

Her whole face brightens and she grins. "Actually, that's a brilliant idea," she says before I can voice my thoughts. "Who better to give me pointers than someone as experienced as you? You know what makes for a great kiss."

"I'm not sure how I'm supposed to take that."

"Take it as a compliment. So will you do it?" Maui could take lessons from Sophie on how to do puppy-dog eyes.

"Are you sure?"

"Very sure."

"All right. But you can't tell anyone."

Because I'll never hear the end of it from my brothers if they find out.

I lean down and brush my lips gently against hers. Yes, they're as soft as expected.

My heart thump-thump-thumps hard and fast in my chest, like a bird caught in a cage, eager to tell the world how great it feels to kiss Sophie.

As if sensing that, Sophie rests her hand over my heart. The heat from her palm ignites a fire low in my belly, the softness of her lips fanning the flames.

I should pull back and tell her the kiss was good. But I know she was referring to a kiss that's more than the brushing of lips. She wants to experience something deeper, more heated, more soul-searching.

I part my lips and give her exactly what she's after.

One hand cups the back of her head. The other moves to her hip. I long to pull her against me, but it's probably not a good idea. I do, though, give in to the other craving...and thread my fingers through her hair.

With my lips still enjoying the feel of Sophie's, I work the elastic free from her hair. I drop it onto the grass and knot my fingers in the silky strands as my tongue continues exploring her mouth.

Somewhere in the back of my head, a voice tells me I've sampled Sophie's kiss long enough to give her a full report. My body and my mouth tell the voice to fuck off. This is the only chance I'll ever have to kiss her. To hell with stopping just yet.

Our tongues glide together, the erotic sensation waking every nerve in my body. I don't remember the last time a kiss felt this amazing.

And I've kissed enough girls to understand the difference.

I'm just about to explore her jaw, the shell of her ear, her neck, when Sophie moans softly—and I'm reminded I need to stop.

She's looking for feedback on her kiss. She wasn't planning on me ravishing her.

I pull away and clear my throat. My heart is still thumping fast, bitching about me stopping so soon.

"So? How was that?" Sophie asks, her breath as ragged as mine.

When I don't answer right away, because my brain isn't currently functioning one hundred percent, she frowns. "That bad, huh?"

I shake my head, still slightly out of it. "No—it was definitely good. You don't have to worry about Ryan thinking you're a bad kisser."

Me on the other hand? I'm ready to punch him in the face if he tries to kiss her.

Mine.

Except she's not mine—and never will be.

I need to remember that.

Sophie smiles, her eyes slightly dazed, as if she's daydreaming about him. Everything inside of me clenches at the thought.

I release a hard breath, attempting to unknot the tension inside me, and glance at Maui. He's passed out at our feet.

"I take it we wore him out." I chuckle. It's a forced laugh, but I doubt Sophie notices.

She settles her hand on my bicep. Her thumb brushes against my shirt sleeve. "Thank you, Jake. Thanks for being such a great friend."

I smile back at her, the movement genuine. "You're welcome. But you're forgetting it's in the job description."

"Job description?"

"Yes, as your fairy godfather."

Sophie kisses my cheek and my skin tingles at her touch. "Well, job description or not, I appreciate it."

This isn't the first time she's kissed me on the cheek. But unlike the kisses in the past, her lips linger a second longer, as if the action means more to her than before.

I shove the thought aside. Clearly when I kissed her a few minutes ago, it short-circuited my brain. Because Ryan is the man she's interested in....I'm just her friend.

Her wingman.

11

"What the heck are you doing?" Noah asks and I startle.

I'm sitting at the solid oak kitchen table. The leather carving equipment I'm using is lined up on the length of canvas in front of me. I'd been so focused on practicing what Andrew had taught me the other day that I didn't hear my brothers enter.

"What does it look like I'm doing? And why are you guys even here?" I level my gaze at TJ. "Aren't you supposed to be with your fiancée and son?"

I turn to Noah. "And aren't you supposed to be hooking up with some girl at Joe's?"

My brothers exchange looks. "If I didn't know better," Noah says to TJ, "I'd say someone here doesn't want us to know what he's up to." The smug grin in his voice is missing from his face. For now.

My response is a you've-got-that-right grunt.

"When did you start doing this?" TJ's tone is more curious than amused. There's also a dose of awe in it that tweaks at something deep inside me. It's a feeling of pride, even though

89

the level of craftsmanship is a long way from what Granddad had achieved.

The horse's head is a simple design, but it's still a challenge when you're learning the different carving techniques. It's far from perfect, but at least you can recognize what it's supposed to be.

"Only recently," I say, answering TJ's question. "Andrew convinced me to give it a try. He's been teaching me how to do it."

TJ picks up the piece of leather from the table. "What does Sophie think of this?"

"Other than Andrew and you guys, no one else knows about it." Well, there's also Mrs. Norris, but I believe the *two* chocolate croissants I gave her were enough to buy her silence.

"And if you guys hadn't shown up while I was working on this, you wouldn't know about it either. I just want to make sure —*before* everyone in Copper Creek finds out about it—that it's something I still want to do in a few months or in a few years."

Noah inspects the leather square in TJ's hands. "I thought you didn't have time for hobbies. Hobbies and getting laid. I thought the only thing you had time for was the ranch."

"Maybe I want something more from life." Andrew had been right about that. I just hadn't realized it until the tools were in my hands, and I discovered what I could do with them.

Noah smacks my shoulder. "Congratulations on finally realizing that."

"So you guys'll keep quiet about this? For now, anyway?"

I already know I can trust them to do that. And I won't have to bribe them with croissants—chocolate or otherwise—to keep them quiet.

"Sure, if it's what you want," TJ says.

"You know we will," Noah adds, taking the piece of leather from him. "How much longer before you can do this on saddles? Between the horse breeding, Sophie's horse-whispering services, TJ's rocking horses, and now custom-designed western saddles, we'd have it made."

I snort a laugh. "You're getting way ahead of yourself, bro."

Noah returns the leather carving to the table. "I don't know about that. I mean sure, not tomorrow. But just think about it. With Violet as our marketing guru, we could have quite the business with all those things. We could even offer riding tours and sell your stuff in our gift shop." Which we don't currently have. "Along with Violet's horse photography. It would be great."

"As much as we appreciate your suggestion," TJ says, "you're forgetting one important thing. While Jake is creating the saddles and I'm building rocking horses, who'll be running the ranch? All by himself." He slaps Noah on the bicep, in case Noah hasn't figured it out yet.

"It'd certainly make our ranch unique compared to Scottsdale," I say, the business side of my brain kicking in. "It's a good idea. Just not feasible right now."

I pick up the leather square and flash the design at Noah—with the less than perfect horse image—reminding him of the other reason his idea isn't feasible. At least not yet.

TJ laughs.

12

---

knock on the office door pulls my attention from the computer screen and the spreadsheet I've been working on for the past hour.

"Come in." I swing the desk chair around to see who it is. It's the only piece of office furniture that isn't antique oak.

The door opens and Sophie enters with Maui clambering behind her. She's wearing her lacy white sundress, but instead of her cowboy boots like she'd planned, she's wearing stilettos. Her long blonde waves tumble over her shoulders and down her back.

Holy shit.

I swallow hard, forcing my mouth to shut. Because I'm pretty sure it's been gaping open.

"How do I look?" She spins on the spot, causing the skirt to hitch up, revealing more of her long, toned legs.

Legs I'm now imagining on my shoulders as I pound into her, stilettos still on her feet.

Yes, we can blame the kiss—the kiss I haven't stopped thinking about—for that fantasy.

Shit, I'm screwed. Royally, fucking screwed.

You can always rip up your company policy, the voice in my head says. I mentally flip it the finger and switch the image of Sophie beneath me with...

Double shit. I can't even come up with anyone to replace her.

Sophie watches me expectantly, waiting for a reply.

"You look great. You clean up nicely." I wink.

She walks over to me.

Do not *look at her legs. Do* not *look at her legs*.

Too bad my eyes and my brain aren't currently on speaking terms.

I push myself from the chair and will my arms to stay by my side. *Whatever you do, don't touch her*.

Because the moment I do, I won't be able to keep from pulling her into my arms and kissing her.

I trace the tip of my tongue along my lower lip, relieving their sudden dryness, reliving her taste.

But while I might be avoiding touching Sophie, the same can't be said about her. She rests her hands on my chest. "You clean up nicely, too."

The heat from them soaks through the cotton of my T-shirt. What happens when oxygen is introduced to fire? It helps feed the flames. And that's exactly what her hands are doing to me. They're feeding the fire that flickers inside me.

Only now those flames aren't just flickering like a campfire. They're threatening to become big enough to burn down a goddamn forest.

But as much as my brain keeps telling me to step back, my legs continue ignoring it.

I reach up and finger a strand of her hair. "I'm sure Ryan will love it like this." *That's good. Focus on her goal for tonight.* "Remember, you get points every time you say a coherent sentence to him."

"Right. And I lose points every time I violate a rule."

I glue on a smile. "You got it." I check the time on the

computer screen. "I'll be down in about ten minutes. I just need to finish something first."

She reaches up and kisses my cheek. "Thanks again, Jake, for doing this."

I'll swear to my dying day her kiss was all it took to short-circuit my brain once again. That's the only explanation I have for wrapping my arms around her and breathing in her straw-berries-and-cream scented hair. "You're welcome."

Shit. I need to get laid. Maybe that's my problem—I haven't had sex in a while. I'm just redirecting my sexual frustration to Sophie.

I release her and sit down.

She turns to leave. Then does another one-eighty. "I forgot to tell you Gertrude is bringing someone. She wanted to know if that's okay."

"Gertrude's got a date?" It can't be Andrew, even though I've caught him flirting with her a few times.

And for an eighty-five-year-old, he sure knows how to flirt.

Sophie shrugs. "I guess so."

"Must mean she's finally gotten over her thing for Ryan Reynolds. Now she's pursuing men closer to her age....You can tell her it's no problem. We have plenty of food."

Sophie leaves and I get back to work. It takes me a little longer than planned, but I finally finish what I was doing.

What was that? Figuring out how best to implement Sophie's idea of rehabilitating horses with behavioral problems.

I shut off the computer and head downstairs. Sophie, Aubrey, and Violet are in the kitchen, talking and laughing and drinking wine.

"Hey, ladies," I say, walking farther into the room. The chattering comes to an abrupt halt, and their expressions morph into a familiar one. It reminds me of TJ's as a kid...whenever his hand was caught in the cookie jar before dinner. "Already getting into trouble, are you?"

Violet is the first one to wipe the guilt off her face. "No, we're saving that for Granny and her friends." By Granny, she means Grandma Meg.

I chuckle. "God save us from whatever those three have cooked up."

Deacon comes barreling into the kitchen, with Maui hot on his heels. Asgard follows them, looking exhausted from keeping an eye on the energetic duo.

And a moment later, Loki enters the room, meowing at them like a nagging wife.

Violet scoops up the big chubby gray cat and hugs him. "Are they getting into trouble again?"

He gives her a smug look and purrs, basking at her attention.

Deacon plonks his butt on the tile floor. Maui clambers onto his lap and tries kissing Deacon's face. The toddler giggles.

I crouch next to the pair. Mostly to keep on an eye on them and to ensure Maui doesn't bite Deacon.

Welcome to the joys of a teething puppy.

The front doorbell rings.

"I'll get it." I push to stand and call for Maui to heel.

Right—that's still a work in progress.

"I'll watch him," Sophie says and takes my spot next to Deacon.

In the main foyer, I open the front door. And almost groan out loud.

Gertrude doesn't have a date. She brought Kennedy along with her. Grandma Meg and Tilly are standing behind the pair.

Kennedy steps in first, wearing her usual style of body-hugging dress. This one is light blue. She leans in and fake kisses both of my cheeks.

"I take it Copper Creek's charms got to you, and you

changed your mind about returning to New York?"

She laughs. "I'd hardly say that. I just decided to extend my visit for a few more weeks, so I can spend extra time with Granny. Believe me, I'm ready to get back to the excitement of big city life." Her gaze scans my body and lands on my package...as if to say big city life isn't the only thing she's ready to get back to.

I know I said earlier that I need to get laid soon, but that won't be happening tonight. Not with Kennedy.

And not with Sophie around.

Yes, I'm aware Sophie and I aren't dating, but somehow the idea of fucking Kennedy—or any other woman—feels like I'm cheating on Sophie.

Which is fucked up thinking in and of itself.

I wave the group into the house and direct them to the kitchen. I barely have a chance to join them before the doorbell rings again.

Maui bounds into the foyer and barks.

"No barking, Maui. Sit."

That goes down well since I have no treats to reward him with. And he knows it. I might as well have asked him to calculate a complex math equation.

"Maybe we should place you in your crate for now," I tell him. He gazes up at me with his happy puppy expression and stays put.

I open the door and let in the next group of guests. And so continues my stint as the ranch's butler. I barely get to leave my station before the doorbell rings again.

The last guest to arrive is Ryan.

With a tall, pretty brunette wearing a short red skirt and white halter top.

Oh, shit.

Sophie and I hadn't considered that he'd bring a date.

A date who doesn't look familiar.

Maybe she's from Golden Falls.

"Jake, Violet was wondering—" Sophie starts to say, entering the foyer.

At the abrupt halt to her sentence, I twist around. She's staring at Ryan and his date, mouth hanging open.

She quickly recovers and smiles. The woman could become an actress. You'd never guess from her expression that she's hurt at how quickly Ryan has already moved on and is dating someone else.

And damned if I don't ache to take her into my arms and do whatever I can to distract her.

I'd even kiss her if that would help.

"Hey, Sophie." Ryan gestures for his date to enter. "Bailey, this is Jake Daniels and—"

"You're TJ's brother?" she asks in breathless excitement.

I nod. *Shit*, I hope she isn't one of the girls TJ screwed around with back when he was single. That would make things slightly awkward when it comes to Violet.

"Wow, you're just as hot as he is."

"Bailey." Ryan's tone resembles that of a mother scolding her son for an inappropriate comment, but there's also affection and amusement in it. "You have to excuse my sister. Her manners are appalling. We'll blame that on her living in New York City for so long."

I glance at Sophie. She's busy staring at Bailey, but relief is now sitting squarely on her shoulders.

"Bailey, this is Sophie," Ryan says. "She's the ranch's horse trainer."

"It's nice to meet you." Sophie extends her hand to the girl.

Bailey shakes it and grins. "So you're the horse whisperer my brother told me about. I don't suppose you know a trick or two to make him less overly protective?" She backhands him on the chest.

Sophie laughs, still looking at Bailey. "I'm afraid not. Horses aren't the same as men. You can't train men the same way...or at all."

"So they don't respond to the whip the same way a horse does, huh?" Something about the way Bailey says it makes me think she's not referring to the whip used for training horses.

She's thinking more along the lines of BDSM.

The thought is echoed by the way her gaze returns to me. It trails down my body as she slowly licks her lower lip.

Oh, Christ.

"What was Violet wondering?" I ask Sophie, just for an excuse to change the direction of the conversation.

"If you've seen the brie baker."

The brie baker in question belonged to my grandmother.

I direct everyone to follow me to the kitchen, where I grab the brie baker and escort the group outside to the patio.

TJ is manning the grill with Violet as his assistant. The picnic table has been covered with a cloth, every available inch filled with food the girls whipped up. A few people also contributed to the selection.

Including Tilly with her deviled eggs.

Ryan and Bailey head over to Aubrey's group.

"You do understand that you don't get points for talking to Ryan's sister while you're avoiding eye contact with him, right?" I ask Sophie.

"I'm just warming up. Don't worry, I've got this, Jake." She lets out a long exhalation. "I think." The last part is mumbled under her breath. "But you do realize it's gonna be hard for me to flirt with him in front of his sister?"

Right, as if she needs *that* added pressure.

"You don't have to worry about that. Somehow she doesn't come off as the type who hangs out with her brother at parties. See what I mean?" I chuck my chin toward Bailey...who is wandering over to the barbecue.

"Didn't Ryan say his sister was crushing on TJ when your

brother was on *Cowboy Most Wanted*?" Sophie asks.

"Do you think he's told her yet about Violet?"

We watch the action unfold—the way you watch a cop hand out a ticket to a driver caught speeding. You can't help it.

Grinning and fanning herself, Bailey says something to TJ.

"What is she doing?" I ask Sophie. "It's not like it's hot out. And she's bouncing like she has to take a whiz."

Sophie snickers. "She's probably fanning herself so she doesn't pass out. And the bouncing is because she's fangirling."

I snort a laugh. "At least you don't do those things around Ryan."

Until now, Violet was talking to Tilly and hadn't noticed Bailey. Tilly walks away, and Violet turns back to TJ at the same moment Bailey throws her arms around his neck. Her large tits press against his chest.

"And you definitely don't do that to Ryan every time you see him," I add. "So from where I'm standing, Soph, you're doing great in the Ryan department."

Speaking of Ryan, he's busy talking to Aubrey. He hasn't even noticed his sister's reaction to my brother.

"Should we do something?" Sophie asks, possibly because Violet looks confused. It's as if she's deliberating whether she should say something to the woman who is zealously molesting her fiancé.

"Nope, TJ's doing great without our help." I chuckle.

"Ohmigod, I can't believe it's you, TJ." Bailey's voice is loud enough for everyone in a ten-mile radius to hear. "I can't believe you didn't end up with Natalie in the end."

Ryan looks over his shoulder and shakes his head like you do when you're mentally talking to yourself.

"Too bad we don't have any popcorn for the show," I say. Sophie giggles. "Okay, after that, your inability to speak in coherent sentences doesn't seem so bad. So how about once he's peeled his sister off TJ, you go talk to him?"

"Okay." Then under her breath she chants, "I can do this. I can do this. I can do this."

"Attagirl. I hear repeating your mantra a thousand times always helps." I grin at her.

That gets me a smack on the arm.

"Hey, no abusing your fairy godfather. You might damage my wings." I exaggerate brushing off the spot where she hit me.

Sophie rolls her eyes.

Ryan manages to remove his sister from my brother without surgical equipment being necessary and points to Violet. He then says something to both women.

Smiling, Violet waves at Bailey. TJ wraps his arms around his fiancée's waist, pulling her to him, his love for her unmistakable.

Sophie tosses back the last of her wine, then tops it up with the open bottle on the table. "All right. I'm ready." She steps forward. I stay put.

She swivels back to me. "Aren't you coming?"

"I was just gonna watch from here."

She grabs my wrist. "No, you have to come with me. You'll keep me from making a fool of myself."

The last part of the sentence goes by in a haze, my mind still stuck on when she said, "Come with me."

I would love to *come* with her.

Come inside her.

Come on her breasts.

Even have her come on my face.

She tugs on my arm, snapping me out of my inappropriate fantasy.

We join Ryan and Bailey, with Sophie practically clinging to me for dear life. And cutting off the circulation in my arm.

As we get closer, she lets go of my arm. I shake it, attempting to be inconspicuous, attempting to get the blood flowing again.

"So how are you enjoying your stay in Copper Creek?" Sophie asks Bailey. She quickly glances at Ryan before returning her attention back to his sister.

Nice try, sweetheart, but you don't get points for that.

Bailey gives me the same once-over she gave me when she found out I was TJ's brother. The one where she's imagining me naked. "I like it. Very much. It's very...scenic." Her gaze shifts to Sophie. "Have you lived here all your life?"

"No, I grew up in Great Falls."

Talk to Ryan, too, I silently tell Sophie. *And goddamn, look at him when you talk to him this time.*

Clearly mind reading is not her superpower. "I moved here after Jake and his brothers offered me a job."

Her gaze briefly flicks to Ryan before returning to his sister.

I cough, hoping she gets my message to talk *to* him.

At least she doesn't have a deficit in points. She's not avoiding him. That's a start.

Taking my hint, Sophie says to Ryan, "Jake I and went to college. Same." She swigs back a healthy mouthful of wine.

A grin forms on Bailey's face, and she tries to hide it behind her fist.

"What did you study in college, Jake?" Ryan asks. "The same thing as Sophie?"

At least he understood what she attempted to say. There's hope for them yet.

"No. Business. I figured it was a good idea for running the ranch."

"But he could have been an astronomer," Sophie tells them. Well, mostly tells Bailey. "He's incredibly smart."

Bailey's head tilts to the side. "Ah, so you're the hot geek type. Have you ever thought of moving to New York City?"

A hand lands on my lower back. "Jake, honey. Can I speak to you for a moment?" Kennedy asks.

I glance at Sophie to check if she's okay with me leaving her alone with Ryan. Well, semi-alone.

Who am I kidding? She's an intelligent woman who doesn't need me playing fairy godfather twenty-four seven.

Besides, what do momma birds do when they're teaching their babies to fly? They push them out of the nest.

Do the babies go splat against the concrete?

Not at all. They fly, just like they're meant to.

Sophie is capable of talking to good-looking men. She just needs a little nudge, like the baby bird.

"I won't be long," I tell her, then follow Kennedy into the house.

She keeps going until we're in the living room. No one else is in the house. They're all outside.

She glances around the massive room. The huge stone fireplace. The numerous windows overlooking the mountains. The overhead support beams with the matching dark honey-colored ceiling and floor. The iron chandelier. The dark-green couch forming an L-shape in the middle of the room.

"Nice place." This is the first time she's been here. We went to her house the two times we hooked up.

"What did you want to discuss with me, Kennedy?"

"I need you to do me a favor."

"What kind of favor?" Suspicion marks my tone like a horse being led to the glue factory.

"It's about Gertrude. I need you to keep an eye on her. Especially when it comes to Tilly and Meg. Did you know they tried to sign up for skydiving lessons?"

TJ had told me something about that. "I heard they weren't allowed to do it because they exceeded the max age limit."

"Thank God for that. But the three of them are operating under some silly notion that because their time on this earth is limited—Granny's words, not mine—they have to complete their bucket list."

"Have you seen their bucket list?" In other words, what

crazy things will I have to save them from?

"No, but I heard rumors about it at the senior center the other day. Apparently the list is legendary there."

"I can imagine. But what exactly are you expecting me to do about it? Get Austin to put her on house arrest until the day she dies?"

Because while I can see him doing that to Grandma Meg—his grandmother—I can't see him doing that to all three women.

Kennedy chuckles. "Good luck with that. Those three might be in their eighties, but they have the mentality of a sixteen-year-old sneaking out to see her boyfriend."

"Good point."

"I'm not expecting miracles, Jake. I'm just hoping that if you hear any rumors of Granny and her gang being up to no good—the kind of 'no good' that could get them into a lot of trouble or hurt—you'll do whatever you can to stop them."

So basically, I've just been promoted from fairy godfather to guardian angel. Hopefully it comes with added benefits.

Like hazard pay—because once Grandma Meg, Gertrude, and Tilly discover I'm supposed to be curtailing their plans to go out in style, I could be in danger.

Note to self: don't eat their homemade goodies.

I'd rather not find out the hard way that they'd slipped laxatives into the batter.

"I'll do what I can. I don't want anything bad to happen to those three any more than you do. But I can't promise miracles."

Or even a money-back guarantee.

Not that there's money involved for my new services.

Maybe I could get business cards made up—complete with a kickass fairy godfather wearing killer wings and a tilted halo.

"That's all I can ask." She flashes me an I-owe-you-one smile...and her gaze drops to my package again.

13

———

Kennedy takes a step forward. I take one back, narrowly missing the corner of the couch.

"Granny's mentioned a few times that Meg is bemoaning the fact that neither you nor Noah is ever going to give her grandchildren."

Not that they would actually be Grandma Meg's biological grandchildren—more like her pseudo-grandchildren.

"At least TJ is willing to do his part to make up for our deficit in the kid department," I point out. Which is a good thing. Her grandson Austin is as interested in settling down as Noah and I are. TJ and Violet will have to make up for his grandchild deficit, too.

Kennedy laughs. "TJ's going to be very busy keeping up with her grandchild demands." She steps forward again. "I can't stop thinking about the last time we fucked. I thought we were pretty amazing together."

I remember it that way as well. Unlike Sophie with her one-time lay, Kennedy is experienced. She knows what she likes, and she knows how to give it as good as she gets.

104

Those are the women I prefer—especially when they aren't interested in a relationship.

But even though that's the type of woman I prefer, a certain beautiful blonde keeps popping into my head. Naked on my bed, hair fanned out. Looking at me with her trusting blue eyes.

I shake the image from my head.

No point going there.

"Like that, is it?" There's a grin in Kennedy's voice the size of the Bitterroot mountain range.

I frown. "Like what?"

"There's someone else."

I grunt. "There's no one else."

She cocks her head to the side like a cat deciding between toying with her prey or pouncing on it. "Maybe you aren't ready to admit it to yourself yet, but there's definitely someone. And for the record, she's a lucky girl."

You know what they say about people who protest? The more they protest something isn't true, the more truth there is to it.

Keeping this in mind, I use the only solution I can think of.

I don't say anything at all.

On that topic.

"We should go back outside before anyone gets the wrong idea."

She grins at me. "You mean like the woman you're in love with?"

I inwardly groan and start walking.

Kennedy follows me, her heels clicking on the hardwood floor. "Can I guess who she is?"

I pick up my pace. "There is no one. I wasn't interested in having a girlfriend when you lived here, and that hasn't changed."

"You're no fun." Her tone holds a pout as real as a counterfeit dollar bill.

I head for the double French doors leading to the kitchen. "And don't go 'round telling people that I like someone when it's not true. The last thing the busybodies need is you giving them something new to obsess over."

Like when people were speculating if Lizzy Mae Curtis was pregnant after she had gained some weight while on her honeymoon.

By the time I return outside, I've been in the house long enough to have quickly fucked Kennedy. But I can't tell from the slight frown on Sophie's face if she's thinking the same...or if her disappointment has more to do with how things are going with Ryan.

On my way to her, I stop at the grill to check on TJ and the food.

He flips a hamburger. "So you and Kennedy, huh? Thought you weren't the kind of guy who did the same girl more than once. Twice if she's really good."

"God, men are such pigs," Violet says. If eye-rolling in the tone were an Olympic event, the judges would have given her a perfect ten.

"One, I'm not a pig. I'm your fiancé, who you love dearly. And two, as you know, I'm a one-woman man."

"Now you are." She backhands TJ's chest. "But that's only because I've tamed you."

He wraps his arms around her waist and pulls her to him. I expect him to tell her he's untamable, like a wild stallion. Because that's what I would say.

That's what the old TJ would've said.

But instead, the new TJ—the TJ who is engaged—says, "And there's no one I'd rather be tamed by than you."

And because that's clearly not enough for them, they gaze at each other like nobody else exists.

Normally, Noah and I walk away whenever they're like this —which is a frequent occurrence with these two.

This time I don't.

"You can get your heads out of the gutter when it comes to me and Kennedy," I tell them. "Nothing happened between us, and nothing's gonna happen. That's all in the past."

TJ miraculously drags his attention away from Violet. "Then why did you guys disappear inside?"

"So she could ask me to keep an eye on Gertrude. She's worried about the bucket list her grandmother, Grandma Meg, and Tilly are working on."

"Can't say I blame her." Violet looks pointedly at the three women in question. "Those three are scheming about something. Austin and I just haven't figured out what it is yet."

"And that's the only reason you and Kennedy went inside?" TJ asks.

"What's with all the brotherly concern about who I bang?"

He flips another burger. "No reason in particular."

I'm not buying it. He's never given a damn about who I fuck before now.

But since I don't give two shits about his sudden need to parent me on my sex life, I don't push him for the real answer.

Asgard is sitting near the grill, giving TJ his infamous puppy-dog eyes. He's hoping a hamburger or hot dog will heroically jump off the burning grill, surrendering its life to make his stomach happy.

It's his typical expression whenever we use the barbecue.

I scratch him behind the ear. "No luck yet, huh?"

He whimpers his answer. I laugh.

"You need any help with the food or anything?" I glance over at Sophie. Aubrey has joined her and Ryan, along with a few other friends, including Brianna from the vet clinic. Bailey is talking to Austin. He's nodding. She's smiling in full-out flirt mode.

"No, we're good," Violet says. "The food's almost ready."

I stride toward Sophie's group, but I'm brought up short when Bailey steps in front of me.

"Jake, can I talk to you for a second?"

Apparently this seems to be the trend for tonight—women wanting to talk to me, preventing me from keeping an eye on Sophie. A coach can't do a good job if he's unable to watch the game and see what skills the players struggle with.

"Sure, what's up?" I ask.

"I was hoping you can help me with something."

"With what?"

But instead of answering me like I was expecting, she reaches up and plants her mouth on mine.

It's a quick kiss. She pulls away before I can react.

My gaze immediately shifts to Sophie. By the time I look back at Bailey, she's gone. I mentally shrug off the kiss and join Sophie's group by the wooden trellis covered with vines. Kennedy is also with them.

She leans closer to me, her mouth only inches from my ear. "I guess that answers my question. And no, it's not Ryan's sister who you're in love with." She chuckles what could almost be an evil cackle—but that too might be my imagination. "But don't worry, I won't spill your precious secret."

I could almost groan out loud. Kennedy hasn't changed much since we were kids. One bored Kennedy equals a shitload of trouble.

For me.

"I have no idea what you're talking about," I growl back, my voice low enough so no one else hears me.

"What is Broadway like?" Brianna asks Kennedy, unknowingly distracting the redhead from her mind games. Distracting her before she gives me another reason to strangle her.

"It's a magical place," Kennedy says. "There's no other location like it on earth."

Sophie's face breaks into a smile, eyes sparkling with excitement. "You mean like Disneyland?"

One night during our senior year of college, while we were celebrating with tequilas, she'd confessed to me that she'd always dreamed of going there.

I don't remember what we were celebrating, but I do remember the Disneyland thing.

"Much better than Disneyland," Kennedy says. "There are stars everywhere. Real stars. Not the wannabe actors and actresses who play the themed characters at the Disney parks."

Personally, I think the only real stars are the ones in the sky.

Sophie glances at me and her lips slide up to one side, as if she's aware of what I'm thinking because she knows me that well.

I itch to ask her how things went with Ryan, but I doubt she can interpret my raised eyebrows—the eyebrows asking if she has talked to him yet.

Rather than shifting my gaze from Sophie's lips, I linger on them longer than necessary. The memories torment me: how she tasted, the echo of her lips against mine, how the kiss left her breathless.

I tear my gaze away. *No more thinking about her lips, dumbass,* I remind myself. *Or even looking at them.*

"Have you ever been to Disneyland?" I ask Ryan, the words spilling out before I have a chance to hold them back.

Deep down, a part of me doesn't want him to know about Sophie's dream of going there one day. It's the special secret between us I don't wish to share.

Unfortunately, that part doesn't have much control over my mouth.

Or rather my brain. My mouth is still busy fantasizing about Sophie's kiss.

"No, can't say I have," Ryan says. "Have you?"

"Yes, once. When I was ten years old." Which Sophie

already knows about. "It really is a magical place. At least it was back then."

Yes, I'm man enough to admit that.

I'm also man enough to admit, "Noah was especially taken by it. And the princesses. He made my parents take him to each one to get a signature."

I say it as Noah joins us.

"What can I say? Even back then, I appreciated the beautiful ladies. Although now I prefer them less fake and sparkly. Anyway, TJ sent me to tell you the food is ready."

Everyone heads to the picnic table. Before Sophie has a chance to join them, I pull her aside. "Are you any closer to winning your prize?"

I know whatever she tells me will be the truth. Lying isn't in her nature.

She nips her lip between her teeth, and for a brief moment I wish it was my teeth doing that to her. That I was the one tugging on her lower lip.

When she doesn't say anything, I give her a little nudge. "Did you attempt to say *anything* to him? And by 'to him,' I mean were you looking at him directly in the eyes and letting him know you're interested in him?"

There are no technicalities on this one. Either she did or she didn't.

"Er, well."

"You didn't, did you?"

"I didn't have a chance. Aubrey joined us after you left with Kennedy, and there's a chance I might've let her do all the talking." Her tone is slightly off at the mention of Kennedy's name.

"Nothing happened between Kennedy and me," I say, feeling the sudden need to clarify.

"That's a relief. Because you weren't gone all that long. I mean, I realize it's called a quickie, but I'd hope you have more stamina than that." A nervous giggle bursts from between her lips.

I move closer to her, my breath brushing against her cheek. "You don't have to worry about me, sweetheart." My voice is low and husky. She inhales softly. "When it comes to fucking, I have plenty of stamina to spare."

Having no idea why I told her that, I pull away in time to see her trace the tip of her tongue along her lower lip. And I come close, once again, to groaning out loud.

I crave to kiss that fine mouth of hers.

Kiss it and savor it. Plunge my tongue inside its sweet heat.

Sorry to disappoint. But that's not happening again in this lifetime. So you might as well get over it.

"That's good to know," she says, her voice rough, her eyes dark. She coughs to clear her throat.

"Do you know what his hobbies are?" I ask, working to get the lesson back on track. "You can always ask questions based on that."

She gives a single nod. "Okay."

"Ask me a question. We'll practice it while everyone's in line, and then you should be able to ask it without any speed bumps."

"Just one question?"

"Yes. Maybe if you can say it to him without any problems, you'll be more confident to ask another one."

She contemplates for a moment. "So, Ryan, what do you do in your free time?"

"That's great. Ask me again."

She does—and I have her repeat it several times.

I pat her shoulder. "You're ready, slugger."

We join the end of the short line at the barbecue and grab our food.

Ryan is standing near the edge of the patio with Grandma Meg, Tilly, and Gertrude. His sister is also there.

"Maybe we should rescue him," I suggest, even though he doesn't look like he needs rescuing. I just figure Sophie might be more comfortable talking to him without the audience.

I get her to practice her question one more time. Again, she nails it.

"Slip in the question as soon as you have a chance," I say as we walk to the group.

"Just the bachelor I need to talk to." Tilly beams at me in a way that puts me on high alert. All right, the bachelor part might have something to with it, too.

"What can I do for you?"

She doesn't answer. She waves Noah over, who is grabbing a beer from the cooler.

He nods and meanders our way. "You wanted to see me?"

"Yes. All three of you, actually. You might have heard that I'm on the committee to help increase tourism to Copper Creek." She puffs out her chest like a proud peacock. "We're working on ways to raise extra money for the marketing. One thing we're doing is organizing a bachelor picnic-basket auction, and this is where you three come in."

The three of us exchange looks. I don't know about Noah or Ryan, but I have no idea what she's talking about.

"Do we want to know what that is?" I finally ask.

"Each participating bachelor will create a picnic lunch. Each basket will then be auctioned off during our special picnic event. The highest bidder not only wins the basket's contents, she gets to eat it with the dreamy bachelor."

"We're not expected to date or marry her after that, are we?" Noah's tone borders on horrified. If it weren't for the part where Tilly is expecting me to also be involved, I would laugh. Tilly's plan is karma for Noah signing TJ up to be a contestant on *Cowboy Most Wanted*, especially since he didn't ask TJ first.

But that's Noah's karma, not mine.

"No, you're not expected to do any of those things. But if you and the lady should hit it off, there's nothing to say you can't date her."

"Are we the only men doing this?" I ask. "Not that I'm saying I will do it."

"Not at all. We're recruiting as many men as possible. Especially the kind of men the women will be eager to bid on. So nice, good-looking men. The more men we have involved, the more money we'll make. And just so you two know"—she levels her gaze at Noah and then me—"you don't have much say in this. I've got enough stories from when you were both little boys that you'd rather didn't go public."

I inwardly groan. I don't doubt she has enough stories to humiliate me for the next ten years.

"You can count me in," Ryan says. "And you don't even have to blackmail me into doing it. I'd love to help out in whatever way I can. Everyone has been friendly and welcoming since I moved here."

"You can count me in, too," Noah says.

Great, which means I don't really have a choice.

Unless I wish to come off as an asshole. "Sure, sign me up as well. When's it for?"

"Saturday, June second." Two weeks from tomorrow.

Ryan's phone rings. He excuses himself for a moment and walks off to take the call. Tilly tells us we'll be hearing from her soon about the auction, then leaves us to rejoin her friends.

"Too bad I won't be around for that," Bailey says. "I wouldn't mind having lunch with a cowboy. Would make a great photo for my Instagram account." She's looking at me when she says it.

Chuckling, Noah slaps me on the back and abandons me to what I'm hoping isn't about to become an awkward situation. With Bailey and Kennedy.

Ryan returns. "I'm sorry, guys, but I need to go. One of the

Scottsdale ranch mares went into labor and she's having complications."

"I hope baby and mother will be okay," Sophie says.

I nod that I agree with her. Scottsdale ranch might be our rivals, but it doesn't mean I want them to lose any horses, especially under circumstances like this.

Ryan does a double take at Sophie and at first, I don't get why. But then it hits me like a ten-ton truck with faulty brakes.

She said a coherent sentence directly *to* him.

Even though I'm her fairy godfather—hired to help her talk to men she's interested in—her newfound success feels like I swallowed a boulder.

And it's weighing my gut down.

Oh, crap.

14

The thing with sports is that when you are learning a new skill, the first few attempts might be an epic fail. You can't quite figure out what the coach is telling you, and your body is content to do its own thing.

With practice, you are eventually able to hit the baseball, score a goal, do a slam dunk. You celebrate because you're positive you'll be the sport's next superstar.

But when you attempt to replicate the results, you're back to square one.

Welcome to Sophie's life when it comes to her new breakthrough.

"Ryan, it nice was seeing me again."

So close.

The corners of his mouth twitch. "You, too, Sophie. I'm sure I'll see you around."

Maybe...but probably not. If things go the way they've been for the past week, she'll go into hiding again.

My job will be to make sure she doesn't.

"You coming?" he asks his sister.

"I can drop her off on my way back to Granny's," Kennedy says.

"That works for me. I'm still having fun here." Bailey winks at me and Kennedy smirks.

Fuck. Why do I have a feeling their new friendship isn't good news for me?

"All right. I'll see you back at the house." And with that, Ryan leaves.

"I need some wine," Sophie says on a sigh and hurries off before I can tell her I'll get her some. Bailey joins her.

"Jake, Jake, Jake," Kennedy says, her voice silky like a spider web. "For someone who doesn't like playing games, why are you playing them with *me*?"

"Again, I have no idea what you're talking about."

She raises an eyebrow. "Don't you? Bailey kissed you and you immediately check Sophie's reaction?"

I snort what I hope is a convincing laugh. "I was checking Ryan's reaction, given that it was his sister who was kissing *me*. The last thing I want is to piss the guy off because he thinks I'm making moves on Bailey...which I'm not."

Good save.

"Well, for the record, you have a better chance with Sophie than she does with Ryan," Kennedy says, completely ignoring my comment. "He might sit more on the introspective side of things, but even he prefers his girlfriends to be able to speak English."

"Hey, Sophie speaks English."

If vultures could smile, I imagine their grin would resemble the one on Kennedy's face. "You know what I mean, Jake. Ryan is a smart man. I mean other than the part where he was dating Shakira Johnson. She was obviously wrong for him. She likes to be the center of attention. Ryan is the opposite. Those two couldn't have been any more like water and oil had they tried."

"What's your point, Kennedy?"

"God, when did you become such an idiot, Jake? Let me make the math easier for you. You and Sophie are close friends. And friends like that usually end up making great lovers. I have a few colleagues who are happily married because they started out as best friends."

"So?" I shrug. "That has nothing to do with Sophie and me. We're just friends and will always be *just* friends. And if she wants to date Ryan or any other guy in Copper Creek, that has nothing to do with you."

"All I'm saying is that you guys should move things to the next level. See where they go. And I can help you if you want." Her smile is hardly reassuring.

In spite of that, I laugh out loud. "*If* I want something to happen between Sophie and me, I'm pretty sure I can figure it out without your help. But thanks for the offer."

"You can't blame me for trying, especially since I've decided to stay in Copper Creek for a few more weeks. This thing between you and Sophie will make things more entertaining. Plus I have another ulterior motive for getting you two together."

"What's that exactly?"

"Granny hopes to be a great-grandmother. And since I'm her only grandchild, the pressure is on me to grant her this."

"What does that have to do with Sophie and me?"

"If you and your brothers start producing lots of kids, Granny will be so busying enjoying them, she won't have time to realize I don't have any."

"Except Noah and I aren't planning to settle down with anyone. So I guess you'll have to talk to TJ and Violet about your scheme. I'm sure they'll be more than happy to help you out." Once they're married and Violet has lifted the sex ban.

Fortunately, Sophie picks that moment to return with two glasses of wine, effectively ending the conversation between Kennedy and me.

She hands one to me.

"Thanks." I take a longer sip than is normally considered acceptable with wine.

"Have fun, you two. But not too much fun." And with that Kennedy strolls off.

"What was that all about?" Sophie asks.

I don't really want to talk about it. Nor do I wish to stick around any longer. "You want to get out of here? Maybe go to the river for a bit?"

"Okay."

We both drain our glasses and bail.

No one calls after us to ask where we're going.

We make it to the edge of the lawn before Sophie reaches down and removes her stilettos. "I swear, I have no idea how some women practically live in these things."

She resumes walking, the shoes dangling from her hand.

"You can't walk all the way to the river barefooted," I point out.

"I'll survive."

I glance back at the patio. No one's paying attention to us, and in another few feet we'll be completely out of view.

I crouch. "Get on. I'll carry you."

She hesitates for only a second before climbing onto my back. Her arms go around my neck and I stand.

"You good there?" I ask.

"Couldn't be better." She breathes against my ear, and an unexpected thrill trembles through me.

I continue walking until we end up on the dirt path that cuts through the wooded area.

Several minutes later, we arrive at the spot by the river where my brothers, myself, and our friends used to hang out when we were kids.

I lower Sophie onto the narrow sandy beach.

The moment her feet touch the ground, she's unbuttoning her dress.

I freeze on the spot, my mouth gaping open. For several seconds, all I'm capable of is staring at her.

"What are you doing?" I ask once I finally locate my voice.

"Getting ready to jump off the tire," she says without pausing for even a second.

When my brothers and I were kids, our grandfather got the idea that hanging a tire from a branch overlooking the river would keep us out of trouble around the ranch. Great in theory—not so much in practice. We still found ways of getting into mischief.

Sophie continues unbuttoning the front of her dress, only stopping once it's open to her waist. The fabric slides apart, revealing her purple bra.

"You do realize the water is cold?" Cold as in, her nipples will freeze off.

"Does this mean you aren't joining me?" Her smile is all kinds of trouble. The kind of trouble that will have me doing anything she asks.

"It's not like I have swim trunks under my jeans."

"Does that mean you're going commando?"

Damn. What was in the wine we finished before coming here? It's making me hear things—because there's no way she asked me that.

"No, I've got boxer briefs on."

She drops her dress to the ground. *Holy fuck*. Her panties match her bra. Her see-through, lacy bra.

My brain commands my head to turn away or for my eyes to close. Neither listens to it.

"You probably shouldn't go into the water, Soph. You're drunk." It's the only explanation I have for why she's doing this.

Or maybe it's because she sees you as nothing more than her friend...her gay friend, Mr. Fairy Godfather.

"I'm buzzed, not drunk," she clarifies.

"Well, I can guarantee as soon as you land in the river, you won't be buzzed anymore. More like numb from the cold."

Her mouth slides into a one-sided grin. "There's nothing wrong with living a little."

I take a step toward her. "Since when did living a little include turning yourself into a popsicle?"

I will my gaze to stay put and not slide south to her tits. It doesn't listen.

The lace obscures a fair portion of her skin, but its strategic placement allows a sneak peek at her pink areola.

And instantly I go hard.

My attention shifts to the river, and I mentally scrub the image from my memory. Or at least try to.

But "try to" fails to solve my current predicament. At this point, even a cold shower would be ineffective.

She doesn't think of you that way, I remind myself.

"Have you figured out who you're taking to Violet and TJ's wedding?" she asks, doing a one-eighty on our conversation.

"I haven't given it any thought." Which is true.

She walks toward the swing.

I follow her. "You're not really jumping from the tire, are you?"

She twists around so she's walking backward. "Why not? I need to learn to take a chance on things. To stop always playing it safe."

"Since when is playing it safe a bad thing?"

"You realize I have no clue what it feels like to have a man go down on me?"

Did I just groan out loud?

"What are you talking about?"

"The one time I had sex, he never went down on me."

That's because he was a goddamn idiot. If I had sex with

her, you can guarantee I'd be eating her out until she was screaming my name.

"So include it on the list of requirements for the next guy you date," I helpfully suggest.

She stops walking. The tire swing is right behind her. "Do you know who Emma Cartwright is?"

I quickly go through the Rolodex in my brain, searching for the name. It doesn't sound familiar. Maybe she was a one-night stand at some point. The benefit of one-night stands is you don't need to remember the girl's name. Just like you don't expect them to remember yours.

Fortunately, Sophie decides to put me out of my recollection misery. "That's my pen name."

"Seriously?" I wasn't even close when I tried to guess it.

"You know what's really sad?" She grabs the tire.

"What's that?"

"I write erotic romances, but I've never had sex anywhere near as hot as what I write. I feel like a fake."

"Do your readers complain that the sex sounds like a phony wrote them?"

"No, I get great reviews about them."

Note to self: Do not look up her books. Do not download them. And do not read them.

All right. That's a complete lie.

Of course I'm going to read what she wrote. I'm a guy. How can I not?

Purely for research, of course.

So I can be supportive.

Yeah, yeah, I know I said that guys don't read romances. But that was before I found out she writes erotic romances.

"But that doesn't mean I don't feel like a fake," she adds. "It just means I've read a lot of great, sexy romances. I've learned from the best."

Don't think about great sex with her. Don't think about great sex with her. Don't think about great sex with her.

She pulls the tire back and jumps onto it, causing the tire to swing forward over the water. At the optimum height, she lets go.

With a shriek.

Probably because she's realizing the water will be fucking cold.

She lands with an epic splash, following the rules of the game my brothers and I dreamed up when we were kids.

She easily scores eight out of ten points.

But that's mostly because the judge is currently sporting a hard-on for her.

Which means only one thing.

With a sigh, I hurriedly remove my clothes, other than my underwear. I grab the tire, and the next thing I know I'm in the fucking freezing water.

But at least my hard-on is no longer an issue.

Right now my cock is cursing worse than a sailor who sat on a thumbtack.

Suck it up, buttercup, I tell it.

I swim back to shore. By the time I arrive, Sophie is standing on the small beach. Her dress clings to her wet body, the white fabric revealing more than it covers.

Which means I'm getting a bird's eye view of her perfect tits. Even the lace bra isn't doing much to camouflage her stiff nipples. Her wet hair is pushed away from her face like a Sports Illustrated Swimsuit model. Teasing. Erotic. Erection-inducing.

Shit.

I stride to where I left my clothes and quickly pull my jeans on.

"Jake, will you kiss me again?"

"Kiss you?" I ask, pulling on a boot, not daring to look at

her. "Didn't I tell you the other day your kisses are fine? You have nothing to worry about."

It's only me who has to worry about what will happen if I kiss her again.

"I know. But I feel like I could use more practice. And since you are my fairy godfather..."

I can't help it—I laugh. "I'm sure Cinderella didn't have that clause in her fairy-godmother contract."

With both boots on, I turn around...and almost land on my ass at the expression on her face. There's a slight desperation to it.

Or maybe that's just how I feel.

Do I crave another kiss? Damn straight I do.

Do I think it's a smart idea to do it?

Not on your life, but that doesn't stop me from being stupid.

Gently cupping her face, I brush my thumb against her cheek. Her gaze is so open, so trusting, it's capable of healing the scar in my chest from my ex-girlfriends' betrayals—if given a chance.

Sophie's eyes are dark and her breath is slightly ragged.

I slowly lean down, giving her a chance to change her mind or for my brain to regain control of my body.

Neither happens.

I lightly press my lips against hers, waiting for her to realize this is a big mistake.

When she doesn't say anything, I shift my hand to cradle the back of her head. My lips part, encouraging hers to do the same.

Her tongue slips into my mouth and glides across my tongue. It feels and tastes as heavenly as it did last time. And a lot better than my memory gave it justice.

My free hand moves to her lower back and I pull her against me. Her wet dress is cold against my bare skin.

I deepen the kiss. Heat flickers where our bodies touch. Flickers and begins to consume me.

I should step away to prevent getting burned, but my body keeps begging for one more moment. Keeps reminding me that this will be my last chance to kiss her. I might as well enjoy it while I can.

Sophie's taut nipples press against my chest, pleading for me to warm them. I move my hand from her lower back and trace my way up along her ribs. She sucks in a soft breath.

Shifting back slightly, I cover her breast with my hand. I'm aware I'm stepping beyond the gray zone when it comes to the company policy....

Who the hell am I kidding?

I was never in the gray zone from the moment I first kissed her. I stepped straight into the I'm-going-to-burn-in-hell zone. Do not pass go. Do not collect a fire extinguisher.

"Is that okay?" My voice teeters on the side of low and husky, ready to go down for the count.

"Yes," she whispers, her tone equally husky. Her beautiful blue eyes continue watching me with the same raw, naked trust as before.

I brush my thumb against her nipple. She whimpers. "How about that?" I ask.

"That's fine, too."

"And what about this?" I pinch her nipple between my thumb and finger.

Fuck, I want to taste her.

She nods, her breaths coming in rapid, shallow pants. "Please show me what it feels like to have a man take my nipple into his mouth."

Warning sirens blare from somewhere in the back of my head. I mentally dismantle them.

I slip the button through the top hole of her dress, a challenge when the fabric is wet. When she doesn't stop me, I continue unbuttoning it. Part of me itches to say, "Fuck it," and rip the dress open the rest of the way.

But I don't—and eventually I get low enough to peel the material away from her breasts and down her arms. She pulls her hands free of the fabric, leaving the dress to gather around her hips.

I brush my thumb over her nipple again, pressing the rough lace against the hard peak. She gasps.

"You like that, huh?" I ask.

"Very much."

Christ, I want to feel just how much she *likes* it. But touching and tasting her nipple is one thing. Running my finger along her pussy to see if she's wet is another.

And since she's only given me permission to suck on her nipples, I won't cross the line further than I have.

I slide her bra straps down her arms, tracing my fingertips along her skin. It's as soft as I imagined it would be.

Goosebumps pebble at my touch. "You're cold."

She shakes her head. "Right now, I'm very warm."

I know what she means. May in the valley isn't particularly hot, but right now it feels like it is.

I unfasten her bra in one easy move. Not wanting to get it dirty, I hold on to it and finally get a good look at her breasts. "God, you're fucking perfect," I say under my breath.

Her breath hitches.

I lean down and swirl my tongue around one of those goddamn perfect nipples. She groans.

I can't believe the one idiot she's ever been with never took the time to worship her beautiful breasts.

A smug voice in my head points out that this is a good thing. She'll remember that I'm the man who made her feel good. The other guy will be nothing more than a fuzzy memory, like a dream when you wake up. Easily forgotten.

Her fingers tangle in my hair, massaging my head, keeping me close.

I take her nipple into my mouth and almost groan at the perfection of it, groan at how right this feels...even when it shouldn't.

I worship the peak, giving it the lavish attention it deserves. While I do that, my hand doesn't stay idle. My fingers tease and pinch the other nipple.

Sophie trembles at my touch. I straighten. "Are you okay?" I ask, my arms around her.

"More than okay," she whispers, voice gritty with need.

It's right then that I realize how much trouble I'm in—the way-over-my-head kind of trouble.

But I don't want to stop....

15

———

ophie smiles at me, her eyes a little unfocused.

I hand her bra back to her. "Not quite the lesson I had planned as your fairy godfather, but I hope it proved useful. As research."

"It was very helpful. Thank you."

"You're welcome. Glad I could be of service. Just let me know if you need any more help in the research department." I wink at her even though I'm kidding.

Mostly.

Helping her doesn't violate the company policies.

Right—I don't believe that either, but I can't find it in me to say no to anything she asks for. If this helps her writing, then it's a sacrifice I'm willing to make.

Surely that's in the employee handbook somewhere. And if it isn't, it should be.

Sophie buttons her dress. I pull on my T-shirt.

I'm not ready to go back to the house yet. And I'm certainly not ready to face Kennedy and Bailey.

Right now I have no idea what those two are up to...or if they're up to anything. And maybe it doesn't matter. Ryan is a big boy. I doubt anything Kennedy says will change his mind about Sophie if he's interested in her.

Unless...he's the kind of man who won't piss on someone else's territory. If he thinks I'm interested in Sophie as more than a friend, he might think twice about asking her out.

Shit.

This means in order to help her win her man, we have to get moving on our lessons. It means the countdown is on for when I'll have even less time with her—because her free time will be spent with Ryan.

At that thought, my stomach clenches, my chest tightens, and my heart feels like a shrinking ray zapped it.

No, no, no. My number one priority is making sure Sophie is happy. That's it. Nothing more. It doesn't matter if she'll have less time for me once they're dating—just as long as she's happy.

I take a deep breath, then I thread my fingers with hers and lead her to the nearby fallen tree trunk. It's perfect for sitting on.

Which is exactly what we do. The world around us is quiet, other than the typical sounds of nature and the occasional splash coming from the river.

"Not that I'm a psychology expert," I say, "but there must be something in your past that caused you to become a basket case around guys you're interested in."

"You're calling me a basket case?"

"You're avoiding the question."

"Technically, you didn't ask one."

"All right, Miss Technically, what happened in your past that turned you into the Sophie who has trouble talking to guys she's interested in?"

She looks away, her gaze focused downstream. Even though I can't fully see her face, I know she's chewing her lip.

"Something happened, didn't it?" I ask. If this wasn't true, her shoulders wouldn't have just slumped with a thousand secrets sitting on them.

"It's not a big deal."

"You know whatever it is, I won't judge you."

She nods, still looking out at the water. "I know." But even then, she doesn't say anything beyond that. She just sits there.

But I can be patient. So I wait her out—knowing she'll tell me once she's ready.

After a minute she releases a long breath. "You won't drop this unless I tell you, will you?"

"You know me well."

It's only then that she looks at me. "That's right, I do. Okay, since you're not going to drop it...it happened back in high school. I was what one would call an awkward teen—braces, skinny, painfully shy. I was happier around horses than around people." She smiles at me, but it's withered at the edges at best. "I just related to them better."

So far, she sounds nothing like the Sophie I know and care about—other than the part about how well she relates to horses.

"Because I was skinny and practically boobless, I preferred oversized sweat shirts and jeans. They saved me from dealing with the boys who thought making fun of me was a sport."

Did I mention boys are dicks?

Well, they are.

"But despite that, I used to read romances. They made me believe that one day I would meet that magical guy who would fall in love with me just the way I was. Maybe if I had read something like *Game of Thrones* instead, things would have turned out differently." She chuckles. But it's not a happy laugh. It's a God-I'm-such-an-idiot sound.

"During my senior year, I crushed on a guy in my English lit class. But then who didn't? Not to sound like a cliché or anything...he was the school's starting quarterback. And to top it off, his girlfriend was the head cheerleader.

"He was a nice guy. His girlfriend was another matter. When she entered the girls' bathroom, the girls in there couldn't bail fast enough. Rumor had it one got stuck in the bathroom window while trying to escape."

Sophie shakes her head, caught up in the memory. "At one point, Caleb dumped his girlfriend...or she dumped him. After that, he became even nicer to me. He flirted with me, did everything he could to make me believe he was interested.

"One day I got it into my head that I should ask him out. I mean, why not? He seemed to like me. He said yes, and I probably spent the rest of the day glowing because of it. We were supposed to see a movie together. He couldn't pick me up in time for it because he had practice, so he told me to wait for him outside the theater building."

Sophie continues to stare out at the water. It's as if I'm not even here. She's telling her story to the breeze.

"I didn't tell anyone about the date—not even my best friend. I had told her about the flirting, and she'd gotten mad at me. She said he was just playing me for a fool." Her tone twists into something mangled, but there's still enough strength in her words for her to keep going. Although at this point, I'm not sure I even want to hear the rest. I already know it doesn't end well.

"Because I didn't own any dresses, I borrowed one from my mom. It didn't fit me like it did her, but it was pretty and it made me feel like a princess. I even left my hair down.

"I borrowed my parents' truck and drove to the theater. As planned, I stood outside and waited and waited and waited. The show started and I was still waiting, convinced that maybe he got caught up at practice. I even texted him. He never replied.

"I eventually realized that he had stood me up. My best

friend had been right. I was about to return to my parents' truck when a blue one I didn't recognize pulled up. Several guys from school were standing in the back. Caleb was sitting in the passenger seat.

"The boys began laughing at me. Caleb leaned out of the window and told me he could never date a girl who reeked of horses and shit. That's when the boys began scooping manure from the back and flinging it at me." Her voice cracks like a fragile piece of china dropped on the tile floor. And each word feels like a sharp jab to the gut—relentless in its mission.

A tear escapes her eye, followed by another and another. I cover her hand with mine and thread our fingers together.

"I couldn't get away. It was like the manure was coming at me from all directions. Some landed on my face. My mom's dress was ruined. It was in my hair. It was everywhere. Then the next thing I knew, there was a screech of tires and I was left standing there alone.

"I couldn't drive home in my parents' truck. Not in the state I was in. And I definitely couldn't call them or my best friend to come get me. So I had to walk the ten miles home."

Fuck. Fuck. Fuckity-that-would-explain-everything-fuck.

I shove my fingers through my hair to keep from introducing my fist to a tree. Because of some shit-headed teen, the sweet and amazing woman next to me struggles talking to guys she's interested in. A shit-headed teen who ganged up on her with his limp-dick asshole buddies.

"Were they punished for what they did?" I ask.

She shakes her head again.

"Why the fuck not?" I keep my tone gentle despite the profanity. What happened wasn't her fault.

"My parents were beyond upset when they found out what the guys did. They couldn't believe I hadn't called them, because no matter what, they would've come for me."

That doesn't surprise me. I've met her parents. They're

funny and smart and caring like she is. Her mother would rather smash the car than drive over even a caterpillar.

"They let me stay home for the next two days because my feet were hardly in a state to walk anywhere. Turns out, walking ten miles in sandals isn't a smart thing to do."

"I can imagine."

"I returned to school after that. But by then, everyone had seen the photos of what I looked like covered in manure. No matter where I went, people would laugh at me and call me horse-shit face. My best friend tried to stand up for me, but people started picking on her because of that. I ended up bailing school and went to the stable where I worked part-time. That's where my parents found me hours later—cleaning the stables, my cheeks tear-stained. If the owners had given me a toothbrush, I would've gladly scrubbed the stables with it, just for the distraction.

"They were the ones who called my parents. They were concerned something had happened to me. My parents called the school, but the principal came up with some bullshit excuse as to why he couldn't do anything. I finished the last two months of my senior year at home, studying for my GREs."

"So that's why your sentences go wonky whenever you talk to a guy you're interested in?"

"Maybe. I'm not the same girl I was back then. I'm more confident, except for when it comes to guys I'm interested in. It's like deep down I can't let go of the humiliation from that night. Maybe somewhere in my mind, I'm convinced he's really Caleb returning to hurt me again.

"I guess my inability to speak coherent sentences is like my own protective force field." She laughs, the sound more on the amused side of the fence than the side with the bitter beauty queen has-beens.

"You do realize Ryan is nothing like that asswipe from high school, right? He would never hurt you like that."

Because I, for one, would beat his ass if he tried.

Or I could arrange an accident. My horse Orion likes Sophie. I'm positive he would help out.

She smiles. "I know. But this has been going on for so long, I'm not sure I can stop talking that way. Maybe they can do brain surgery for cases like mine." She wipes her face dry with the back of her hand.

Her wet eyelashes sparkle in the early evening sunlight. Even after telling the most gut-wrenching story, she's still beautiful. The tears only heighten her beauty—the same way morning dew turns everything fresh and magical.

Her gaze drops to my lips and holds there for the longest moment. When she looks back at me, I see it in her eyes. She wants me to kiss her again.

She gives an almost imperceptible nod, as if she knows I'm deliberating the pros and cons in my head.

Pros

1. She wants me to...and I'll do anything for her.

2. I long to kiss her—and keep on kissing her (but that's a given).

3. I could help her for a moment to forget the past I made her dredge up, all because I thought it would fix the problem.

4. Because maybe if I kiss her enough I'll finally get her out of my system...which is the right thing to do.

Cons

1. It's against our company policy—a policy I've already violated a few times.

2. ?

3. ?

4. ?

So far the Pro side is winning, but I'm sure it will be a close competition. Eventually.

Remember how I said I was a patient guy? Confession time. I'm not as patient or as smart as I should be.

I lower my lips to hers. I don't bother being gentle this time —beyond the first teasing kiss. This time it's hard and possessive. It's sublime.

Our tongues fight for domination, tasting, feeling, challenging. Sophie fists my T-shirt with both hands and pulls me closer. I give her everything she needs to help her forget the past. That dumbass is probably now nothing more than a washed-out NFL wannabe. With a beer gut and a receding hairline. Dreaming about the glory days.

A small fire ignites low in my gut. I keep kissing Sophie, adding more fuel to the flames. I cup the back of her head. But touching her this way isn't enough. I crave to be inside her— and I'm not just talking about my cock. I long for so much more than what we've been to each other up till now.

Company policy be damned.

Sophie pulls back slightly. Our panted breaths mingle and become one.

Her gaze explores my face for a moment. "Make love to me, Jake. I want to know what it feels like. I write erotic romance and I still don't know what it feels like when a man gives you an orgasm. I'm guessing it's not quite the same as a do-it-yourself job."

Usually I'm not a fan of the phrase "make love." Unless you're in love and you're actually making love, call it what it really is. Fucking.

But my usual allergic reaction to the term doesn't make its presence known when Sophie says it. No warning alarms blare.

"Are you sure about this?" I ask. "If I say yes, will that wreck our friendship?"

Have you ever watched *When Harry Met Sally*?

No, I didn't watch it voluntarily. It's one of Sophie's favorite movies. So I've seen it at least once—that I'm admitting to.

Anyway, Harry claims that men can't be friends with women. Why? Because the guy will always be thinking about having sex with her.

And it's true. For the most part.

On top of that, the moment you have sex with a female friend, things change. Expectations change.

Friendships are never the same again.

"We won't let it change anything," Sophie says, answering my question.

"Are you positive?"

"Absolutely." She starts pushing up the hem of my T-shirt.

"What are you doing?" I look pointedly at her hands, then back to her face.

She tilts her head to the side. "You don't want to be naked for this?"

I cover her hands with mine. "Not this way, Sophie. Your first time was crappy. I'm not letting your second time be just as crappy. I mean, how will that help you as a writer?"

"Okay, so what's the plan?"

"We're not doing it here. Not that I'm against outdoor sex. Assuming no mosquitos are around." Pounding into a woman isn't quite the same when you've got a hungry mosquito playing target practice with your ass. "And for the record, I also have nothing against shower sex, counter sex, sex in the back of the truck. But I do have to say no to sex on the sand. I don't think you have to ask why."

Sophie laughs, the sound neither nervous nor shy. "So...are we really doing this?"

Yes, we're really doing this.

I just hope it doesn't screw up our friendship.

I just hope it doesn't fuck up so much more.

16

In an ideal world, Sophie and I would've magically appeared in my room once we decided we were going to fuck.

But in the real world, we still had to walk back to the house —where a few stragglers were hanging out on the patio. She and I had already vanished long enough to leave some people wondering what we'd been up to. No need to feed the rumor mill by disappearing into the house together.

"Sophie," Grandma Meg says, "I haven't seen much of you this evening."

"That's probably because you've spent it with your rambunctious great-grandson," I say with a laugh. "I'm surprised he hasn't worn you out yet."

She huffs and fists her hands on her hips. "I'm not *that* old, Jake. I still have plenty of fire left in me for you and your brothers to give me a truckload of little ones to grandmother." The spark in her eyes claims she's about as irritated by my comment as honey is spicy.

And I don't doubt the part about her having plenty of fire in her. She's like the Energizer Bunny of grandmothers. Her batteries aren't fresh from the package, but they've got plenty of power left in them.

"So what do you think of Copper Creek's new vet?" she asks Sophie.

"He's very nice."

"Yes, he *is* nice. But I've also noticed he's quite the hottie."

My mouth slides up to one side. "Isn't he a little young for you?"

She playfully backhands me in the chest.

"Ouch." I rub the spot in mock pain. "You've been eating your Wheaties again." The breakfast of champions.

"I was thinking more like he's quite the hottie for our sweet Sophie." She smiles at the woman I'm lusting over...and I almost groan out loud. Talking about Ryan is the last thing I want to do.

"He's very nice," Sophie says, stuck in repeat mode.

"Well, I'm going to see to it that something special starts up between you two. I think he would make a good husband for you."

Where's duct tape when you need it?

Not that I would actually use it on Grandma Meg, but the temptation is there if she doesn't stop talking about Ryan. Especially when she's scheming to hook those two up.

Right—because thirty minutes ago you weren't interested in being anything more than friends with Sophie, an annoying voice in my head says. *And now that you're a horny bastard who can't wait to get her into your bed, you don't want her to end up with Ryan—the reason you're playing her fairy godfather to begin with.*

I remind the voice that it's not like that and mentally give it the finger.

"Oh, you don't need to worry about that." Sophie says it faster than a rabbit chased by a hungry coyote. "I'm sure if Ryan and I are meant to be, things will work out without you helping us."

"Nonsense. Sometimes these things just need a little extra push in the right direction. Men can be so dense at times." Grandma Meg looks at me. "Present company excluded, of course."

I nod my head in thanks while at the same time mentally zipping her mouth shut.

Unfortunately, mentally zipping someone's mouth shut isn't enough to keep them from talking.

"They miss all the obvious clues that a woman is interested in them," Grandma Meg continues. "They have to be batted over the head with it. And that's where the girls and I come in."

Yep, I'd say the panicked expression on Sophie's face is more than justified.

And why does it feel like Grandma Meg has inadvertently fired me as Sophie's fairy godfather? Maybe I should consult with my union rep.

Assuming fairy godfathers have a union.

And a rep.

Sophie gives her a nervous smile. "You really don't need to do that."

"Meg," Tilly says, approaching us. "Are you ready to leave yet? We don't want to miss the beginning of *The Amazing Adventure*."

Grandma Meg checks her watch. "Oh, heavens. Is it really that time already?"

They aren't the only ones who leave a few minutes later. Gertrude and Kennedy do the same, taking Ryan's sister with them.

After the last guest departs, my brothers and I—along with Violet and Sophie—put the food away and load the dishwasher. As we work, we keep an eye on Deacon while he plays with Maui and Asgard.

The energetic puppy rushes around the kitchen, chasing the ball that Deacon rolls across the floor. His excited yaps make the little boy giggle and he tries to imitate him. His toddler version of a bark causes us all to laugh.

TJ wraps his arm around his fiancée, her back against his chest. He whispers something in her ear and she laughs softly. If I were a betting man, I'd say he's trying to convince her to give up her plan to be a born-again virgin for their wedding.

She gives him a quick kiss over her shoulder and shakes her head.

That's right—looks like someone still has to wait a few more weeks before getting laid.

I chuckle.

But seeing them like this makes me wish I could do the same with Sophie. I want to find out what it feels like to have her in my arms that way. To have her sweet ass pressed against my length.

"What do you say, Deacon?" TJ says. "Time to hit the trail and for me to return you and your mommy home?" Their home, for the time being, is an apartment near Grandma Meg's house.

At least until the wedding. After that, this place will be a little more crowded. Fortunately, it's a huge house.

Fortunately, Noah and I have no plans to get married.

Deacon hugs Asgard good-bye and waves at Maui. "Bye-bye, Owie." Then he walks over to TJ and stretches his arms above his head. "Daddy, up."

Violet beams at the pair. TJ might not be Deacon's biological father, but you would never guess it. The similarities between the two are amazing. Only Violet knows what his real father looks like.

Deacon rests his head on TJ's shoulder.

"Bye, Deacon." Sophie waves at him. He waves back. And with that, Deacon, TJ, and Violet head out.

That leaves Noah, Sophie, and me in the kitchen.

"I'm meeting with friends at Joe's," Noah says. "Either of you wanna join me?"

Which means he'll be gone for a few hours. The same with TJ. Translation: Sophie and I will have the house to ourselves.

"No, I'm good," I reply.

"Yeah, me too," Sophie adds.

"You want to stay and watch a movie for a bit?" I ask her. The question is more for Noah's benefit. It's not like I'm planning to stick around long enough to finish it.

"Great idea."

"Have fun. Don't do anything I wouldn't do." Noah chuckles and walks out of the kitchen.

"That leaves things wide open," I murmur so only Sophie can hear.

She laughs.

Since we'd already taken Maui outside not long ago to relieve himself, Sophie and I settle down in front of the large-screen TV in the entertainment room. While we wait for Noah to leave for Joe's, we pretend to discuss what movie we want to watch.

Only, he's not in that big of a rush to depart.

Sophie and I pick a movie we've already seen and sit next to each other on the couch. Her strawberry-and-cream scent invades my space, tormenting me. I itch to pull her onto my lap...but I don't.

I patiently watch the movie as I strain to hear when Noah leaves.

And the moment he does, it takes all but five seconds before I have Sophie straddling my lap...and then we're kissing. I lean my head back on the couch, encouraging her to deepen the kiss.

My hands move to her hips and continue up to her breasts. I cup them in my palms and knead them.

Sophie is busy with her own exploration. And by exploration, I mean she's rocking her hips and grinding her core against my hardening length.

Holy shit. My cock hardens to the point where it's almost painful.

A small bark pulls me from the moment. Maui and Asgard are watching us, their heads tilted to the side.

"Sorry guys, but we're not a peep show," I tell them. They keep watching us.

"Maybe we should continue this in my room," I tell Sophie, then turn to the two dogs sitting next to the couch. "*Without* the audience."

Asgard gives us a doggy grin.

Besides, what I have planned for the next few hours is better done in my room. I don't want to risk either brother coming home while I enjoy getting Sophie off.

She climbs off my lap and we head upstairs. But not before I tell Asgard to keep an eye on Maui. He barks what I'm hoping is a "Yes, sir!"

In my room, I shut the door, flick on the bedroom light, and lead Sophie to the bed. I don't want to waste another second without her in my arms.

My mouth is against hers from the moment we stepped into the room, and even though I'm capable of navigating the way to my bed in complete darkness, it's a different matter when you're kissing someone.

I bump into what I'm guessing is the foot of my bed. I'm too busy to look up and take inventory of the situation.

I shift directions. My hands, in the meantime, have their own mission. They fumble with the buttons on her dress. Caveman me itches to rip open the front to save time. But I doubt Sophie would appreciate that, even though I'm positive a few of her heroes have done the same.

I eventually unbutton enough of them to peel the dress away from Sophie's shoulders and down her arms. It doesn't fall to her feet—which would've been preferable—but the fabric does make it to the swell of her hips.

A moment later her sexy purple bra is on the floor, and I finally remove my lips from Sophie's mouth and take in the perfection before me. My room is warmer than the air was when we were by the lake, but her nipples are just as hard.

"What's that?" Sophie asks, her gaze on my oak dresser.

I pause what I'm doing to check what she's talking about.

She picks up the piece of leather with flowers on it. The latest simple project I'm working on with Andrew's guidance. It's far from perfect, but it's definitely better than my last attempt.

"This is really good," she says. "Where did you get it?"

"It's mine."

"Yours? As in someone gave it to you?"

I shake my head. "As in I'm currently learning how to carve designs in leather. I figured it's about time I have a hobby."

She stares at me as if I've just uttered a foreign word. "Jake Daniels, the workaholic, has a hobby?"

"Ha, ha. I'm not that bad." At her yes-you-are look, I let out a long exhale. "Okay, I *am* that bad. But that's why I decided it was time I got a hobby that involves my hands. And just so you know, leather carving isn't the only thing I like to do with my hands."

I brush my thumb across her nipple. It hardens some more —and my new hobby is quickly forgotten. I don't think I'll ever grow tired of playing with Sophie's breasts.

Unfortunately, this will be the last time I get to enjoy them. We're only doing this for research for her novels. After today, it's back to Sophie and Jake, employee and employer.

Why can't you be more than just employee and employer? She's obviously into you enough to want to have sex with you.

I ignore the annoying know-it-all voice. For now, anyway.

There's only one thing I want to focus on—and that's making this an evening Sophie won't forget anytime soon.

Unable to wait another moment before getting to taste her again, I pop one nipple into my mouth. Not wishing for the other one to feel neglected, my fingers toy with it. Teasing. Pinching. Rolling.

Sophie's body dips slightly, as if her knees are threatening to buckle. I wrap an arm around her, supporting her.

That's when I realize her dress is no longer on her. She's standing there in only her purple lace panties.

My other hand releases her nipple and glides down her body to the waistband of her underwear. Sophie sucks in a sharp breath. My fingers keep moving, eager to discover how hot and wet she is.

They slide along her slick seam, hidden under the silky fabric. There's no doubt that I'm affecting her, if her rapid breaths are anything to go by.

"Just how fucking wet are you, Soph?" I practically growl. "Should I check?"

She whimpers her confirmation, along with a brief nod of her head.

I slip my fingers under the elastic of her panties. They glide effortlessly along her already swollen lips. "Christ, you're so fucking ready for me."

Here's the thing with women. Some don't get off on dirty talk. It's taboo to them and they don't like it. Whereas other women get even more aroused by it, even if they're not dirty talkers themselves.

Can you guess which one Sophie is?

She groans, the sound more erotic than anything I've heard before.

"I want to taste you so badly." I hook my thumbs on the waistband of her panties and slide them down her legs. She steps out of them and I toss them to the side.

I glance up at her, taking in the beauty in front of me. The awkward teenager she was talking about earlier has long since vanished.

Now she's standing here confident...and there's nothing more desirable than that. I don't care what size you are or what you're wearing, nothing beats confidence. It's sexy—plain and simple.

I push myself to my feet and kiss her naked shoulder—because I can. Then my mouth is on hers again, and I kiss her long and hard.

Sophie's hands are far from idle while our tongues reunite. Her fingers deftly pop my jeans button through the hole. The sound of a zipper sliding down tears through the air, and the next thing I realize, my jeans and boxer briefs are caught up around my ankles.

Her fingers wrap around my cock. At her touch, it's ready to sing a round of hallelujahs.

Not so fast, cowboy, I tell it. *This isn't about you.*

She pumps her hand down my length. My cock hardens some more in reply.

I cover her hand with mine. "Not yet, Soph. I want to taste you first. And I won't last much longer if you keep that up."

Usually I have great stamina. But usually the women aren't Sophie. Something tells me the rules are about to change... much like the company policy that I'm conveniently ignoring right now.

I kick off my jeans and underwear, remove my T-shirt, then lead her to the brown leather armchair by the window. "Sit here and put your feet up on the armrests." I lean down, my mouth a breath's width from her ear. "I want you to open yourself to me."

She looks over her shoulder at me. Her eyes are dark with desire, dark with need. And that has raised her sexiness factor to code red.

She lowers herself onto the seat and does as I ask.

And the breath in my lungs leaves in a single *whoosh*.

The low-lying sun shines on her from the side and lights her up like an angel. An erotic angel who will now be starring in my upcoming fantasies.

I stare at her, etching her image into my brain.

Her mouth twists into a mischievous half grin. "I'd say take a photo—it will last longer—but I wouldn't want to risk the photo accidentally going public. Even though I trust you with my life, the risk is still there."

Smart girl.

My cock gets even more excited—and it has nothing to do with the way she looks. It's due to what she said...due to how she trusts me with her life. Those three words mean more to me than anything else she could've said.

"Don't worry about my memory," I say. "It's not going to forget this anytime soon."

Sophie's lips part as if my words surprise her. But I can't figure out why she would be surprised, so I let it pass.

Besides, I've got more important things to do.

I kneel in front of her. She watches my every move. To ensure she's got the details right in her scenes? Who knows?

But at this point, I'm trying not to dwell on it—trying not to wonder if she's comparing me to one of her heroes.

I knock the thought away. As her fairy god-lover (because no way in hell am I referring to myself with the other term for now), it's my duty to give her a lesson in an area I know something about.

Helping Sophie land a guy who she's interested in? Not my forte.

Helping her experience the sensation of a man going down on her? That's more in the realm of possibility.

I run the tip of my tongue along one lip of her pussy. She tastes every bit as good as I thought she would. I repeat the move on the other side. She makes a sound that's a cross between a whimper and a moan.

I flick my tongue against her clit, and the sound from her mouth is upgraded to a full-out groan.

Her fingers knot in my hair, keeping me close to where she needs me. Keeping me close to where *I* need to be.

I look up at her. Her eyes are closed and her lips are slightly parted. "Watch me, Sophie. I want you to watch me make you come all over my face." My tone is low and demanding. Challenging.

She opens her eyes, which are heavy with desire. My dirty talk is getting to her like I had hoped. There've been a few times in the past several months when I've dreamed of being with Sophie this way. But nothing compares to reality.

Nothing compares to the way she's looking at me—like I'm her world.

I continue teasing her, my tongue relishing the taste of her. Then I shift my focus. My thumb replaces my tongue and my tongue delves inside her.

She squirms in the seat but continues watching me with heated eyes.

This—this vision in front of me is more spectacular than all the nebulas combined. And I, for one, am enjoying every second of it...every gasp, every moan.

I settle my free hand on her hip, keeping her somewhat still. My tongue continues worshiping her—and taking Sophie to new heights, if her begging is any indication.

"Oh. God, Jake," she releases on a moan. Her hands tighten in my hair and pull on it. My cock hardens some more, to the point where I'm close to coming.

"Oh, God. Oh, God. *Oh. God.*" With that, her soft heat clenches around my tongue and her body jerks up. This is followed by the aftershocks, her body jerking less than before but still moving.

As she returns from whatever solar system she was catapulted to, I lower her feet to the floor. She appears content, if not a little dazed.

It's an expression I've never seen on her before—but one that looks good.

One I wouldn't mind seeing on her again real soon.

If I can....

17

A languid smile appears on Sophie's face as she sets her feet back on the floor. She's still seated in the armchair. "Wow. Just wow. I mean I've had orgasms before. But my self-induced ones are nothing like that."

Normally, I don't need a woman to tell me she enjoyed herself. I don't require the reassurance some men crave. I can tell if I've satisfied her or not.

But hearing those words from Sophie means everything. I pull her up to stand, and I crash my lips against hers.

Sophie leans into me and brushes against my cock. She pulls her mouth away from mine and glances down. "We definitely need to do something about that." She starts to drop to her knees.

I grab hold of her shoulders. "The only thing I want to do is be inside you, Sophie." More than she can possibly imagine. "And as much as I love blowjobs, it's not your mouth I want to be inside of right now."

I guide her to the bed.

She places her hands on my chest. I was turned-on before. That was nothing compared to this. "I want to ride you like a cowgirl." Her tone is low and rough and naughty, all my favorite fantasies rolled into one. "I want to tie your hands to the bed and ride you long and hard."

That groan? It might have been me...at the mental picture she planted in my brain.

How many times have I let a woman tie or handcuff me to a bed? Zero. It's not that I've never been interested in trying it. It's just being tied to a bed requires a level of trust I've never had with another woman.

Especially not after what my ex-girlfriends did.

But the idea of doing this with Sophie...?

"That sounds really tempting...with you. But for now, I want to touch you while I'm inside you, and I can't do that if I'm tied to the bed."

"That works for me too." She smiles, but then for a second her sexual confidence seems to falter, and a light blush creeps onto her face.

I lightly kiss her. "Are you still okay with us doing this?"

She nods. "Absolutely." And just like that, the confidence is back.

I grab a condom from my bedside-table drawer and sit back against the pillows.

Sophie joins me, straddling my legs. I quickly open the foil package and roll the condom on.

She positions the head of my cock against her entrance and slowly lowers herself so only the tip is in her, allowing her body to adjust to my width.

She sinks, inch by inch, until I'm fully seated inside her. Her tight heat holds on to me as if it never wants to let me go—and I'm perfectly content with that. I would stay inside her for all eternity if it was possible.

The guys can run the ranch and phone me if they have any questions.

Totally works for me.

Sophie rocks her hips forward. I'm surprised the tight friction doesn't cause me to blow my load. She continues shifting her hips back and forth, the movement both sensual and erotic. For a moment I enjoy the sight of my cock sliding partially in and out of her. It's an incredible sight...right up there with the aurora borealis.

Maybe even more so.

I shift my hand to her clit and apply just enough pressure to bring her closer to seeing the stars.

"Do you want me to fuck you harder or slow down?" she asks.

"Christ, Sophie. You don't know what you're doing to me." I growl out the words, rushing to the brink of euphoria. Usually I have great control, but she's doing a bang-up job of testing it.

I don't remember the last time sex felt this intense, this mind-numbing.

"I'm not going to last much longer," she says on a moan.

"Let go whenever you're ready. I'll be right with you." Because there's no place I'd rather be.

The pressure in my lower region grows stronger and stronger. I rub her clit, spreading the slippery wetness around.

And then I feel it—the beginning signs of her impending orgasm. "That's it, Sophie." My voice is husky with need and determination and lust. "Give in to it."

That seems to be all it takes.

Her muscles clench down on me. I raise my hips in several jerky moves, using all the leverage I can muster.

My orgasm grasps my body and I'm flying skyward. *Up. Up. Up.*

It takes a moment for me to regain my senses. My hands are still on Sophie's hips. She has a dopey, satisfied look on her face —no doubt a reflection of my own.

"Wow, that was definitely better than my one-and-only other time." Her smile widens. "At least I've been truthful in my books when it comes to what it's like to have a man inside you."

I laugh. "Do you usually spout such poetic words after you have sex?"

She giggles. "Sorry. The writer side of me chose to join us in bed."

"Now that's the weirdest threesome I've ever heard of. Are you normally into that kinky stuff?" I wink at her and she blushes.

"Not me personally. But as for kinky, the kinkiest my characters have ever done is being tied or handcuffed to the bed. There's no BDSM or anything like that." Her tone sounds like mine whenever I talk about the ranch...all business.

She carefully climbs off me and looks around the room. Uncertainty clouds her expression. I've been with enough one-night stands over the years to recognize the look.

Some women don't expect anything else after fucking you. They're just looking for a good time, nothing more. They're the ones who make a hasty retreat, uninterested in overstaying their welcome. They know the one-night-stand rules and live by them.

Other women aren't so familiar with them. They confuse *one* night with sleepovers. And usually when a woman plans to actually *sleep* in your bed, deep down she's also hoping for something more—something long-term.

And I'm not referring to being the guy's fuck buddy.

Sophie is neither of those types—but we're also standing on new territory...and the rules no longer apply.

At least not the way they were written.

"Hey, I hope you're not planning on going anywhere just yet." I'm not even close to being finished with her.

I exit the bed and deal with the condom. Then I return and coax her to lie next to me.

I kiss her deeply, still unable to get enough of her. "Unless you have to be somewhere, there's still a lot of research we should cover while you're here."

I kiss her again. This time it's just a teasing kiss.

"What about your brothers?"

"What about them?" I murmur. I kiss her shoulder, then trail my mouth along her skin to her neck.

She shifts her head to the side, giving me better access. "What will they think about what we're doing?"

My tongue flicks against her soft skin. "Who cares what they think? But don't worry if you don't want anyone to find out. They won't say anything." Mostly because I'll knock their lights out if they do.

And they know it.

But I also know they would never do anything to purposely hurt her.

She stiffens slightly but then lets out a breath and nods.

I pull away from her neck and gaze down at her. "What's wrong?"

She shakes her head. "It's nothing. I was thinking about something else." Her lips slide into a reassuring smile and she trails her fingertips down my chest. "So, about that research..." Her eyes—honest and open and vulnerable—look into mine as if searching for something.

"Is there anything specific you're interested in trying?" Because there are about a thousand things I would like to do to her...and not all of them have to do with sex.

As soon as that thought makes its presence known, I realize something. The something I've probably known for a while but was too much of a stubborn ass to admit it to myself.

I'm in love.

I don't mean I'm falling in love.

I've already fallen and hit the ground hard.

Tell her, my heart implores. *Tell her how you feel about her.*

My brain gives me the opposite advice. The phrase "Don't be an idiot" might have been tossed into the mix.

"I'm open to almost anything," she says.

"Okay." I lick the shell of her ear, distracting myself from how I feel about her. "I'm up for that."

Literally.

My cock has been ready for action since she brought up doing more research.

And it has every intention of helping her out in whatever way she needs.

THERE'S ONE THING I'LL SAY ABOUT SOPHIE: SHE'S AN EAGER student and a great learner.

The woman has stamina...plus a healthy appetite for sex.

But that's what you get from suffering through a sexual drought for the past six years.

Yes, you heard correctly. Six. Years.

Now she's sleeping in my arms, her back against my chest. I finally wore her out a few minutes ago.

I kiss her lightly on the shoulder, not wishing to wake her.

But while I might have worn Sophie out, the same can't be said about me. I'm wired.

And what do I usually do when I'm wired? I pace or go for a ride. But it's dark out and while my horse might be named after a constellation, he won't be too impressed if I expect us to go for a ride now.

I could pace, but I don't want to risk waking Sophie. So I just lie next to her and deliberate the pros and cons of telling her I love her.

So far, there are no winning sides.

There's too much at risk.

But in the end, as the dawn peeks above the horizon, there's one thing I'm certain of: I need to tell Sophie I love her.

I fight back the urge to wake her up now and tell her. But tomorrow—well, more like this afternoon—I'll let her know how I feel. I'll take her to the river and tell her that I'm no longer her fairy godfather.

I'm going to tell her I've had enough of being the one behind the scenes, doing my best to ensure her dreams come true.

I'm going to tell Sophie I want to be her prince charming.

Her happily ever after.

18

The first thing I'm aware of as I stir awake is that my room is a lot brighter than when I normally wake up in the morning.

Even with my eyes shut, I can tell the sun has been above the horizon for a few hours.

Fuck.

I look at the alarm clock. It's eight a.m. *Fuck. Fuck. Fuckity-fuck.*

I can't believe my brothers let me sleep in.

I scramble out of bed—and become aware of point number two.

Sophie isn't lying next to me anymore. I'm used to waking up alone following a one-night stand, but I had hoped this time would be different.

Hell, I was positive this time would be different—because there was no reason for Sophie to bail without waking me up first.

Except she didn't know that, I remind myself. As far as she knew, last night was a one-time thing.

I quickly dress, take a whizz, and hurry downstairs to the kitchen to grab coffee and a quick bite.

A piece of paper, with my name written on the front, sits tented on the table. I pick it up and open it:

Morning Sleeping Beauty,
Your breakfast is in the fridge!
Signed,
Your thoughtful Brother Noah
PS
Hope you had pleasant dreams.

Sarcasm drips like oil from each word. I don't have to hear his voice to know what he was thinking when he wrote the note.

And given that he would've seen Sophie's car last night when he got home—but didn't find us in the entertainment room—it's not too hard to figure out what exactly he pieced together.

Same deal with TJ.

I check the fridge and find the breakfast omelet and hash browns Noah made. Half the time my little brother can be a pain in the ass, but there are times—like this—when I'm ready to skywrite that he's the best brother in the world.

I heat the food in the microwave and quickly devour it. Afterward, I take Maui out to relieve himself, with promises that I'll play with him soon.

TJ is in the stable, cleaning the stalls, when I arrive. Each of us has daily chores. Some chores are enjoyed by only one of us, so that person always does it. Then there are those chores none of us enjoy, so we rotate them on a weekly basis; that way no one is stuck always doing them.

Cleaning the stalls falls under that category.

TJ looks up, shovel in hand. "Well, if it isn't Sleeping Beauty himself," he says on a chuckle. "Late night, huh?"

"You can wipe that smirk off your face. Have you seen Sophie?"

"She slipped out of the house this morning when she thought Noah and I didn't notice. Does this mean we can expect an updated version of the company policy soon?" He scoops up a pile of soiled pine shavings from the mound on the floor and dumps it into the wheelbarrow.

"Look, I'd rather you don't mention it to anyone. And that includes Violet."

"You want me to lie to my fiancée?" The way he says it, you'd think I'd asked him to run down Main Street naked.

During rush hour.

Which, when I think about it, doesn't really amount to much, other than a few cars and a truck...but you get the picture.

I shrug. "No. Just don't mention it to her. That's not lying."

He pauses his shoveling. "Omission of the truth is still lying. Besides, she and Sophie are close. You're deluding yourself if you believe those two haven't already gossiped about what happened between you and Sophie last night."

"All right, how 'bout this? You don't bring it up unless she does. But even then, it's only on a need-to-know basis, and I really don't believe she needs to know."

"Right—you keep believing that." He scoops up another pile of shavings. "What's going on between you two anyway?" When I don't answer, he asks, "Was last night a one-time thing, or can we expect you to sleep in most mornings?"

He's kidding about the last part. We run a ranch. There is no sleeping in, even on the weekends.

But since I don't wish to discuss my feelings when it comes to Sophie until I've talked to her first, I go for option two.

"I've been working on the business plan for our new endeavor when it comes to Sophie's talent for horse whispering. Now I need to discuss the marketing side of things with Violet. Is she coming over later?"

I already know the answer, but I figure bringing up his fiancée is a great way to steer him from the original conversation.

"Yes, she and Deacon are due here later this afternoon."

"Perfect." I leave him to his chores and enter the tack room. I grab my toolbox and go out back to start repairs on the barn.

"HEY, JAKE."

I turn around, hammer in hand. Ryan is standing behind me, carrying his medical bag. "Hey, Ryan. Can I help you with something?"

"Noah called and asked me if I could check on one of your mares."

"He never mentioned anything to me about it." Probably because I was still sleeping after my marathon sex with Sophie. "But I can take you to the pasture where he's working, and he can help you out."

"Sounds good."

We stride toward where Noah's currently working.

"I bumped into Sophie this morning," Ryan says. "She was visiting Aubrey at the clinic."

That would explain why I haven't seen her yet.

"It's funny," he says, "but every time I've tried talking to her, she'd get her words mixed up whenever she said anything."

"I noticed. I wouldn't take it too personally. It's just something she does around certain guys." Like the kind of guys who remind her of the bully and his friends from high school.

"Well, that's the thing. She came into the clinic this morning and it was like someone had waved a magic wand."

"What do you mean?" The sinking sensation in my gut? Just ignore it. I'm sure it's nothing.

"She had no problem talking to me this time. It was like a miracle. Before this morning, I'd been thinking of asking her out."

My stomach starts its free fall.

Down.

Down.

Down.

"But until this morning," Ryan continues, unaware of what he's doing to me, "I had been hesitant to do so. I didn't know what to make of her reaction to me. Anyway, I asked her out."

I didn't groan out loud, did I?

Hopefully not.

Don't worry. Just because he asked her out, it doesn't mean she's interested anymore. That was yesterday. Before she and I made love.

A voice in the back of my head bursts out laughing. *She might have called it that, dumbass, but it doesn't mean she's in love with you. She was doing research for her novels.*

I laugh at Ryan's comment. The sound is about as real as the Easter Bunny—not that Ryan would realize this. "I'm guessing she said yes since you're telling me this?" I do my best to sound happy for him.

He studies me for a second like I'm some sort of exotic bacteria he's examining under a microscope. Then he nods and smiles. "That's right."

I plaster a happy smile on my face while my heart wonders if being stomped on by Orion would hurt as much as this.

But I can't blame Sophie for what happened. She has no idea I'm in love with her. And it's not like she's ever given me a hint that she sees us as something more than friends.

If anything, I should be thrilled and mentally high-fiving

myself. I did my job. Last night I got her to bare her soul to me, and I helped her move on after all the pain the football-player-asswipe had caused her.

Now she can finally have the happily ever after she deserves.

Right—and if I repeat this enough times, I'm sure my heart will agree with me. Eventually.

Or not at all.

"That's great. Congratulations. But you do realize that as her friend, it's my duty to remind you that if you do anything to hurt her, well…?" I leave my words hanging.

He knows I'm jesting.

For the most part.

"Not to worry. I really like Sophie and her happiness is important to me." He holds out his hand and I shake it.

At least we're in agreement about her happiness. I can't hate the guy for that.

Much.

"Hey, Noah," I say, as we approach him. "Ryan said you called about one of the mares?"

"Yes. Thanks for coming on short notice," he says to Ryan.

I leave them to talk. Under different circumstances, I would've gone with them to see the mare in question. Our horses' well-being is as important to me as it is to my brothers. But right now, horse talk is the last thing I'm interested in.

Not when it reminds me of Sophie—horse whisperer extraordinaire.

I head back along the path to the stable. As I get closer to the building, I spot Sophie in the training ring working with one of the younger mares. Even when it's the weekend, she usually comes over for a few hours to work with the horses while I complete my chores. Then we hang out together if she doesn't have plans with Violet and Aubrey.

She's smiling at the horse...and just like that, my insides turn to melted chocolate ice cream.

Her smile normally affects me, but this is the first time it's felt like this. Only now I'll have to share her smiles with Ryan.

I walk to the wooden fence and watch her perform her magic.

It'll be okay. We're still friends. She promised nothing would change between us once we had sex. Of course when she said that, I hadn't realized I was in love with her. But hey, if I can fall in love, I can just as easily fall out of it.

It can't be that hard.

Right?

I fold my arms across the top rung of the wooden fence.

The sunlight shines off Sophie's long blonde waves, turning her into an angel. But instead of the sexy vixen of an angel who I made come several times last night and early this morning, she's back to your common variety angel.

The problem? They're both hotter than hell.

I bang my forehead against my folded arms. *Idiot. Idiot. Idiot.*

"Are you okay?" Sophie's sweet voice breaks through my thoughts.

I straighten as if I haven't a care in the world—like last night meant nothing to me. It was just sex.

Hot, amazing, the earth-is-shaking-under-me sex.

You're not helping yourself here. "I just saw Ryan. He came here to check on one of the mares."

She smiles. And I do my best to focus on anything but her lips...and her eyes.

Which leaves me with the top of her head.

Perfect.

"He said he was coming over this afternoon," she says. "I hope Merryweather will be okay."

"I'm sure she will be....So, I heard about your great news."

A slight frown forms between her eyes. "What great news is that?"

I chuckle. "How many pieces of great news do you have to keep track of? I'm referring to how my therapy session yesterday cured you. With the wave of my magic wand, I fixed it so you can talk to Ryan without any of your previous issues."

I lightly fist my hand, blow on my fingernails, and polish them against my plaid shirt. "I knew I was good—I just didn't realize I was that good. Does this mean I get a fairy-godfather promotion? Like an upgrade in wings? Or like how Gandalf in *Lord of the Rings* went from being Gandalf the Grey to Gandalf the White?" There's a slight chance I might be babbling.

She laughs. *Christ*, I love that laugh.

"You definitely deserve a promotion. And I do owe you big-time, Jake. You helped me realize something yesterday. And then when I talked to Ryan at the clinic this morning, I realized I'd been an idiot all this time. I'd let the bully define me. For all these years I'd let him win." She grins. "But no more. I'm a new woman."

She steps to the side, her feet shoulder width apart, and fists her hands on her hips. Like a blonde Wonder Woman. In jeans, cowboy boots, a hat, and a long-sleeved T-shirt.

I always thought the dark-haired version was hot.

I was wrong.

"And *this* woman knows what she wants," Sophie says, "and she's not afraid to go after it." She scrapes a front tooth against her lower lip and her eyes drop to my mouth. Then her gaze moves away.

It happens so quickly that I'm positive I imagined it. I'm the one remembering what it felt like to kiss her—not the other way around.

"So what's next, Cinderella? Does your fairy godfather need to turn your rags into a ball gown and a pumpkin into a golden carriage? And maybe I can conjure up glass cowboy boots."

She cringes. "A glass slipper sounds uncomfortable enough. Could you imagine taking off boots made from glass?"

I laugh. "You have a point. So you're saying you don't need any of that stuff? That there are no royal balls in your future?"

"I guess it depends on whether you count Violet and TJ's wedding as one. There's going to be dancing and girls in pretty dresses."

Shit, I'd forgotten about that.

"So, you're bringing Ryan as your plus one?" Great, then I'll have to find a date for sure.

"I haven't asked him yet. I'm gonna wait a little longer. See how things go."

"Good plan."

And the number one reason why I was worried about having sex with Sophie lumbers into the training ring: the smug, unwanted white elephant.

For the first time in forever, an awkwardness settles between us. Only in my case, the cause of it isn't because we had sex. It's because I'm in love with this woman, and she's now going out with her prince charming—a prince charming who isn't me.

Well, you know what they say about love?

It sucks.

"And you?" Sophie asks, then does the lip-chewing habit she always slips into when she's uncertain. "Are you bringing anyone?"

"Yeah. Sure."

Her eyes widen. "Who?"

Good question. But because my brain isn't working at full capacity—thanks to my broken heart—I blurt the first name that comes to it. "Kennedy."

If I thought Sophie's eyes were wide before, that's nothing compared to now. "I thought she was returning to New York next week."

"She was. She extended her stay for a few more weeks." And since she doesn't live in Copper Creek anymore, she won't misinterpret my invitation to mean we have a chance at our own happily ever after. Together.

The thought of Kennedy stirs up a nest of hornets in my gut. With the help of Ryan's sister, she figured out that I'm in love with Sophie—before I realized it myself.

Maybe I got lucky last night and convinced her she has it all wrong. If I did? Problem solved.

And if I didn't?

She and Bailey could ruin everything when it comes to Sophie and Ryan.

19

A few hours later, I park my truck in front of Gertrude's house. She lives on a quiet residential street not far from Grandma Meg. The house is small and well-maintained, as is the tiny garden out front.

I walk up the path to find the front door open and Kennedy's soulful singing voice drifting from inside.

I ring the doorbell. A moment later, she appears, looking the way Kennedy normally does...ready to strut the runway.

She's wearing the heels that most guys fantasize about when they're attached to a pair of never-ending legs. This is usually accompanied by said legs wrapped around the guy's hips.

Only, in this case, that fantasy isn't paying me a visit. Not unless those legs happen to belong to Sophie.

Don't go there, idiot. She's dating Ryan now.

The rest of Kennedy is wearing a short, flirty, flowery dress. Her long red hair is pulled up in a messy bun.

She grins—the cat to the canary. "You're the last person I expected to see, Jake. And please don't give me that crap about being in the neighborhood."

165

"You do realize Grandma Meg is nearby, right? So the 'I was in the neighborhood' excuse is still feasible."

"Feasible...but unlikely. So let's cut to the chase. What is it you're really here for? Because we both know it isn't for sex." She gives me a smug look. I roll my eyes.

"I'm inviting you to TJ and Violet's wedding...as my date."

She looks at me for the space of ten seconds and bursts out laughing.

"What's so funny?"

"First, that's got to rank up there as the worst way a guy has asked me out on a date. And second, I happen to know a certain hot vet asked out a certain pretty blonde. So, you want to make her jealous so she'll see you as more than just a friend, and you're hoping I'll say yes."

"Sophie likes Ryan, and as long as he treats her well and isn't an asshole, I'm happy for her." That's the God-given truth. "She deserves to be happy, and she deserves to be with a guy who wants to settle down and have a family."

Kennedy's mouth twists into a you're-such-a-freaking-liar smirk. "Sorry, not buying it, but if that's what you want to keep telling yourself, who am I to argue?"

"Is that your way of saying you won't be my plus one at the wedding?"

"No, I'll be your date. It'll be fun."

Why do I have a feeling she's not referring to the actual wedding and reception?

"Good, I'll let my brother know."

"Does that mean, as your date, we'll get to kiss?" The smirk on her face is still there.

"Of course not. We're not going as a real couple, and we're not actually dating."

"So if we're not actually dating and your goal isn't to make Sophie jealous, then why do you need me to go as your date?"

Good point. It's not like Violet is forcing me to bring someone.

"I just figured since your grandmother will be there, you might want to go, too."

Her grandmother has a date lined up, and according to the guest list, the man happens to be Andrew.

"All right, I'll go as your fake date to *not* make Sophie jealous." She winks at me.

I let out a hard breath. "For the hundredth time, you have it all wrong. Which means you need to make sure Bailey also doesn't have the wrong idea. If Bailey tells her brother what she *thinks* is the truth, Sophie will be the one hurt the most."

Kennedy tilts her head to the side, studying me, puzzling out what makes me tick. "You really do love her. No matter how much you claim otherwise, Jake, I can see it in your eyes. The fact that you're trying so hard to make her happy, even when it means sacrificing your own happiness, just proves it."

"Thought you were an actress, not a shrink," I grumble.

I feel like I'm standing in front of her naked, and she's examining my soul. Normally, I don't have issues with the naked part. It's the second part that's unnerving.

She laughs. "I'm a woman of many talents....Now if you don't mind, unless you've changed your mind about earth-shattering sex, I need to get back to practicing my lines for the upcoming Broadway show."

"Have fun doing that."

I return to the ranch in time to see Violet pull up in front of the house. Naturally, TJ is sitting on the front porch, unable to wait another second before his fiancée is in his arms again.

At the reminder of what I'll never have with Sophie, regret kicks me in the heart like it's a soccer ball. But since I'm ninety-five percent certain I'm not experiencing a heart attack—or at least not a fatal one—I ignore the pain and park my truck in the garage.

Yeah, I know what you're thinking. There are plenty of other fish in the ocean, and in time I'll get over Sophie and move on.

Well, you know what? That saying is a load of crap.

Whoever came up with it had clearly never been in love before.

I walk around to the front of the house, where TJ is unbuckling Deacon from Violet's car.

"Hey, big guy," I say. "How about you and I mosey over to the pasture to check on the colts?" I give the little boy my best fake Texan drawl.

Deacon waves at me. "Hi, Uncle Jake."

TJ removes him from his car seat and hugs him. Deacon flings his arms around his daddy's neck and squeezes tight, possibly cutting off TJ's oxygen supply.

My brother lowers him to the ground, and Deacon hurls himself at me. Laughing, I pick him up. "How about we give your mommy and daddy some alone time?"

Deacon nods like a bobblehead even though he has no clue what I'm talking about.

I lower him back down. "You wanna help me train Maui for a few minutes, and then you guys can play together?"

Again, Deacon nods. I lead him into the house to where Maui is waiting for me in his crate. TJ and Violet stay outside.

I put Maui's leash on him; then Deacon and I take him into the backyard, to the large stretch of lawn beyond the patio.

Deacon assists with Maui's training. Well, assists as much as a two-and-a-half-year-old can. Because he's more interested in playing with Maui, and Maui is more interested in playing with Deacon, I keep the training time short.

We switch to Deacon tossing Maui's favorite ball onto the grass and Maui tumbling after it.

"You're a natural with kids," Violet says behind me. "I hope you're planning to have some one day."

I snort a laugh. "You're only saying that because you want Deacon to have cousins." It's not like Austin—her only sibling —is looking to settle down and have a family.

"Maybe. And maybe it's because what I'm saying is true. I know you're not interested in falling in love and settling down, but I really hope you don't ignore what's in front of you just because you're so stubborn."

I chuckle. "I'll be sure to keep that in mind. But I wouldn't hold your breath. Anyway, in case you wanted to know, Kennedy is going to be my date for your wedding."

Violet's mouth drops open before she recovers herself. "I didn't realize you guys were dating."

"I'd hardly say we're dating. She's in town while visiting her grandmother and decided to extend her stay a little longer. And since I have no one else to ask"—because my someone else is asking Ryan—"I figured I'd ask Kennedy."

Which I'm already regretting.

"Okay, I'll mark that down. So...TJ said you want to discuss the marketing plans for Sophie's horse-training services?"

Deacon appears at my feet with Maui's ball. He holds it up to me. "Throw ball."

I reclaim it from him and toss it farther than he can throw it —but not too far that Maui can't see where the ball went. He and Deacon go bounding after it.

"That's right," I tell Violet. "I'd like to get that up and running as soon as possible. Sophie and I thought she could take on a client or two at first to start building her reputation. Word of mouth will be key for the program's success. The goal is to gather accolades to post on our website, to develop a list of happy clients for future clients to contact for recommendations."

"That's a good idea. Maybe we can aim locally to begin with. It would be easier and cheaper for all concerned if Sophie can help a local owner with their horse. It won't necessarily be a tough behavioral problem, but it'll be a start. After word gets out, you might hear from owners who are at the end of their rope when it comes to their horse. Those are the ones she's hoping to eventually help."

Maui trots back to us with Deacon hot in pursuit.

"What do you suggest we do to find those initial clients?" I ask.

Violet scoops up her son and blows a raspberry on his exposed stomach. He giggles.

"We can talk to people in town and tell them about Sophie's plans," she says, placing him back on the ground. "People love her. If they know someone she could possibly help, they'll get the word out. For now, I think that's her best bet.

"Plus I've already talked to Mayor Wineberg. She's bringing it up at the next town council meeting."

And this is why I wanted to talk to Violet. I knew she'd be able to help us.

"Once we have enough recommendations built up," she says. "I'll work with Sophie on setting up a website."

"Another website?"

"I know the service is supposed to be part of the ranch's business model, but it would be better to treat them as separate entities. This way you can cross-promote each other's services. Once Sophie's business gets some roots set in, I can create a page on your website for it. The ranch can promote her training program and provide a link to *her* website. She can do the same with her website when it comes to the ranch. It will be an extra source of traffic for you guys. Plus this will help keep your website simple."

I grin at her. "All I can say is that I'm glad you're marrying my brother and not marrying Chase Scottsdale. That's a brilliant plan." Chase is the grandson of the owner of our rivaling ranch in Copper Creek.

Violet smiles back at me. "Trust me, it's *not* my marrying

your brother that you should be thankful for. It's the fact that you hired Sophie and managed to keep her that you should be thankful for. Don't believe for a second that Walter Scottsdale hasn't tried to lure her to the dark side."

"He has?"

Violet nods. This time she isn't smiling. "He's been quite insistent about it, actually."

Fuck.

My heart points out that if she's Walter's employee, my company policy when it comes to dating won't matter anymore.

I remind it that's a moot point if she's dating and falling for Ryan. She's already picked him over me. I was only good enough to kiss and have sex with...as a learning tool.

"Is she considering it?" I ask.

"You'd have to ask her."

Damn straight I will.

20

It's one thing to plan to do something, it's another when the forces of the universe have other ideas.

It's been a week since Violet told me Walter Scottsdale has been lusting over Sophie.

As his horse whisperer.

You would think that because she's a ranch employee and my friend, it'd be easy to ask her about it.

This is where the universe is conspiring against me. Here's a quick rundown of how it flipped its middle finger at my plans:

Sophie was late for work because of a flat tire the first morning after Violet's revelation.

Which Ryan fixed after rushing out like a knight in shining armor when she called him.

Even though I would have done the same if she had called me.

Then, she had to leave early because of a medical appointment.

She slept in a few days, which is unusual for her. No, it's not because she stayed up late having sex with Ryan. Or at least that's what I keep telling myself.

And then, Violet and Aubrey kidnapped her several times during lunch. Something to do with Violet's wedding and Sophie being a bridesmaid.

They also kidnapped her after work before I had a chance to talk to her.

And when she wasn't otherwise preoccupied with the universe's plan to keep me from talking to her, I was super busy running the ranch.

Before she dated Ryan, I got to see and talk to Sophie several times a day. Now she's like a drug, and I've been forced to go cold turkey.

And there's not a single part of me that's happy about it.

Hoping to finally see her, I walk to the training ring where she would normally be working. No one is there.

I stalk to the stable to see if maybe she's there. She's not.

But Noah is.

"Have you seen Sophie?" I ask, entering the tack room. He's inspecting the horse supplies in the metal cabinet against the wall.

He turns around, a tub of vitamins in his hand. "She didn't make it in today. Something about her being sick."

"She's sick? How come this is the first I'm hearing about it?"

He shrugs. "TJ told me. Maybe Violet told him. I thought you knew."

"Do you know what's wrong with her?"

He returns the vitamins to the cabinet. "I have no idea. I figured if it was something serious, you would've told me...but that's when I thought you knew she was sick. Maybe TJ knows."

"Any idea where he is?"

"Well, given that Violet has the no-sex-before-the-wedding rule, I can guess where he *isn't*." He snickers. "He said something earlier about fixing the fence on the other side of the mares' pasture."

I pull my phone from my back pocket and text Sophie, asking if she's okay.

While I wait for her reply, I text TJ.

A minute later, he responds, telling me his location. I climb into my truck and drive to the far end of our property. He's busy hammering a nail into the wooden crossbeam when I pull up.

Even though my phone didn't ding while I was driving over, I still check it in case Sophie texted me. Nothing.

"Noah told me that Sophie's sick," I say, walking over to him. He turns to face me. "Any idea what's wrong with her?"

"Violet said something about her puking."

"And no one thought to tell me this?" I growl out.

"Sorry, bro. Thought you knew."

Normally I would have. Normally Sophie would have called to tell me she wasn't feeling well.

Well, this fairy godfather is still on the clock...even if Cinderella has landed her prince.

I climb back into my truck and keep driving until I'm parked in front of Sophie's house.

Her car is in her driveway.

I stride to her front door and ring the doorbell. No one answers. Nor is there any movement or sound to indicate someone is alive inside.

What's one perk to being Sophie's best friend? Well, not so much a perk as a privilege. I know where to find her spare key. She knows not to hide it under her doormat or a statue or plant pot by the front door. It's under a rock in the front yard.

Which, I might point out, doesn't work very well during the snowy winter months.

Fortunately, being late spring, there's no snow on the ground. I casually walk to the leafy bush near the sidewalk, glance both ways down the street, then crouch beside the shrub and remove the spare key from under a rock. If anyone's looking my way, it just appears as though I'm inspecting the plant.

I return to her front door and unlock it.

"Sophie?" I call out before stepping inside.

A faint groan comes from the direction of the bathroom.

I shut the front door and head for the room. The door is open a crack. I widen it to find Sophie on the floor, hugging the toilet like it's a trophy.

I kneel next to her. "Hey. I'd ask you if you're okay, but I already know the answer. What happened? You're not pregnant are you?"

I was joking but then a sudden thought hits me. What if she is pregnant...with my child?

We used condoms, but accidents happen.

A tiny tremor of excitement runs through me. It's so unexpected, it almost knocks me to my knees—if I wasn't already there.

Since when do I want kids?

Once again, the image from before, of a little girl who looks like her mother, but with my blue eyes instead of Sophie's brown ones, visits.

Sophie shakes her head. Just a fraction of an inch, but enough for me to notice. "Nope, not pregnant. I went out with Ryan last night and must have eaten something that didn't agree with me."

My grandmother used to believe in signs. She would always tell my brothers and me that signs were God's way of guiding us. Great, if you believed in God and if he provided a manual for interpreting the signs. Because let's face it, some signs are so obscure they could mean anything.

I mean, what if you thought the sign was suggesting that you get a vasectomy, but it was really hinting that you were due for a haircut?

Do I believe in signs? Not at all. But if I did, I'd conclude the food poisoning is a sign that Ryan and Sophie aren't meant to be. That I'm the man she's destined to be with.

Does Sophie believe in them? I have no idea, and now's not the time to ask her.

Besides, like I've pointed out, signs are always open to interpretation. She might not see the food poisoning as a sign that she and Ryan aren't meant to be.

I gently stroke her lower back in soothing circles like my mom did when I was sick as a kid. "How long have you been like this?"

"Since around midnight." Her voice is weak and her face is pale. My heart aches seeing her like this.

I push myself to my feet and grab a washcloth from next to her sink. I wet it with cold water and return to Sophie.

In time to witness her dry heave into the toilet.

Once she's finished, I press the cloth against her slightly fevered skin. "All right, Cinderella. Time to get you to bed."

I place the cloth on the counter, then scoop her up in my arms and carry her to her bedroom. Her bed covers are messily pulled to the side, but other than that, her room is exactly as I remember it from the one time I've seen it. The walls are light brown, with several large canvas photos hanging on them. My favorite is of Orion, who is galloping toward the camera. Horses in action—Violet's specialty.

"You don't need to stay." Sophie's voice is a dry whisper. At hearing it, my heart is caught in a clammy, clenched fist. "I'll be fine. I just need to sleep off whatever it is."

"Let me be the judge of that." I carefully lower her onto her bed. "We need to get you rehydrated. Do you have any ginger ale?"

She makes a small whimper that I interpret as a "no."

I could go get her some, but I don't want to leave her alone. So I text Violet, asking her to drop off some ginger ale and soda crackers.

She responds less than a minute later.

Violet: I'm on my way.

I text my brothers to inform them what's going on and not to expect me until Sophie is healthy again.

Both get back to me a few minutes later, letting me know not to worry. They'll finish my chores for me. They also both wish her a speedy recovery.

I return to the bathroom to grab the washcloth. I rinse it again with cold water and walk back to Sophie's bedroom. She's curled up on her side, already asleep, when I enter.

I sit next to her on the bed, doing my best not to wake her. Even in her current state, she's still beautiful. My heart squeezes like a broken accordion. *Fuck*, Ryan's a lucky man. I only hope he realizes how lucky he is.

The devil pops up on my shoulder. *Ryan, Shmyan*, he says. *You're the one she kissed. You're the one she made love to.*

He snickers at the "made love to" part. Yeah, the devil is all about fucking and less about loving.

Your point? the angel on the other shoulder asks. She looks suspiciously like Kennedy—who, if you ask me, is as far from angelic as you can get.

My point is, the girl obviously has a thing for our boy, is the devil's reply. *He needs to pick up his balls and fight for her.*

Except she hasn't shown any interest in him, other than as a friend, the angel points out. *I vote we let the hottie vet have her.*

It's official. Whatever ailment Sophie has, I'm now coming down with it.

Don't listen to the old blowhole, the devil tells me. *You saw her first. Finders keepers.*

The angel rolls her eyes.

My phone pings.

Violet: I'm here!

Me: Door is unlocked.

Ignoring the devil and the angel, who are still disagreeing about who should have dating rights to Sophie—Ryan or me—I head for the front door.

Violet is standing in the foyer when I arrive, a fabric grocery bag in her hand. A two-liter bottle of ginger ale is cradled in the other arm.

"How's she doing?" She hands me the items.

"Asleep. Did you want to see her?" *Please say no.*

"That's okay, I'm sure you're doing a great job as her sexy male nurse." She gives me the familiar smug smile I saw a lot of back when we were teens.

I laugh, the sound low so as not to wake Sophie. "I doubt she thinks of me as sexy."

Violet rolls her eyes, mirroring that of the angel a few moments ago. "I swear," she mutters, "how can men be so oblivious?"

I feel a frown form between my eyes. "What are you talking about?"

"Over two-thirds of the women in this town think you're sexy."

I blink, then laugh again. "What—someone do a poll I wasn't aware of?"

"Not an official one."

"You mean even the married women and the women over the age of sixty feel that way?"

Never attempt to pull one over on a numbers guy.

"*Especially* the women sixty years and older. There are some horny older women in this town." She giggles. "Just a warning, you might consider keeping your window closed at night, or else some of them might attempt to scale the tree outside your bedroom window."

She laughs harder at what is no doubt a disbelieving expression on my face. "I'm telling you now, Jake, you underestimate the effect you have on some women." Her gaze shifts briefly to the hallway leading to Sophie's bedroom. Then she looks back at me. "Tell her once she's feeling better to give me a call."

"Will do."

She leaves and I take the supplies to the kitchen. I pour the ginger ale into a glass, carry it into Sophie's bedroom, and park it on her bedside table.

For a moment, I study the woman I'm in love with. Her face has a slight flush to it and there are dark circles under her eyes. But despite all of that, she's still beautiful. My heart lets out a longing sigh—right before it curses me for being so stupid and coming up with the company policy, even though it was initially written to protect her from Noah's playboy tendencies.

She's not interested in me that way, I remind it. *You can't make someone fall in love with you if they're not interested.*

The need to touch her burns deep inside. I don't bother to fight it. This might be the only opportunity I'll have now that she's with Ryan.

I caress her cheek with my thumb. It's hot to the touch.

Her eyelids flutter but her eyes remain closed.

"Soph, I know you're tired, but you need to drink some ginger ale."

She mutters something but her eyes stay shut.

I gently shake her shoulder. "Sweetheart, I need you to wake up."

"Five more minutes, Mom," she mumbles. "I'm having a good dream."

The corner of my mouth jerks to one side. "Mom? My masculinity and I will try not to be too insulted by that." I lean down and kiss her forehead. "Come on, Sleeping Beauty, time to wake up. You just need to have a couple of sips of the ginger ale. You can go back to sleep afterward."

Her eyelids finally drift open and I help her sit up. I prop her against me and bring the drink to her lips. She manages a few tiny sips, then tells me that she wants to go to sleep.

"Okay, for a few minutes. You'll need to drink some more fluids after that."

She gives a faint nod and within seconds of lying down, her eyes are closed, her breathing even.

I remove the knitted throw from the end of her bed and cover her with it. She doesn't stir.

I head for her living room to retrieve a chair to sit on while I watch over her. As I pass the open door to her office, I'm drawn to the room the way a moth is drawn to a lightbulb. I've only been inside it one other time—back when she first moved into the house.

The small room is nothing like my office back at the ranch, with furniture from Ikea instead of oak antiques. The view is nowhere near as spectacular either.

Two bookshelves stand tall against a windowless wall, and I scan their contents. Three of the shelves contain a number of reference books on writing novels, characters, descriptions. There's also a shelf containing books by Emma Cartwright. Sophie's books.

I remove one titled *Enslaved* and check the back cover. Definitely not my typical read, but hell if I'm not giving it a go.

A short time later, I'm sitting in an armchair next to Sophie's bedroom window, all shades of turned-on. My cock is hard in my jeans, frustrated that the hero in the book is getting more action than I am.

And I'm *only* on Chapter Two.

I'll give Sophie this...she's a damn good writer. The moment I started reading, I got sucked into the story.

The suspense might have something to do with it, too.

I turn the page, eager to find out if the former SEAL can track down the heroine's missing sister. The man reminds me of Austin, Violet's brother. He also served with the SEALs... until he left and became Copper Creek's sheriff.

Interesting.

Now that I think about it, she did have trouble talking to him when she first moved to town. But he has that effect on most people—unless you know him.

I finish reading the chapter, then park the book on the seat and kiss Sophie's cheek. "Hey, Soph, it's ginger ale time."

She mutters something in her sleep. A something that sounds a lot like "...love you."

Is she dreaming about Ryan?

My heart yells *Incoming*, and free falls onto my stomach.

My stomach lets out a disgruntled *Ugh!*

Tell her you love her, my heart implores.

I ignore it. That's the last thing she's interested in hearing, especially when she's sick. Talk about all levels of awkward once she's healthy again and remembers what I said.

Unable to help myself, I stroke my thumb against her cheek again. "Hey, sunshine, it's time to wake up and have something to drink."

This time she does open her eyes. Then her eyes widen some more. "What are you doing here?" she whispers. "What time is it?"

"I'm taking care of you." I glance at her alarm clock. "And it's one thirty in the afternoon." I remove the glass from the bedside table. "Time to drink a little more. And if you keep this down, maybe you can try some crackers."

She nods and attempts to sit up. I help her and hand her the drink. This time she swallows slightly longer sips before she's had enough. She waits a few minutes, then has a cracker before leaning back on the pillows I've fluffed for her.

"Feeling a little better yet?" I sit next to her.

"Depends."

"On what?"

"If feeling like a zombie is better than feeling like a semi hit you." The corners of her mouth twitch up. Not a whole lot, but enough to prove she's not dead. And enough to reveal the humorous side of her I love so much.

"Point taken." I brush a strand of hair behind her ear. "You can go back to sleep if you want. I'll be sitting over there reading if you need me." I nod toward the armchair.

I'm really hoping she doesn't tell me to go home, that she's okay now. And if she does? Her living room couch is just as comfy as the chair, maybe even more so.

Until I'm positive she'll be fine, I'm not going anywhere.

Because that's what friends do.

That's what you do for the people you love.

"You're just gonna watch me?" Her tone holds a teasing lilt to it. "Don't take this the wrong way, Jake, but you really need a life."

"Hey, what can I say? Until you're feeling a lot better, you are my life. You and Cade Mathews."

She blinks, and her face scrunches in confusion. "Who's Cade Mathews?"

I exaggerate a gasp...faked, of course. "How can you forget the incredibly hot Cade Mathews?" I push myself off the bed and walk to the chair. "Please tell me he and Angela end up together." I pick up the novel I'm reading and show her the cover.

She groans. "Please tell me you aren't really reading that."

"Of course I am. What can I say? I was curious about what you write. Did you realize Cade sounds like Austin?"

This time her groan is a lot louder. "I'm going to puke." Only she doesn't sound like she means it.

"No need to do that. And for the record, I'm enjoying it. So don't tell me if Cade and Angela find her sister. I mean, I'm assuming they do because this a romance and not a thriller. But either way, I don't want to know until I get to that part."

Sophie gapes at me.

"Now if you don't mind, I'd like to get back to the story while you sleep." I sit back on the chair and flip to where I was before I had to wake Sophie up.

"You know you don't have to read it, right?"

I wink at her. "I know. But I will anyway."

And I'll *try* not to imagine that Angela is really Sophie and she's doing those things to *me*.

Something tells me that before I finish the book, I'll need quite a few cold showers.

21

———————————

B y the fourth sex scene in Sophie's book, my cock was begging for mercy.

That's if you can call a massive hard-on begging for mercy.

"Wow. I can't believe how realistic your sex scenes are, given you were practically a virgin when you wrote them." I say it quietly so as not to wake Sophie.

It's no wonder those few times she and I fucked, I ended up having orgasms to rival all others.

She fucked like a pro.

"I take it you like the book...or at least the sex scenes," she says, startling me.

I glance up to find her regarding me, a soft smile on her face, and I close the book. "Sorry, didn't mean to wake you."

She slowly pushes herself to sit. "You didn't. I've been awake for a bit, watching you read."

"Hah! And you accused *me* of not having much of a life." I walk to her bed, rearrange the pillows for her, and pass her the almost empty glass of ginger ale from her nightstand.

184

Once she finishes it, I take the glass and pass her two crackers. "I'll get you some more ginger ale. How are you feeling?"

"Better. I still feel like a zombie, but a zombie who has a chance to be converted back to human form."

"That sounds like a major step up to me....Do you need anything else while I'm in the kitchen?"

She shakes her head.

I return a few minutes later to find her still in bed, staring out the window with a faraway look on her face.

"Hey, where are you?" I ask. Or maybe I don't want to know. Maybe she's daydreaming about Ryan.

She opens her mouth to say something, but her phone rings from the nightstand, halting her words.

She reaches for it, checks the screen, and accepts the call. "Hey." Her voice is still weak, but there's a level of cheerfulness that was missing earlier.

I'd like to say that I don't strain to hear who it is. I'd also like to say that I don't pray it isn't Ryan—the guy who's the equivalent to Snow White's Wicked Queen.

Yeah, yeah, I know. The queen actually tried to murder Snow White; Ryan wasn't trying to kill Sophie. But the queen did poison Snow White...and Ryan paid for the food that gave Sophie food poisoning.

So in my professional opinion, that's pretty much the same thing.

"No, I'm feeling better now," she says to the unknown person. "It wasn't your fault. I'm just glad you didn't get sick, too."

Oh. Ryan.

For a second, I wonder if I'm supposed to hide in the closet so he doesn't realize I'm here.

I quickly kick the notion to the wayside. It's not like they're Skyping. He has no idea I'm in her house.

"He's here now...."

Okay, so much for that theory.

"All right." She holds the phone out to me and mouths, *He wants to talk to you.*

I take the phone from her. "Hello?"

"How's she doing?" Ryan asks.

"She's still sick but getting better."

Now for the billion-dollar question: how do I want this to play out?

Do I hope that he rushes over to take care of her? In other words...be her loving boyfriend.

Or do I hope that he's a douchebag and leaves her alone in her hour of need.

Right, she's not dying, but you know what I mean.

"That's good to hear," he says. "Are you sticking around until she's better?"

Huh? There's not even a smidgeon of jealousy or cavemanness in his tone. If our places were reversed, I'd be fucking jealous if some guy was taking care of my girlfriend, unless...

He isn't concerned about me being his competition. The same way you wouldn't be worried about a gay guy stealing the heart of your girlfriend.

"That's right," I say.

Sophie smiles, and a familiar warmth spreads throughout my chest. I smile back.

"Well, let me know if there's anything I can do to help."

Maybe it's just me, but if Sophie was my girlfriend, I'd be racing to her side if she were sick.

Which is what I did.

And she's not even my girlfriend.

What wouldn't I be doing? Happily pawning her off on her friend—male or female.

"Will do." I hand Sophie back her phone.

She talks to him while I fetch the ginger ale and crackers from the kitchen. Anything to avoid listening to her talk to him.

She's off the phone by the time I return...with a box containing Monopoly. I found it on top of her fridge.

"You want to nap some more or play this?" I hold the box up for her to see.

Mischief gleams in her bright blue eyes. "Prepare to lose to the Monopoly champion, Daniels."

"Dream on, sweetheart. You forget I have magical powers. You don't stand a chance."

She laughs, the sound more in the evil-cackle category than anything else. "You're on."

I set up the game next to her on the bed and move the armchair over. "I'll be the banker."

We've been playing for a while when I casually say, "I hear Walter Scottsdale is trying to woo you to the dark side."

I say it partly to find out if it's true...but mostly to distract her from the part where she's winning.

She wasn't kidding when she said she was the Monopoly champion. The woman is ruthless when it comes to the game.

She rolls the dice. "There might be a chance he's doing that." Her tone sounds distracted, but I can't tell if that's because she's sizing up her next opportunity to strike and annihilate me, or because she's attempting to sidetrack me from the conversation.

"How big a chance is it that you're considering his offer?"

"None at all. I love working for you and your brothers. Walter heard about my new horse training services. He was impressed and offered me more money if I set up camp at his ranch."

"What kind of money are we talking about?"

She picks up the tiny metal dog and moves it five spaces, past Go, and lands on her property. She holds out her hand. "Two hundred bucks, please."

I dole it out and wait for her reply. When she still doesn't answer, I push a little harder. "You might as well tell me, Soph. I'll find out one way or another."

She sighs. "Fine. Double what you're paying me."

Shit.

"But like I said," she hurriedly adds, "I'm not interested in working for him. My heart is with your ranch. Always will be." She hands me the dice.

I roll them...and land on one of her properties.

Her very, *very* expensive property. Which she owns all the hotels and plots of land for.

She grins. "What did I tell you? Monopoly Champion. Right here." She points to herself with both thumbs.

I chuckle. "Gloat much?" I gather the money I owe her and hand it over.

"So, how's the planning going for your picnic basket?" she asks as she rolls the dice.

"Planning? I'm supposed to plan it?" Heck, until she mentioned it, I'd forgotten about it.

Yes, I know—for someone who loves to plan and create lists, you'd think I'd already have it figured out.

"Absolutely. You need to create a basket no one can resist, and then all the single women will be scrambling to outbid each other. The more money raised from the event, the better for Copper Creek."

"Are you telling me that just winning the opportunity to eat lunch with me won't be enough?" I wink at her.

Her gaze slowly skims down my body, and she lets out a barely noticeable sigh. Except with Sophie, I notice everything.

"You've got a point. All you have to do is show up, preferably shirtless, and women will be vying to win a date with you, even if your basket is empty."

"I was actually kidding."

She cocks her head to the side and smiles softly. "I wasn't."

Time to change topic. I'd rather not think about other

women being interested in me. There's only one woman who I want lusting over me.

Too bad what I want and reality aren't on the same page— or even in the same book. "I guess Ryan doesn't have to participate now that you guys are dating."

Lucky guy.

In so many ways.

"No, he's still participating."

"He is?"

"He wants to help the town because everyone's been so great to him since he moved here. He wants to do whatever he can to give back to the community."

"Even if he has to date another woman while he's dating you?" Because I can guarantee if I was dating Sophie, I wouldn't be interested in going on a date with anyone else. She'd be it for me.

She laughs. "It's not like he would be cheating on me. For one, I would know about it."

"What if she tries to kiss him?" I'm pretty sure he wouldn't be fine with it if I kissed Sophie...like I did before the two of them began dating.

"As long as he doesn't kiss back, I'd say it's fine. And again, it's to help out the businesses, our friends." She chews on her lip and her gaze drops to my mouth. It lingers there for a moment. "Does this mean you're planning to kiss the winner of your basket?"

"No." That's the honest-to-God truth. It doesn't matter who bids for my basket, I'm not interested in kissing anyone.

Not while Sophie still has my heart.

"Not even if she's hot?"

"Since all the hot women in town are either married or dating, I doubt that'll be an issue."

The corners of her mouth quirk up. "You haven't heard?"

"Heard what?"

"Tilly isn't just promoting the auction to Copper Creek residents. Violet arranged promotion to expand the reach. From what I've heard, there's lots of excitement about all the sexy bachelors here. Tilly's even hoping to get some rich cougars interested in attending." She laughs—which might have more to do with the horrified expression on my face than anything else.

"By cougar, I'm guessing you aren't referring to the mountain lion variety?" I say.

She laughs even harder, indirectly answering my question.

Any other time I'd be a grumpy-ass about all of it. But with Sophie now looking healthier and happier than a few hours ago, I keep the grumpy-ass at bay.

I pick up a pillow and gently smack her arm with it.

"Nope," she says, giggling. "Definitely not the mountain lion variety. But it doesn't mean you have to go out with them. Just wiggle your sexy ass on stage. That will help the cause."

I raise an eyebrow. "You think I have a sexy ass?"

A light blush sweeps across her face. "Who doesn't think that?"

I snort a laugh. "I'm pretty sure TJ, Noah, Austin, and Ryan don't agree with you there."

"True. But the women in Copper Creek certainly do."

"What about you? Do you consider my ass sexy?" My voice is low and husky, instead of the playful tone I was aiming for.

"There's a good chance I might agree with that assessment." She swallows. Hard. "You know what? I'm feeling much better now, and I could really use a shower. Do you mind if I do that before we finish the game?"

She doesn't wait for a reply—and can't scramble off the bed fast enough.

"Go ahead. Then I can read more of your book while I wait."

Her gaze drops to the end of the bed where I've put it. She

lunges for the book, but she's on the other side of the bed and too far away to easily reach it.

I snatch the book up before she can touch it.

"You really don't have to read it," she says. "In fact, you can leave now if you'd like. I'm sure you've got plenty of other things to do back at the ranch. Actually—that's a brilliant idea. That you leave. Now." Her words get faster and faster with each one, and she shifts her weight back and forth between her feet.

I didn't think it was possible, but she's even hotter when in a near state of panic. I'm not talking about the kind of panic where you're close to having a heart attack. It's more on the comical side....Just don't tell her I said that.

I make myself comfortable on the seat and grin at her. "No, I'm good with sticking around. I want to make sure you're one hundred percent healthy again."

She opens her mouth to protest.

"Sorry, Soph, but you're not getting rid of me that quickly." I prop my feet on the bed and resume reading the book. "Besides, I need to find out where Angela's sister disappeared to." I wave her away with my hand.

She pauses for a moment, then gathers up her clothes and bolts from the room, leaving me to wonder about her reaction earlier. Her reaction to when we were talking about me kissing the winner of my basket.

Leaving me to wonder about the way her gaze studied my lips for longer than considered normal...unless you're contemplating kissing the person.

Get a grip, dumbass. You probably had a crumb on your lip or something.

It's official. Being Sophie's fairy godfather has fried my brain.

22

Two days after the food poisoning incident, Sophie is back to work. The temperature is warm outside, which means she's wearing her denim shorts, soft pink T-shirt that skims her curves, and her cowgirl hat and boots.

She's in the training paddock, lunge line in hand, as the young horse trots around her in a wide circle. I lean against the top rail of the fence, watching the magic between them.

She eventually brings the horse back in to her and rewards him with a treat. The pair then walk toward the gate as I open it for her.

She's a few yards short of it when she pauses, removes her phone from her back pocket, and checks the screen.

She taps it and puts the phone to her ear. "Hi...Meg?" Her eyes widen. "You're where?...Do I *want* to know why you're in Golden Falls Jail?"

My heart slams on its brakes.

I stalk the remaining distance between us and grab the phone from her hand. Sophie doesn't protest.

I increase the volume so she can hear what Grandma Meg has to say.

"It's really a silly story. Well, more like a misunderstanding..." Grandma Meg's voice fades away.

"How about you start by explaining what you're doing in Golden Falls jail," I say.

"Jake?"

In the background, I make out a younger voice saying, "Hurry up, bitch. I have to call my lawyer."

This is followed by: "You'll get much further in life, young lady, if you use your manners."

"Is that Gertrude?" I ask Grandma Meg on a groan.

"That's right. And Tilly's here, too."

Why am I not surprised?

"When you told Sophie you're in jail, you didn't actually mean *in* jail, right? You're just visiting a police station for the heck of it." *Christ*, please tell me it's that.

"More like the first option."

"All three of you are in jail?" *What the fuck?* Who would arrest three sweet little grannies? "Why are you in jail?"

"Because of our bucket list."

Double Christ. I run my hand down my face. "Your bucket list? Why the fuck do—"

"Language, young man." The tone is one I remember from when I was a kid and I did something wrong. It's the tone usually accompanied by a cookie afterward.

I start toward the house. "Why do you have 'Land in jail' on your bucket list?"

Sophie joins me, the horse walking alongside her now on the lead rope.

"Well, technically, it's not on the list," Grandma Meg says. "But we might have to add it to get bonus points for our stay here."

I inwardly groan once again. "So what's on the list that resulted in jail time?"

"We might have borrowed a car and gone for a joyride." There's a cringe in her tone at the last part.

"Borrowed? The definition of joyride is, the vehicle is stolen and the individuals are racing it."

"It was more like we borrowed the convertible Mustang and were planning to return it when we got back to town, but..."

"But what?"

"Have you ever ridden in a red convertible Mustang, Jake?"

In the background, there's an audible groan and a "for fuck's sake." Presumably from the inmate who Gertrude berated for the lack of manners.

"Do I want to know who you stole it from?"

"Not stole, *borrowed*. It belongs to Andrew's grandson."

"Ohmigod," Sophie says with a level of enthusiasm the situation doesn't call for. "I *love* that car. It's gorgeous."

I shoot her a look to tell her she's not helping. She shrugs and mouths, *Sorry*.

"Isn't it?" Grandma Meg says. "And it drives like a dream."

"Andrew's grandson loaned you his car?" I ask.

"No, Andrew did."

I let out a breath I didn't realize was still sitting tight in my lungs. At least Grandma Meg and her merry band of misfits aren't in trouble for larceny.

"But I'm not sure he told his grandson this." The previous cringe in Grandma Meg's tone is back. "It would seem his grandson reported the car stolen."

I drop my head in my hand and shake it in disbelief...or maybe denial. "They arrested you for possession of a stolen vehicle?" That can't be good.

"That, and because we might have slightly exceeded the speed limit."

"By slightly, how much are we talking about?"

"Nothing much. Maybe ten miles an hour over the limit. Like I said, the car drives like a dream. Sophie, maybe Chris will let you borrow it so you can try it out."

Sophie and I groan. The horse whinnies.

"How come you're calling Sophie and not Austin?" I ask.

"Because we're hoping you two will come get us...and...and we were hoping my grandson doesn't have to find out."

Right—because the Golden Falls sheriff won't be dying to rub this in Austin's face. Those two haven't exactly seen eye-to-eye ever since Austin won "best ribs" at the county fair for three years running.

"You do realize there's no way you can hide it from him?" I say.

"Does that mean you aren't coming to bust us out of jail?"

"No, it means I'm coming to *bail* you out of jail."

"Is Sophie coming, too?" Grandma Meg asks a little too eagerly.

"Yes, I'm coming, too. I just have to return the horse I was training to his pasture."

"Good, so we'll be waiting for you. And thank you!" With that, Grandma Meg ends the call.

And Sophie and I are left staring at the phone for a few seconds.

"Are you going to tell Austin?" Sophie asks.

"Eventually. Once we get them home."

She strokes Aries's nose. "I wonder why she didn't call Violet and TJ."

Good question. "Probably because she doesn't want to worry Violet." But she could have called TJ. Like me, he would've helped them, as would Noah.

But instead of asking my brothers, she specifically requested that Sophie and I save them.

Warning alarms go off in my head.

"They're up to something," I mutter to myself.

"Who's up to something?"

I shake my head. "It's nothing. Why don't you return Aries to the pasture while I contact Andrew?" His grandson needs to inform the Golden Falls police that Grandma Meg, Tilly, and Gertrude didn't steal his car.

THE THREE OF US—YES, THREE INCLUDING ANDREW—EXIT MY truck outside of the Golden Falls Police Station.

We enter the building and approach the front desk.

"I'm Jake Daniels. I'm here for Meg Brooks, Tilly Douglas, and Gertrude Brouwer."

The officer on duty, who's in his late fifties, doesn't even bother to hold back his smirk. "Ah, yes—the three troublemakers."

He can't even begin to imagine how right he is about that. "Yes, that would be them."

"Can I see some ID?"

I remove my wallet and produce my driver's license.

He checks it and nods. "The charges for possession of a stolen vehicle have been dropped. But there is still the matter of the speeding ticket." He passes it back to me.

Holy fuck. "Just how fast was she going?"

"The officer clocked her at sixteen miles per hour over the limit."

So, not quite what she had claimed.

Andrew laughs. "Well, what do you know? Gertrude is quite the little hell-raiser. I'm just sorry I missed it."

"Are they still under arrest?" Sophie asks the officer. "Do we need to bail them out or something?"

"No, they're free to leave."

The three of us turn around and check out the small waiting area. We're the only individuals here.

"So, where are they?" I ask.

He picks up the phone. "You can tell the three trouble-makers their ride is here." He chuckles at whatever the person on the other end of the line says. "I don't doubt it."

He hangs up the phone. "They'll be out shortly."

A big burly officer escorts the threesome into the waiting area a few minutes later. He would've been more intimidating if not for the huge grin on his face. "If the three of you are ever interested in annoying the hell out of our detainees again," he says to the elderly women, "just give us a buzz."

"Annoying? What the heck were you doing?" I ask.

"Singing," Gertrude states matter-of-factly. "Have you ever seen the movie *Bridget Jones: Edge of Reason*?"

Have I? It's another of Sophie's favorite movies. So what do you think?

"No."

Sophie giggles softly and I fight the urge to glare at her.

"Well, in it, Renee Zellweger is thrown in jail in Bangkok because the police thought she was smuggling drugs. And there's this one scene where she's teaching the inmates to sing 'Like a Virgin' by Madonna."

"Oh, I *love* that scene," Sophie says.

"Me too," Tilly replies. Grandma Meg and Gertrude nod in agreement.

"So that's what we were doing." Grandma Meg explains.

I'm almost tempted to ask Officer Burly if there's a video of this. "You were teaching the inmates the song?"

"Not exactly. We were just singing it to them." Gertrude starts singing the lyrics.

And I do my best not to cringe. Now I understand Officer Burly's comment about annoying the hell out of the detainees.

For a reason I can't fathom, the three of them decide it's a good time to reenact the movie scene. Complete with the dance moves.

But unlike Bridget Jones, Grandma Meg, Tilly, and Gertrude look like eighty-year-old pinup girls from the sixties, wearing floral dresses I vaguely remember seeing before and with scarves covering their hair.

Grinning again, Officer Burly crosses his arms and leans back against the counter. Clearly, he's entertained by the show.

As are Sophie and Andrew.

I've never seen anyone beam as much as Andrew as he watches the trio perform.

Once they're finished, Andrew and Sophie applaud. Officer Burly pats me on the back. "Good luck with those three." Then, chuckling, he strolls back to the doorway he'd escorted the three troublemakers through earlier.

"All right, ladies," I say to the trio. "Time to get you home."

"Or better yet. While we're in Golden Falls, we can check off another item on our bucket list."

How about we don't do that and call it a day?

"What's next on the old list, girls?" Andrew asks—because he's apparently braver than me...or more foolish.

"Hitting a nightclub and busting some moves," Tilly says, practically clapping her hands in excitement.

"Why would you want to do that?" I ask.

"Because we didn't get to experience it when we were younger. So we want to see what it's like."

"Loud." That's my helpful response.

"You could always go to Joe's," Sophie suggests.

"Except Joe's only plays country music. We want to get our dirty on with the dance music kids listen to these days."

Seriously, who stole Grandma Meg and her friends and replaced them with these facsimiles? They might look same as the real deal, but they're definitely not sounding like them.

"I think that's a splendid idea," Andrew says. "I'd like to

pretend I'm in my early twenties again. Sign me up for this adventure."

Sophie jerks her shoulders at me in a *What-can-you-do?* shrug.

"Okay," I say on a sigh and turn to Grandma Meg. "But if your grandson kills me for this, it's your fault."

"Don't worry. He won't kill you, Jake. He might try putting me on house arrest after this, but it'll be worth it." She faces her friends. "All right, girls. Let's get this party on the road. Or should I say, in the nightclub."

"I don't know about you, ladies. But I could use some nourishment first." Andrew pats his stomach. Everyone else agrees with him, and we set off for a nearby diner.

Fortunately—or unfortunately, depending on whose point of view we're talking about—Golden Falls has the type of nightclub the three elderly women are looking for.

"We're only staying an hour and that's it," I tell the group after we leave the diner. Andrew salutes me like a teenager giving his parents attitude.

I release an I'm-too-old-for-this sigh.

"You do realize this is a dance club?" the nightclub bouncer asks, his brow furrowed, as his gaze studies our motley group. But given our ages, that's hardly surprising.

"We are aware of that, young man," Andrew says. "We're looking forward to learning some new moves." He does a quick little dance step—arm actions and all—that looks better suited for an old timer's movie...like...*Singing in the Rain.*

From the corner of my eye, I catch Sophie covering her mouth with her hand and her shoulders shaking from held-back laughter.

"We don't want any trouble," the bouncer says. Ah, he must be familiar with Grandma Meg and her merry band of misfits.

"We won't be any trouble." I cluck my chin at the four seniors. "They're only here to dance for a few songs."

Still frowning, he steps aside. "All right."

The loud beat of the music greets us as we enter the club, and we weave our way through the crowd to the dance floor. Without a word to each other, the trio of grandmothers disappears into the mass of bodies. Andrew joins them.

Sophie takes one look at my face and laughs.

"What's so funny?"

She reaches up and runs her thumb across my brow. "You've got a grumpy face on. Aren't they allowed to have fun?"

"Sure. But the kind of fun more suitable for their age. Like lawn bowling and bingo."

Sophie grabs my wrist. "C'mon grumpy pants. You're dancing with me."

I should tell her no—but we all know that never happens when it comes to the woman who has my heart. She just has to ask, and I'll do it.

I let her lead me onto the dance floor, away from the rest of our group. The bodies writhing to the music barely leave any space for us. Sophie doesn't seem to care. She wraps her arms around my neck and moves to the music. And naturally, my hands can't help themselves. They pull her closer.

Her scent is intoxicating, the feel of her body against mine hypnotic. Before I know it, my body is moving in time with hers, absorbing her heat, absorbing everything about her that makes her Sophie.

She smiles at me as she moves with complete abandon. Everything around us, other than the music, fades away. She turns around and presses her ass against my groin. My cock perks up. She stretches her body slightly forward and gyrates her hips. My groan is swallowed by the music.

Somewhere deep in my head, a voice suggests I move away, but it's half-hearted at best. I ignore it and shift my hands to her stomach. My thumbs accidentally-not-so-accidentally slip under the fabric of her T-shirt. They might have also "accidentally" stroked her silky skin.

Her arms stretch behind her and she cradles the back of my head. At her touch, my scalp tingles in a yearning sort of way. Yearning for this to never stop. Yearning for a million other things I shouldn't be thinking.

I ignore the last thought and give in to the craving to kiss the soft skin on her forearm. *Christ, this is better than heaven.*

The fast-paced music switches to a slow song. Sophie shifts to face me, and her arms return to around my neck. Our bodies sway to the gentle beat. Her eyes are dark and open, like she's allowing me a glimpse into her soul. Or maybe that's how I feel about the way she's looking at me—like she longs to learn everything that makes me who I am, down to my very core.

We continue swaying and watching each other. Then my body completely takes over for my brain—that's the only explanation I have for what I do next.

I cup her cheek with my hand and brush my thumb against her lower lip. Her lips part slightly, and the tip of her tongue licks the end of my thumb.

My heart begins racing, my lungs draw in a sharp breath, and a five-alarm fire bursts to life deep inside me.

I remove my thumb from her lip—and before I can blink, I crash my mouth against hers.

Ignoring all wisdom, I pull her tight against me so she can see what she does to me. She continues kissing me like I'm the air she needs to breathe.

But then my party-pooper brain flashes an image of Ryan, reminding me I screwed up. I'm kissing his girlfriend.

The girl he cares about.

Somewhere in the back of my mind, a voice points out that she's kissing me as much as I'm kissing her. I mentally accuse it of being wrong. I'm the one who's taking advantage of her, even if I don't mean to.

I release my hold on her and step away. "Fuck, I'm so sorry. I don't know what I was thinking." And because I'm having an impossible time telling my mouth to shut up, I add, "It was a mistake. It won't happen again."

Cursing myself under my breath, I walk away, leaving Sophie on the dance floor.

I keep walking down the hallway and out the main entrance. I pace around the block until Grandma Meg, Tilly, and Gertrude are ready to leave.

Which, fortunately, is fifteen minutes later.

I give them a lame excuse about the strobe lights getting to me. No one questions it.

The trip home is spent with me silently cursing myself for being such an idiot when it comes to Sophie.

Cinderella's fairy godmother never realized how easy she had it.

23

The next day, Sophie sails into the kitchen, looking sinfully hot in her yellow floral sundress and sandals. Maui barks and scrambles toward her, his legs unable to move fast enough.

I set my glass of water on the counter and watch the pair.

She fusses over the excited puppy, and a burst of jealousy pumps through my veins. *Pathetic, Daniels. You're getting jealous of a puppy.* Of course she's going act that way around him. He's like a magnet for all things estrogen. Women can't help but fall for him.

She gets him to perform a few tricks we've trained him to do. Like sit.

"You ready for tomorrow's picnic?" she asks me after she's finished giving Maui all the attention he's clamoring for. It's as if the kiss last night never happened. Like it was nothing but another opportunity for her to practice.

"I have a picnic basket. Is that close enough to being ready?" I say, following her lead when it comes to ignoring the kiss. "And I've got jelly beans."

That was Grandma Meg's suggestion when I borrowed the basket from her.

Sophie laughs. "Jelly beans? Who are you expecting to get to bid on your basket? The Easter Bunny?"

"Hey, who doesn't like jelly beans?" Other than me.

Sophie scrunches up her nose.

Make that other than the two of us.

I lean against the kitchen island and fold my arms—mostly so I don't try to touch her or pull her into said arms. "What do you suggest?"

"You need to make it romantic, and you need to pick foods that are delicious. Preferably something homemade. Otherwise, the women could just go to the grocery store and buy it."

I frown. "Homemade? Like what?"

Yes, I cook. TJ and Noah and I take turns cooking, but none of us do it because we enjoy it. We cook because it beats starving to death.

"How about—for starters—chicken salad? Who doesn't like that...with fresh crusty buns? You can include a sampler of cheeses from Cora Ridge Creamery. And brownies for dessert." She's practically drooling as she talks.

Why? Because they're some of her favorite foods.

"I don't know how to make chicken salad."

"Not a problem, I can help you. And I can help you with the dessert." She starts riffling through my fridge and cupboards. "We'll need to go into town and buy the ingredients. We can order buns at the bakery and pick them up tomorrow on the way to the auction."

She grabs her car keys from her purse. "I'll put Maui in his crate. You want to drive or should I?"

"I'll drive my truck." Where I can continue to pretend the white elephant in the room doesn't exist. The elephant that showed up when I kissed her yesterday while we were dancing and only I seem to notice it.

Denial? My new best friend.

AT COPPER MILLS MARKET, WE WANDER UP AND DOWN THE aisles on our quest for the items we'll need.

"Well, if it isn't my favorite couple," Tilly says.

I open my mouth to remind her that Sophie and I aren't dating.

I don't get that far. Tilly waves me off. "Yes, yes, I realize you two aren't actually dating. Which is a shame. You're a good-looking couple."

She moves closer to us and lowers her voice as if sharing a state secret. "And thanks to you not cooperating with my plans for you to marry each other last year, I lost a bet I had with Gertrude."

"You bet that Jake and I were going to get married?" The disbelief in Sophie's tone mirrors the one in my head.

But probably for different reasons.

"We're eighty-year-old women living in a small town. What else do you expect us to do?"

"What's wrong with lawn bowling?" I say on a chuckle. "Or playing cards?"

"We were playing strip poker for a while, but then we moved the game to the senior center, and they got all uppity about the stripping part."

Sophie squeezes her lips together, doing her best not to laugh out loud. I don't even bother holding back my laughter. There's no point.

"I swear, living in a small town wouldn't be the same without you, Grandma Meg, and Gertrude," I say.

Tilly grins. "You got that right, young man. So, how about

you two do me a favor? Get married this year and have a little girl named Jessica."

"Another bet you've made?"

She shrugs. "Maybe."

"You even bet on the baby's name?" There's more disbelief in Sophie's tone than there was for the marriage question—which I didn't believe was possible until now.

"I'm not answering on the grounds that it could get me in a lot of trouble. But do me a favor and don't name her Sarah or Brittany."

I level my gaze at Tilly. "Let me guess, those are the names Grandma Meg and Gertrude picked?"

She nods. "Mary Jo picked Jocelyn, and Andrew picked Samuel."

Mary Jo Hellman (aka Miss H) was my high school English teacher.

"This is just a wild guess," Sophie says, "but you guys said the baby would be a girl, and Andrew voted a boy?"

"Wait, you have no problems with them predicting the name of our fictitious kid," I say, "but you have an issue with Andrew betting it will be a boy instead of a girl?"

Tilly snickers. "That's the name he picked for your daughter. Of course, it's also the name he picked for your future son."

"You do realize you're all wasting your time with these bets, right? Sophie is dating Ryan, the vet." At the word *dating*, my stomach clenches like a prune during a heat wave.

"So I've heard, but as nice as I think he is, my money is still on you two having your happily ever after together." She taps her temple. "I have ESP. I know things."

No, that isn't the first time I've heard it. About the ESP.

How many of her predictions have come true?

Let's just say Austin won't be hiring her anytime soon to help him solve his next crime.

Not that Copper Creek has many crimes.

"Does your ESP tell you who's gonna win my picnic basket tomorrow? And if they don't mind that it'll be empty because Sophie and I still have to buy food for it?"

Tilly pinches my cheek like she did when I was five. "Now, don't you go making fun of me, Jake. And yes, I know exactly who'll have the winning bid." Her gaze shifts to Sophie and back to me. "But I also don't want our sweet Sophie starving tomorrow because you haven't bought any food, so I'll let you two get back to work." She turns and shuffles away, humming a happy tune.

Sophie's cheeks are adorably flushed. "Well, that was interesting."

"As you know, there's never a boring moment when Tilly and her merry band of troublemakers are around. But don't worry. Like most people, I doubt Ryan will take what she said seriously."

Assuming he finds out what she said.

Sophie gives me a small smile, but something's slightly off about it.

"Are you okay?" I lightly tug a strand of her hair. "Honestly, you don't need to worry about Ryan thinking you're interested in me. He knows you and I are friends. Nothing more."

Ignore the sensation of a hot butter knife being stabbed in my chest. It's nothing, really. Just a minor inconvenience.

Sophie looks at her phone—and our shopping list on it. "We need to get chicken breasts."

And the butter knife turns in my chest.

We're here to buy ingredients for the picnic, I remind my heart. *We're not here so I can get down on one knee and tell her I love her.*

Why not? my heart grumbles.

We resume our hunt for the ingredients we'll need for the food. I also buy a bottle of white wine, as per her suggestion. Afterward, we head to Copper Creek's bakery and order Sophie's favorite buns for tomorrow.

"Is there anyone who you are hoping will bid on your basket?" Sophie asks as she chops the celery into tiny pieces.

You. "Not really. Preferably someone who's only interested in the food." And nothing else.

We both reach for the mayonnaise jar on the counter at the same time. My fingers brush against her hand. The usual hum of electricity vibrates through me.

Sophie gasps softly. I jerk my hand away as if I'd been electrocuted—which would've been preferable.

What I really need is a power outage when it comes to Sophie and the effect she has on me.

I step back, but like the sky shortly before a lightning storm, the air feels electrically charged, crackling with unspent energy. There's no escaping it without leaving the room.

I wait for her to finish with the mayonnaise, then I add some to the brownie batter.

Shit, I really want to kiss her.

But I can't do that.

So, I do the next best thing...I begin pacing.

"Are you okay?" she asks, repeating my question from the store.

"I'm fine. There's a storm coming. They usually make me antsy."

That's a lie and she knows it.

"I should probably take Maui out while I still can." Then I can pace outside and give myself time to pull myself together.

Great idea.

"I'll work on some off-leash training with him while we're in the backyard," I tell her. "We won't be long. You want outside, Maui?"

The nine-week-old puppy is busy attacking his favorite toy near the kitchen table. At my question, he gives a little bark and charges toward the hallway leading to the back door.

Sophie laughs. "That would be a yes."

I follow him and open the door.

"So, Maui, you have any relationship advice for me?" I ask once we're outside. Sophie is still in the kitchen.

He sniffs the ground, ignoring me.

"All right, not so much relationship advice—more like advice on how to get over the woman I'm in love with."

Maui barks.

"Right—not your area of expertise."

A flash of lightning streaks across the cloudy sky. This is followed a few seconds later by a low rumble of thunder.

Maui gives a little yelp and scrambles in the opposite direction of the house.

I follow him. "It's okay, boy. Daddy will keep you safe."

"Is everything all right?" Sophie calls out from the open door.

At that moment, the sky decides we need hail thrown into the mix. I chase after Maui, except I can no longer see him.

Shit. He must have disappeared in the long grass.

I call his name as I scan the area. Stinging hail hits my bare skin. Clearly having unfulfilled fantasies about Sophie isn't enough—the storm is upping my punishment.

"Where did he go?" Sophie asks.

Her dress is soaked and clings to her. And because God hasn't finished tormenting me, her taut nipples poke through her thin bra and the fabric of her dress.

"I don't know," I call out over the noise. "He couldn't have gotten too far."

"Do you hear that?" She's looking away from me, toward where the grass is longer, wilder, and marks the beginning of the slope. It's steep enough that my brothers and I can't be bothered to mow it. To attempt to do so, could lead to disaster, even with a ride-on mower.

Before I can say anything, Sophie takes off running. Even in sandals, she can move fast. I follow after her—but she already has a head start on me and is closer to the direction of the faint barking.

With a startled shriek, she disappears from view. I arrive at the edge of the incline in time to see her half tumbling, half sliding down it.

She lands in a pile on the ground next to Maui, who is barking excitedly at his rescuer. She scoops him up and cuddles him close.

I race down to the pair, doing my best not to join her fate, and crouch beside her. "Are you okay?"

"I'm fine," she says, still cuddling Maui.

He reaches up and licks her face.

"Okay, you two. Let's get you both back to the house." I help Sophie to her feet, but it quickly becomes obvious that her ankle isn't on speaking terms with her.

Before she can protest, I scoop her up in my arms. She's still cradling Maui.

"Why, Willoughby," she says in a fake English accent. A badly faked accent. "What would I ever do without you?"

Willoughby? Ever seen the movie *Sense and Sensibility*? The one based on the book by that British chick who died well over a hundred years ago? It had Emma Thompson and Kate Winslet in it.

That's the one.

Yes, I might have seen it once or twice—all right, three times—because it's another of Sophie's favorite movies.

That's how I know she's referring to the scene where Kate Winslet tumbles down the hill during a storm and sprains her ankle. Willoughby rescues her and carries her home.

Even though he turns out to be a douchebag in the end, this scene always has Sophie sighing.

"Great. I get to be the douchebag? Does that mean Ryan gets to be Colonel Brandon?" Spoiler alert—Colonel Brandon gets the girl.

"She ends up with the Colonel because Willoughby couldn't marry her due to circumstances out of his control. He did love her in his own way."

For the first time since seeing the movie, there's a part of me that actually sympathizes with the asshole. Although in his case, he could have still married Kate Winslet if he had really loved her. He just loved money more.

I carry Sophie and Maui back to the house. The hail has slowed by the time we step into the mudroom—which is currently aptly named, given that both Sophie and I are wet and muddy.

I remove my boots and carry her to the couch. Maui is still in her arms, enjoying the attention. Her warmth seeps through our wet clothing, heating me to the core.

Not that I need heating. I was already hot from having her in my arms. Her touch is like a match when struck. It's enough to ignite a fire.

"You can't put me on the couch, Jake. It'll get messy."

"Then where am I supposed to put you? I need to check your ankle."

"I'd rather shower first." Her tone warns me that she's going to be goddamn stubborn about this.

I'm about to argue, but she parks her finger against my lip. Without meaning to, I inhale her sweet strawberries-and-cream scent.

It's like kryptonite to Superman.

My weakness.

"I really need to shower first," she says. "Can you help me with that?"

I swallow. Hard. "Help you? How?"

"Help me get into the shower."

"How are you going to stand in the shower with a sprained ankle?"

"You'll need to help me there, too."

Shit. "I can't do that. You're dating Ryan."

She tilts her head to the side like a curious cocker spaniel. But that's not what makes me feel like I'm being sucker punched to the nuts. It's the casual way she says, "You've seen me naked before and didn't have an issue with it."

"Yes, but you and I were having sex at the time...and you weren't dating Ryan."

"And that's the difference. I won't be having sex with you. I'll stay in my underwear if that makes you feel better."

There's something in her eyes—hope, maybe—that prevents me from saying no.

But no way in hell am I getting out of my jeans. I see her half-naked, and I'll be going full mast.

She doesn't need to witness that.

In the bathroom, I set her ass on the counter.

That alone gets my cock more excited than it should be.

Down boy.

It's as cooperative as Maui when he's learning a new trick.

I release an I'm-totally-screwed breath and remove her sandal. Her ankle is swollen but not overly so. Yet.

I start helping Sophie out of her dress. The fabric clings to her body, unwilling to let go. Like me, it believes this is a bad idea.

A minute later, it lands on the floor with a splat, and Sophie is left sitting on the counter in only her white lacy bra and panties.

I recite the brownie recipe in my head, making up half the ingredients—because hell if I know how to bake brownies. I never finished the ones I began prior to taking Maui for a walk.

Before Sophie has a chance to see the effect she's having on me, I move to the shower and turn it on.

"I'll be back in a second," I say, heading for the bathroom door.

"Where are you going?"

"To get you dry clothes." Not that I have anything that will fit her.

By the time I return with my old university sweat shirt and sweat pants, steam fills the room. Fortunately, this includes the mirror. Now I won't have to see the reflection of the number one idiot in here: me.

I remove my socks and shirt, turn on the shower and adjust the temperature, then make a move to pick her up.

She gently pushes my arms away. "Aren't you taking off your jeans?" Her gaze drops to them.

"It's not like they'll get any wetter in the shower." They're already soaked.

"Good point."

With that said and done, I pick her up and carry her into the tub. There's not a lot of space in it. Our bodies are practically touching.

She rests her hand against the wall, keeping her weight off her injured ankle.

"Not quite how I remember it in the movie," I say. "Although I'm sure Willoughby wouldn't have minded being in the shower with Marianne."

Sophie laughs, the sound echoing in the steamy room. "I don't think they had showers back then. They would have soaked in the bathtub."

Even better.

Maybe we should've used TJ's shower. Being the oldest brother, he has the master bedroom with the large walk-in shower.

I pick up the bottle of shower gel and show her the label.

"Sorry, this is all I have."

This being more on the manly side than the sweet scent of strawberries and cream that permeates every part of her.

"That's fine. I happen to like the way you smell," she says... and shit if my cock doesn't grow harder.

"I happen to like the way you smell, too." *Oh, crap. I didn't say that out loud, did I?*

Time for a change of topic.

Fast.

"I'm guessing Cinderella's fairy godmother didn't shower with her, huh?" *Yes, dumbass, because that was so much better than the last comment.*

"Not unless it's a porn adaptation of the fairy tale."

I almost groan out loud at that.

You're really not helping my situation here, Soph.

I pour gel on my palm and rub my hands together to create lather.

Remember when you lost your virginity and you weren't sure what you were doing? It was awkward and unnerving.

Welcome to showering with Sophie—when I shouldn't be thinking about touching her, shouldn't be thinking of how her skin feels next to mine, shouldn't be thinking of caressing her breasts and the area between her legs.

Okay, I can do this. I can be professional about it.

A voice in my head cracks up...and asks me in what part of the company policy does it say showering with an employee is okay.

I take a deep breath and gently wash Sophie's body. I avoid touching anywhere near her bra and panties. Her arms and legs are dotted with mud and bits of grass. I focus on those parts and only those parts.

"You're really good at this." Her voice is slightly breathless, as if I'm actually affecting her—which couldn't be further from the truth.

I give her a nod in thanks and quickly finish the task. I rinse out her hair, fighting the urge to grab the shampoo and massage her scalp.

I turn off the water, grab a towel, and quickly dry her. Then I use the damp towel on myself—which is pointless given the state of my jeans.

I scoop Sophie up in my arms again—while reciting in my head the names of all the constellations, just so I have something to distract me—and carry her out of the shower. Water streams from my jeans and creates a sloppy wet trail behind me on the tile floor.

I lower her to her feet and help her put on my sweat shirt and pants. Both are oversized on her, but damned if she doesn't look sexy anyway.

For the first time since she asked me to help her with the shower, she suddenly looks shy, uncertain.

"Don't worry, nothing happened between us." I've known her long enough to venture a guess that's what she's worried about. "Besides, Ryan knows I'm more like a brother to you."

She smiles softly. "You're right." Her gaze shifts to the bathroom door. "We should get back to making your picnic now. I don't know about you, but I have a sudden craving for brownies. With ice cream."

"We can do that...right after I check your ankle. And you won't be helping me make the picnic. You'll be sitting on the chair with your foot elevated. But you do get to be the backseat driver in the kitchen."

"What about the brownies?" She pouts—and I long to kiss it off her face.

"Don't worry, you'll still get your brownies and ice cream. If you let me check out your ankle, I'll bake them first."

Her smile brightens, and my heart squeezes in celebration at how I put the grin back on her face. "You've got yourself a deal."

24

The stage for the picnic auction was set up last night in the park near the town hall, with dozens of chairs arranged in neat rows in front of it. Noah and I join the rest of the bachelors backstage who are involved in the event.

I scan the group of twenty or so men. We're all dressed differently. I'm wearing jeans, a white button-up shirt rolled up at the sleeves, cowboy boots, a black cowboy hat, and a belt buckle with several stars etched into it. It was a Christmas gift last year from Sophie.

One guy is wearing a suit. All I know about him is that he moved to Copper Creek last month to replace one of the retiring family physicians. Some of the guys are wearing slacks and shirts. Others are wearing jeans and worn-in T-shirts.

"Where's Ryan?" I ask my brother. He's the only guy I knew was participating who isn't here yet.

"He had a medical emergency," Noah says. "He had no idea if he would be back in time, so he had to withdraw from the auction."

At least now Sophie won't have to worry about other

216

women kissing the man she's dating. Not that she'd seemed concerned about it.

Tilly claps her hands to get our attention. "All right, gentlemen. On the other side of the curtains are some very *hungry* women." She winks at us, then explains how the auction will work. "Any questions?"

We shake our heads, and she herds us into a single line. By the time it's my turn to go onstage, ten guys have already been auctioned off.

"Good luck!" Tilly tells me as I approach the curtain. I stroll onstage, relieved to finally get this over with. Another hour or so, and I can get back to the ranch, forget about the picnic, and throw myself into my chores.

Not a single empty seat is available at what has become a standing-room-only event. Violet wasn't kidding when she warned me that the entire Beaver Ridge County knew about it. Even though the men involved in the auction range in age from nineteen to thirty-five, women of all ages are here—and I'm not counting Grandma Meg and her band of troublemakers. They've joined Tilly at the bottom of the stage steps.

The women in the seats are talking and laughing among themselves. Behind them, a large group of boisterous men are standing, laughing at me, mocking me, and eating popcorn. *Where the heck did they get popcorn?*

And that's when I spot her. Sophie. Looking gorgeous as ever. Her hair is loose and she's wearing my favorite lacy white sundress. The sundress I have mouth-watering memories of removing from her body a few weeks ago before making love to her.

If you had asked me a few minutes ago what scent I could smell in the air, I'd have said the faint but not-so-pleasant clash of different perfumes. And now? All I can smell is strawberries and cream. All I can smell is Sophie.

I release a long God-I'm-screwed sigh as Mayor Wineberg lists the contents of my basket.

A few non-single guys call out smartass comments. I mentally flip them the bird, abiding by the rules of keeping things family-friendly.

"How about we start at twenty-five dollars?" Mayor Wineberg asks.

At some point in her former life, the mayor must've been an auctioneer. Damn, I've never heard anyone talk that fast.

Two dozen or so women bid on me. As the bidding climbs to fifty dollars, the number of women raising their hands begins to diminish.

"Turn around so they can get a better view of your tushy," one guy I recognize yells from the back. Based on his smirk, "tushy" is not the word he's really thinking.

A chuckle ripples through the audience. I twist around and wiggle my ass, which gets me a louder laugh.

Nope, I'm not competitive at all.

Leaves rustle in the nearby trees—as if they too are eager to bid on the men involved with the auction.

"Do we have fifty-five dollars?" Mayor Wineberg asks.

Six women raise their hands.

Kennedy sashays up to the back row and stands next to the chair at the end. The woman sitting on it says something to her. Kennedy nods and the woman vacates the seat. I guess being a Broadway actress must garner you all kinds of privileges in Copper Creek I didn't know about.

"Do we have sixty dollars?" Mayor Wineberg asks.

This time three hands go up...including Kennedy's.

What the hell?

Sophie's gaze takes in the women in her vicinity; then she twists in her seat to look behind her.

"Do we have seventy dollars?"

Kennedy's hand shoots up...and so does Sophie's.

What the double hell?

Sophie turns back to face the stage. She's chewing her lower lip, and I can tell from the way her body is moving that she's bouncing her knee. It's her tell that she's nervous.

But I can't imagine what she would be nervous about.

And while we're listing things I can't imagine...I can't imagine why she bid on me. Maybe she's trying to push up the winning amount to help Tilly out with the auction.

And Kennedy's expression? She looks as casual as can be—like she's sitting back and enjoying the show with a martini.

Which, for some reason, gets my hackles on high alert.

"Do we have seventy-five dollars?"

Kennedy and Sophie put up their hands. Sophie doesn't even look behind her this time to double check that Kennedy is still bidding on me.

What the fuck is she doing? Don't get me wrong. It's not that I'm against Sophie bidding on me. I'm more than happy to have lunch with her. I just don't understand why she's bothering. I mean, I get that we packed her favorite foods, but she doesn't have to bid on the basket to eat them. There's plenty of leftovers back at the ranch.

And she knows this.

She also knows that it's not like I need rescuing from Kennedy. Much.

The woman is my date for TJ and Violet's wedding, after all.

"Do we have eighty dollars?"

Both women raise their hand.

"Eighty-five dollars?"

Again, both women acknowledge the bid.

"Do we have ninety dollars?"

This time only Sophie lifts her hand.

"Ninety dollars going once...going twice...and gone to Sophie West."

The audience applauds.

With her gaze locked on me, Kennedy's lips tug into a smug grin, and her eyebrows do a quick dance. She pushes herself off the chair and walks away, leaving the area without even a second glance.

The audience is still clapping for Sophie, but the noise is nowhere near as loud as Grandma Meg, Gertrude, and Tilly.

Grinning, Grandma Meg and Gertrude hand Tilly what looks to be money. Then Tilly turns to me and taps her temple like she did in the grocery store. I inwardly roll my eyes.

I'll never live this down when it comes to her prediction. Not because it's true...because it isn't. It's because she thinks she correctly predicted that Sophie and I will end up together.

"Next up, we have Noah Daniels," the mayor announces.

Which is my cue to go backstage and for Sophie to pay for her expensive lunch.

I wait in the back with the other guys. Once the auction is over, we return onstage and Mayor Wineberg announces how much money was raised. We're then free to have lunch with our "dates."

I wander through the crowd, searching for Sophie. Several people stop me to congratulate me for winning lunch with "such a sweet and wonderful girl."

I finally locate her by a group of tall bushes, and my heart drops like an elevator that had its cable cut.

Ryan is with her.

And she's hugging him.

He hugs her back.

What do you expect, dumbass? They're dating. Of course they're going to be hugging.

Just be happy they're not making out in front of you.

As if sensing me watching them, they both turn to me. Ryan says something to Sophie. She nods. He kisses her.

I groan and repeat what is now my new mantra—*they're*

dating, they're dating, they're dating—in my head as I walk over to join them.

Fortunately, the kiss doesn't last for more than a second.

"So? Are we making this a threesome?" I ask and then cringe. That didn't come out the way I'd planned.

Sophie's eyes widen and she splutters, "You're into threesomes?"

Ryan cracks up. "Yeah, you can definitely count me out."

"Sorry," I say, "that's not how I meant for it to sound. I just meant is Ryan joining us for lunch?"

He shakes his head. "I've got other plans. I just wanted to see how the auction went before I headed back to the clinic." He smiles at Sophie and she nods, the movement small.

He holds out his hand to me. "Congratulations. Enjoy your lunch."

Slightly confused at why he's congratulating me, I shake it.

"I'll talk to you later," he says to Sophie, then walks away.

"Where do you want to eat?" I ask her.

She points to a quiet spot under a tree near the town pond. "Over there."

We head to the patch of grass. Sophie's limping slightly.

I stopped. "Are you sure you should be walking? Your ankle's still hurt."

She resumes walking. "I'm fine. It's a little stiff, that's all."

"You sure you don't want me to carry you?"

She laughs. The sound isn't her normal laugh. It's more on the nervous side of things, which doesn't make sense. "I'm sure."

At the tree, I spread out the blanket and start removing the food from the basket.

It takes me a moment to realize that Sophie hasn't joined me. She's pacing back and forth in front of the blanket, the limp still there.

"Are you planning on pacing a hole to Australia?" I ask.

She keeps moving.

"Soph, what's going on? Does this have to do with Ryan?" I know she was counting on bidding for his basket, but his canceling because of an emergency wouldn't bother her. She'd understand.

"I like you, Jake." She continues pacing.

"I like you, too. But you know that because we've been friends since college."

"No, I mean I *like* like you." She doesn't pause her pacing for even second to tell me this. "I have for a while now. Even back in college."

The wind picks up, sending the water soaring up from the fountain flying. It lands with a loud *plop, plop, plop* and a gurgling noise. The leaves in the tree rub harshly against each other.

I blink, replaying her words in my head—positive I'd misheard them—and push myself to my feet. "Why are you telling me this? You're dating Ryan. He's your boyfriend."

A strand of hair blows into her face. She shoves it behind her ear and keeps walking. "Ryan isn't my boyfriend. He never was. We weren't even dating. At least not beyond the one date."

My heart beats a new sound: *what the fuck, what the fuck, what the fuck?* Accompanied by the parade in my head of women over the years who have played games with me to get what they wanted.

I grab her arm to stop her. "If you aren't dating, then why did you just kiss him?"

We'll ignore the part where a few weeks ago I was kissing her even though she and I weren't dating either.

But that was different. She wanted me to kiss her so she could ensure her kisses were good enough for Ryan or any guy.

"Because I didn't believe you were interested in me as more than a friend," she says.

I frown and release her arm. "So what? You kissing him was

a test?" My voice sounds dry to my ears, like two pieces of sandpaper being rubbed together.

She winces. "It was Ryan's idea. He said your reaction would prove if you're interested in me."

Seriously, what do they teach at vet school? 'Cause that isn't covered in business school. Not even close.

"So let me get this straight. You like me but instead of telling me the truth, you used Ryan to make me jealous? And not only that, you asked me to help you land him as a boyfriend even though you liked *me*?"

"No. It's nothing like that, Jake. I was scared. I—"

"What? You were scared of me? Nice try, Sophie. We've been friends for years. All you had to do was be honest with me. But apparently that was too much for you."

I trusted Sophie, but she hadn't trusted me enough to tell me the truth. She was like all those other women who'd been happy to play games with my head. Only in Sophie's case, there'd been more than just my head involved. My heart had been unwittingly dragged in, too.

I feel a frown form between my eyes. "Is that why you wanted me to help you in the shower yesterday? And why you took your dress off at the lake the night of the barbecue? Because you like me as more than a friend?"

She steps forward. "I thought if you saw me like that, you'd finally notice me as a woman and not just a buddy to hang out with."

"So you were trying to seduce me?"

She nods. "Very poorly, apparently."

I shove my hands through my hair, attempting to lasso in my thoughts. "Let me guess. All that stumbling over your words when you're interested in a guy was nothing more than an act? And the story about the football player was a lie?"

"No, all of it was true."

"Except you've never had trouble talking to me."

"That's not entirely true. When we first met, I was just as tongue-tied around you as I was with those other guys. You just never realized it. By the time we became friends...well, I'd learned my lesson with Caleb—"

"And you instantly figured I was the same as that lowlife." My tone is calmer now, like the eye of a hurricane. But my emotions—anger, happiness, betrayal, joy, foolish pride, desire —are all caught up in the hundred-and-ten mile-per-hour winds.

"I swore I'd never make the same mistake with you, even when I started caring for you more than I should." She resumes her pacing. Maybe she can send me a postcard once she reaches Australia. Because the way she's going, that's a strong possibility at this point.

"What about Ryan? Were you just using him?"

She can't even look at me when she replies. She just continues walking back and forth, back and forth. "No. Never. Even though I like you, I knew you would never be interested in me the same way. Not when you had your stupid company policy about dating employees. Ryan's a nice guy and caring and sweet. Plus I want to have a husband and kids one day. Ryan was interested in those things, too. You're not."

I fold my arms across my chest. "If that's true, why are you telling me this when you could be planning your wedding and having lots of babies with him?"

"Because he figured out you're the only man I'm interested in. And after what happened with his ex-girlfriend, he decided that he and I were better off as friends."

This is why I have the company policy.

Okay—that's not entirely true. The policy was to prevent a future girlfriend from stealing from me the way Lisa had done back in college.

The no dating policy, in general, was because I'd been afraid of trusting the wrong person again.

Yet, despite that, I still made the same mistake.

Lather. Rinse. Repeat...and all that crap.

I begin backing away. "Look, I can't do this. Whatever game you thought you could play didn't work. I thought you knew me better than that, Sophie."

I turn and stalk to where my truck is parked. I don't bother to look over my shoulder to see what she's doing—and she doesn't bother to call me back.

I remove my phone from my rear pocket and send Aubrey a text, telling her where she can find Sophie.

Turning off the ringer, I climb into my truck and drive as far from Copper Creek as I can get.

I need space to think things through.

I need time to figure out my jumbled emotions.

25

The next two days are spent throwing myself into my work—and not allowing myself time to think.

Because thinking is a bad thing.

When it comes to Sophie.

I'm channeling the frustration and the feeling of being manipulated to create a super-productive self. I'm like Superman: no task is too big or too small.

And I keep telling myself this as I shovel Orion's horse shit from his stall.

Is this mindless, less-than-pleasant chore cathartic?

What do you think?

The dull, rhythmic thud of cowboy boots against concrete approaches. I don't bother to look up to see whom it belongs to.

"So what's going on between you and Sophie?" Noah's tone is somewhere between amused and *What the fuck?*

I glance up and frown. "Don't you have your own chores to do?"

"Sure I do. And as soon as you answer my question, I'll get to them." He crosses his arms and flashes me a warning look about trying to feed him bullshit.

Which is actually funny coming from him, given he's the king of bullshit.

"There's nothing going on between us," I say. "You know that. We're just friends."

"So as her friend, did you know she was planning to resign as our trainer?"

Fuck. "What are you talking about?"

"She gave me her resignation letter this morning, effective immediately."

I release a hard breath. "She must have accepted Walter Scottsdale's offer to work for him."

"But why? Wasn't her horse training business going to be here?"

"He must have offered her something she couldn't say no to." Something she knew we couldn't afford.

"Fuck."

"Exactly."

Noah's eyebrow quirks up. "Are you sure that her leaving us had nothing to do with what happened at the auction?"

"Why would her bidding on my basket have anything to do with that?"

"You tell me."

There have been plenty of times when I've silently cursed Noah for being more of a playboy than someone interested in the business side of the ranch.

This is not one of those times.

Right now, I'd rather see the easygoing guy than the brother who currently believes he's training to be an FBI interrogator.

"There's nothing to tell."

"Is it possible she accepted the offer because then your stupid company policy wouldn't apply to her anymore?"

And suddenly shoveling horse shit doesn't sound so unappealing.

"Why should that make any difference? It's not like she and I were anything other than friends."

Noah barks a laugh. "Is that what you're telling yourself? Because I've seen you two together. You haven't been *just* friends since she started at the ranch. You've just been too goddamn stubborn to see it, Jake."

"Why don't you tell me what you really think."

He shakes his head. Noah doesn't often do disappointed, so being on the receiving end of it smarts like a wasp stinger in the ass. "I have a question for you."

"What's that?"

"You violated your own policy the moment you had sex with her—and don't try to deny it because both TJ and I know it's true. So what's your punishment gonna be?"

I move my shoulders in a hell-if-I-know shrug. "I do each of your chores for tonight."

Which is actually a brilliant idea. That'll keep me too busy to think about Sophie.

I'm about to pat myself on the back for my sheer brilliance when Noah decides to burst my bubble with a jackhammer.

"Oh, I've got something much better." The way he says it sets off sirens rivaling that of a tornado alert.

Why do I have a feeling I would rather face a tornado than what he has planned?

And the devious grin on his face confirms it.

26

"Do I really have to do this?" I ask, standing next to Orion on Main Street, the numbness and anger from the picnic faded like an old scar.

Orion neighs...or snickers.

Roxy Bliss, formally known as Robert, pats my cheek. "You look darling in my dress, doll. Just make sure you don't damage it. I need it for my show this weekend."

The dress in question? It's sleeveless, light blue with lots of tulle (according to Roxy, because hell if I knew what tulle was before this). It's also long, with the hem almost brushing the ground. In its former life, it might've been a prom gown—for a six-foot girl.

It's a complete contrast to the pink T-shirt—with the Good Creations Bakery emblem on the chest—and jeans that Roxy is wearing.

"Shouldn't you at least stuff a couple of gym socks down your bra?" Noah asks with a smirk in his tone. "You're flatter than an eleven-year-old girl."

I give him the stink eye with a heavy dose of mental cursing. He laughs.

229

"Don't forget the finishing touch." Roxy crouches in front of the squat, cylinder-shaped case on the curb. She straightens a moment later with something sparkly in her hand. "Your tiara."

It's official…my man card just got revoked.

Right—it was revoked the second I put on the glittery dress.

She fastens it to my head. "You look like Cinderella. And that would make me your fairy godmother."

Noah cracks up, almost doubling over from laughing so hard. He knows about me being Sophie's supposed fairy godfather.

I level him with another stink eye.

Confusion lands on Roxy's face. "Are either of you going to explain to me why Jake is dressed like Cinderella? And why he's planning to ride down Main Street in my dress while on his horse? Is there a parade I missed the invite to?"

Yeah, a parade of one: me.

"Jake lost a bet with TJ and me."

The truth has nothing to do with a supposed bet. This is my punishment for costing the ranch a brilliant horse trainer.

Roxy's gaze darts between us, her jaw ajar. "Wow, you boys are really harsh. Remind me never to make a bet with you. The worst I can expect from the folks at the senior center is having to sing one of my show songs to them. And that's as much a hardship as having one of my chocolate éclairs."

She checks me over and nods. "You look fabulous, Jake. I mean, you aren't the picture of femininity"—this gets a snort out of Noah—"but you still look fab-u-lous."

Noah's mouth jerks to one side. "Other than the part where you're still flat-chested, she's right. You do look good. The sparkly blue eye shadow is a nice touch." He presses his lips together, attempting to hold back a laugh. More for Roxy's benefit, I suspect, than mine. But that's as effective as opening a vigorously shaken soda bottle.

The laugh erupts from his lungs, and I glower at him.

Roxy grins, shaking her head. "I should get back to the bakery before Martha accidentally burns down the store." She parks her large makeup case on top of her suitcase and picks up her tiara box from the curb.

"Don't forget to tell your customers to look out the window in a few minutes," Noah says, "and to take lots of photos to post on social media."

"I will." She smiles and walks away, pulling her suitcase behind her. Her long legs quickly eat up the distance to the store.

"You know I'm going to kill you for this, right?" I don't even bother looking at Noah when I say it.

"Hey, a deal's a deal. You screwed around with Sophie, breaking your own policy, and lost us an amazing trainer."

I drop my head in shame because he's right.

Have I even attempted to talk to her or tried to convince her to come back?

No, because I have no idea what to say to her.

It's easier being a coward than to admit I'm afraid of trusting the wrong person. Trusting the wrong person and end up losing everything, including the ranch.

"Any idea how I'm supposed to ride a horse while dressed like this?" Heck, I have no clue how to even get on the horse while wearing a ball gown.

"No idea. It's not like Grandpa told us when he taught us how to ride."

I gather up the skirt so it's midthigh. "You're gonna need to help me up."

Noah looks at my bare legs and cringes. "Christ, I can't even begin to imagine the nightmares this will cause me. Your hairy legs aren't exactly what I'm used to when paired with a dress."

I shove his shoulder. "I'm not shaving for your benefit, so get over it."

Somehow, I manage to mount Orion. I'd like to say all my dignity is kept intact, but that would be a lie.

"Yes, I definitely foresee nightmares in my future," Noah says with a chuckle.

"Good. It will serve you right for making me do this." I scan the area. "So where's your partner in crime anyway?"

"TJ? He's a little preoccupied right now."

Given that sex is off the table for him for another week, I guess I know what he's currently *not* doing.

"All right, let's get this over with." I give Orion a kick and we start walking down Main Street. Fortunately, it's one in the afternoon on a Thursday. It shouldn't be too busy right now.

In theory.

Too bad I hadn't factored TJ into the so-called theory.

"Shit," I mutter to myself. When Roxy had mentioned a parade, I thought she was joking.

I was wrong. *Very* wrong.

The sidewalks are filled with people watching me. Someone yells out a catcall. Another person wolf whistles. Because there are also kids watching, I can only mentally flip him the finger—and wave like I'm royalty. The genuine Cinderella would be proud.

Luckily, I don't have to worry about either brother telling anyone the real reason for the ball gown...beyond the fictitious bet I lost.

No one needs to know about the company policy I violated.

No one needs to know with whom I violated it.

I approach the veterinary clinic. Ryan and Aubrey and the rest of the staff are standing out front, taking photos and laughing.

But even though Aubrey is laughing and cheering and whistling at me, I know her too well. I recognize the disappointment in her eyes, which has nothing to do with me being in a dress.

I don't know Ryan all that well, but I swear the same emotion is echoed in *his* eyes.

So now Sophie is no closer to falling in love and having the family she wants than when we started this whole mess, a voice in my head says.

Not my problem, I remind it.

How has Maui dealt with Sophie's absence? Like any young child after his parents divorce, he misses her. Just like I'm sure she misses him. She hasn't returned to the ranch since dropping off her resignation.

Copper Creek's population is just over three thousand, and I'm positive every single one of them is currently on the sidewalk, watching me look like an idiot.

And that's when it hits me.

TJ and Noah aren't making me do this because I violated my own company policy. They're making me humiliate myself because of what I've cost the ranch.

What I've cost our future.

Sure we'll get another trainer, but we won't get another Sophie.

I won't get another Sophie.

27

____

nce Orion and I reach the town hall, I dismount him as he eyes the stretch of green grass in front of the building. Small birds in the nearby trees tweet their chuckles at how ridiculous I look. And I'm positive if Cinderella's mice where here, they'd be doing the same.

Fortunately, the parade of spectators has already disbanded, returning to whatever they were doing before my humiliation.

"Well, that was definitely interesting," Aubrey says. I turn to her. "How the heck did your brothers convince you to ride through town while wearing a prom dress? Or would I rather not know?"

"Does it really matter?"

She doesn't answer. Instead, her gaze slides down my body, taking in the dress with its less-than-flattering neckline, the top that sags due to my lack of tits, the tulle skirt, and she nods. "It's an interesting look on you. But I must admit I prefer your cowboy hat over the tiara." I have to agree with her there.

"Pray do tell...is this what you're wearing to the wedding

234

instead of a suit?" She gestures at the dress and throws in a smirk as an added bonus.

I snort a laugh. "Violet will kill me if I even consider it." And not because I'll upstage the bride—which I won't.

"You might be right about that."

Okay, time to cut to the chase. "What is it you really want, Aubrey? I'm sure it's not to discuss my choice in princess wear." I remove the tiara from my head. Shit, how do little girls even survive these things?

"You mean other than the part where you made one of my best friends cry, and I want to kick you in the nuts because of it?"

I inwardly flinch on behalf of my package. But I guess I deserve it. "Yes, other than that."

"Do you know why I was trying to set Sophie and Ryan up?"

"Because you figured they were a perfect match?"

"Partly that. But mostly it's 'cause I knew she really liked you, Jake. Only you never saw her as anything more than a friend. I thought at least if you saw them together, you might get jealous and realize that you and Sophie could have a future together as more than just friends. And if that didn't happen, I figured things would eventually work out between Sophie and Ryan...once she became comfortable enough around him to speak in coherent sentences."

She punches me on the arm. Hard.

"Ouch!" I rub the spot. "What the hell was that for?"

"For being such a dumbass and for not seeing what was in front of you."

Except I did. I just never thought she felt the same way about me.

"How was I supposed to know that she liked me as more than a friend? Unlike with Ryan and the other guys she was interested in, she never had trouble talking to me."

Aubrey makes a God-you're-such-an-idiot sound. "You obviously don't know her as well as you think you do. She told you she was practically a virgin before she had sex with you." Her tone isn't angry. It's matter-of-fact. "You knew she wasn't into one-night stands. Yet you never questioned why she wanted to have sex with you or why she wanted you to kiss her."

"Shit, women really do talk, don't they?"

And they accuse men of being bad.

"Yes, we do. But she didn't tell me after it happened. She told me after you walked away from her on Saturday." Aubrey punches me on the arm again. Even harder than before.

"Shit, would you stop doing that?" I step back, fearing she might boot me in the calf next.

"And she would have kept it a secret for longer if Violet and I hadn't gotten her drunk and pried it out of her. But that's neither here nor there. The point is, not once did you question why she wanted to have sex and make out with you."

"I assumed she was telling me the truth. I believed her when she said she needed pointers so she wouldn't make a fool of herself when she kissed Ryan."

Aubrey makes the God-you're-such-an-idiot sound again, but this time it's been upgraded to me being a douchebag as well as an idiot.

The attitude is also in her tone when she says, "She could have asked for pointers without actually kissing you and having sex with you." Her tone then softens. "Women aren't like men, Jake. We can't just screw a guy and have an orgasm. Emotions are a big part of it. So do you really believe that Sophie—who doesn't do one-night stands and who doesn't go around randomly kissing men—would have wanted to fuck you if she didn't feel something for you?"

I open my mouth to respond but then snap it shut. No matter what I say, it won't make a difference.

Besides, whatever I have to say needs to be said to Sophie. And only to Sophie.

"The sad thing," Aubrey says, "is that I really do believe that Ryan would be perfect for her. Like I said, they want the same things."

She shakes her head like a teacher who caught her best student cheating. "Look, I understand that your ex-girlfriends fucked around with your head, and that's why you've been avoiding relationships. But this is Sophie we're talking about. She's not like those women you dated."

"Wow, when did you become a therapist?" The sarcasm in my tone is thicker than peanut butter in a blizzard.

"You don't need to be a therapist to figure out what your problem is, Jake."

"And let me guess, you and the girls have discussed your theories about that."

"Not exactly. That would be Gertrude and her gang's department. But if it makes you feel any better, their theories on why I'm still single are crappier than anything they came up with for you."

"What theories did they come up with for *you*?"

She pats my arm. "Let's just say that information is locked away in the vault, never to be heard from again. Now back to you, since it's your love life we're dissecting and not mine. You trusted the wrong women in the past and got burned. But Sophie isn't one of your ex-girlfriends."

"I know that."

"Do you? Because from the looks of it, I'd say you're afraid to truly trust someone who you could possibly love—other than your brothers. Deep down you're always waiting for the woman to betray you. But that's not Sophie. You know her, Jake. You know she would never do anything to purposely hurt you."

I don't say anything because I have a feeling Aubrey hasn't finished.

And I'm right.

"But your fears are the reason you two are perfect for each

other, in an odd way. Sophie is also afraid to fully trust with her heart. She's afraid of being hurt and humiliated again. Her heart knows this and her head knows this, and that's why she has trouble talking to guys she's interested in. Except for you. She trusted you, and in the end, you hurt her worse than those assholes who threw horse shit at her. So she did what she does best...she ran."

Hence her quitting her job at the ranch and going over to Walter Scottsdale's side of the fence.

"Okay, I'll admit it, I screwed up." I bundle Roxy's skirt around my thighs.

"What are you doing?"

"I'm going to talk to Sophie."

"In that dress?"

Hopefully not for long. Because after I tell Sophie how much I love her, I plan to prove it to her. And I won't be in this goddamn dress for that.

28

I arrive at Sophie's house and knock on the front door. No one answers. I try again. Still no answer.

But that's hardly surprising. Her car isn't in the driveway.

She's at work.

At Scottsdale ranch.

Like Pine Meadow ranch, Walter's place isn't in the heart of town. Which means I have to ride Orion there while still in Roxy's ball gown. Most sane men wouldn't go to their rival's ranch while wearing a light blue gown.

But no one's ever claimed that love makes you sane.

Besides, I'd ride there naked if I had to.

This same thought revisits me as I gallop through field after field after field to the ranch. Logic tells me my dignity might have a better chance of staying intact if I show up naked instead of in a dress. Except, Walter's wife might not appreciate it.

Sophie's car isn't on the curved driveway when Orion and I finally arrive at the rustic estate ranch house.

But while her car might not be in the driveway, Chase Scottsdale's, Walter's grandson, is.

239

And he's standing next to his jeep and grinning at me...or more specifically, he's grinning at Roxy's dress.

I dismount Orion and lead him over to Chase.

"Wow, would never have guessed, Jake. Nice color choice. It really brings the blue out in your eyes." A snorted laugh sits squarely in his tone. "Or is this your Halloween costume? What are you? A zombie princess?"

"Try Zombie Cinderella and we have ourselves a winner. Maybe I can get Roxy to set you up with one of her other gowns." One that doesn't smell like horses and look like Cinderella wore it while cleaning the fireplace.

That's right—Roxy's going to kill me.

Luckily for me, she's also a sucker for happily ever afters.

I just need to give her one and she'll forgive me. That, and I'll have to pay for a new dress.

"I need to talk to Sophie."

Chase stares at me as if expecting me to say more.

I try again. "Where can I find her?"

"She's *your* close friend. Why would you think I'd know where she is?"

"Because she works here."

"She does? That's news to me. My grandfather's been chomping at the bit to get her to work for us, but I didn't realize he'd finally succeeded."

"How could you not know? It's not like she's hard to miss. Gorgeous. Blonde. Just how many women fitting that description does your grandfather have working for him?"

Chase chuckles. "Right. But I've been away for a few days and returned an hour ago. I was about to go search for the old man when you showed up. Did you come from your ranch?"

"No, downtown."

His gaze regards Orion, his love of horses evident on his face and in his smile. "Let's get your horse some food and water. We'll probably bump into Sophie on the way."

Orion whinnies his agreement. "We'd appreciate that," I say. "Thanks."

"So what's been going on with you since college?" I ask as we stride along the wide path leading from the house to the stable. On either side of us is a narrow stretch of manicured lawn, which I'm positive Orion is hungrily eyeing from behind me. Beyond that is a white picket fence. "I haven't seen much of you lately."

Chase and I used to be friends in school, but we both left town to attend different colleges and our friendship faded over time. He only returned to Copper Creek about a year ago to help his family with the ranch. From what I've heard, he was working for some fancy-ass high-tech company before his grandfather's heart attack.

"I've been busy working on some projects," Chase says. "And I started my own company."

"You did? Does that mean you'll be leaving for good soon?" The Chase I knew had always been a computer geek. He's never been interested in running the ranch.

"Nah, the old man needs me. But he and I came to an understanding. I'm here to help out, but my company is still my first priority. So as you can imagine, that means long hours for me."

Hence my not seeing him around town as much anymore.

We approach the training paddock. Their usual trainer is there working with a horse. He's good, but he's definitely not Sophie.

"Hey, McBride," Chase calls out to him from the other side of the fence. "Do you know where we can find Sophie?"

"Sophie West?"

"Yes, that Sophie."

The trainer shakes his head. "The last time I saw her was when he"—he points at me—"and I were participating in the charity event you weaseled out of." His voice is heavy with barely suppressed laughter.

"Let me guess," I say to Chase, loud enough for McBride to overhear. "The real reason you were away until today was so you could get out of the event?" I laugh, as does McBride.

"Are you kidding me?" Chase says. "When I heard Abigail Kincaid had set her mind on bidding for my lunch, there was no way I was sticking around."

Abigail is one of those girls who's turned beauty pageants into a career, starting from when she was five years old. Just like her Southern-born momma had done before that. Let's just say Abigail has grown into a spoiled brat—a beautiful spoiled brat —who always gets what she wants.

Would I have skipped town if I'd heard she was planning to bid on me? You'd better believe it. Fortunately for me and the other guys in the auction, she didn't show up.

It then hits me what McBride said and what it might mean.

It's the same thought that must have also occurred to Chase. "Do you know if my grandfather hired Sophie to work here?" he asks.

The trainer shakes his head. "Not that I've heard."

"Okay, thanks."

Chase and I continue walking toward the stables. "Are you sure she said she's working here?" he asks.

"She said your grandfather had been pushing hard lately for her to join the staff. He found out that she's starting a training program for horses with behavioral problems."

"That sounds like Granddad. As good as McBride is, he isn't Sophie. But I thought she was working for you."

"She was but she resigned the other day. I assumed she'd decided to take your grandfather up on his offer. He can be very persuasive."

Chase chuckles, knowing how persuasive Walter can be.

"I'm just surprised she resigned. I got the idea she loved working for you guys."

That makes two of us.

But then again, given what I said to her after the auction, I'm not surprised she quit. I hurt her and she ran—like she always does whenever a guy wrecks her.

I kick an unsuspecting stone on the path, pretending it's my dumbass ego from the day of the picnic. "What can I say? Shit happened, and now I need to make things right with her."

We arrive at the stable, and I lead Orion to the water trough. While my horse drinks, Chase calls Walter and asks about Sophie.

A moment later, he ends the call. "He said he hasn't heard from her since she turned down his latest offer last week."

So if she's not working here and she's not working at Pine Meadow ranch, where the heck is she?

I send Violet a text.

> Any idea where Sophie is right now?

I also text Sophie.

> I'm really sorry about everything, Soph. I need
> to talk to you. Where are you?

While I wait for one of them to reply, Chase and I catch up.

"So, you and Sophie, huh?" he asks out of the blue. "I always figured there was something going on between you two...even if you hadn't figured it out yourselves."

"And how did you come to that conclusion?"

"Because every time I talked to her last year, you looked at me like you were imagining a meteor falling from the sky and flattening me."

Yes, Chase knows about my love of astronomy.

And yes, he might have read the situation correctly.

I shrug because I was hardly admitting the truth. "To be honest, I have no idea what's going on between us. That's why I need to talk to her."

"I don't suppose this has anything to do with your new look." He gestures at Roxy's dress.

"Yes and no. It's a long story, and it's a story you'll never hear. Let's just leave it at I lost a bet with TJ and Noah, and this was their payback."

This time he does laugh. "And that's why you were riding your horse along Main Street in your princess finery?" He waves his phone at me, letting me know exactly how he found out.

Damn social media.

"Yeah, something like that."

My phone buzzes. I check the screen and my heart slouches in my chest.

> Violet: She said she was going away for a few days, but she'll be back for the wedding.

> Me: Where?

> Violet: I don't know, Jake.

A moment later I get another text from her.

> Violet: She said she needed time to work a few things out.

> Me: And you really don't know where she is?

> Violet: Not at all. And just so you know, she forgot to take her phone charger. Her battery was almost dead the last time she texted me.

I text Aubrey and get the same response.

Me: How come you never told me she'd gone away when I talked to you?

Aubrey: Because I thought it would be more entertaining to watch you go charging after her while in that dress. But don't worry, I took pictures. ;)

So that's it.

I'll have to wait until TJ and Violet's wedding to talk to her. And even then, I'll have to hope Sophie will listen to me and give me a second chance.

But at least I'll be wearing a suit and not a dress.

Because I need to win her heart back—and dressing like Roxy's ugly stepsister just won't cut it.

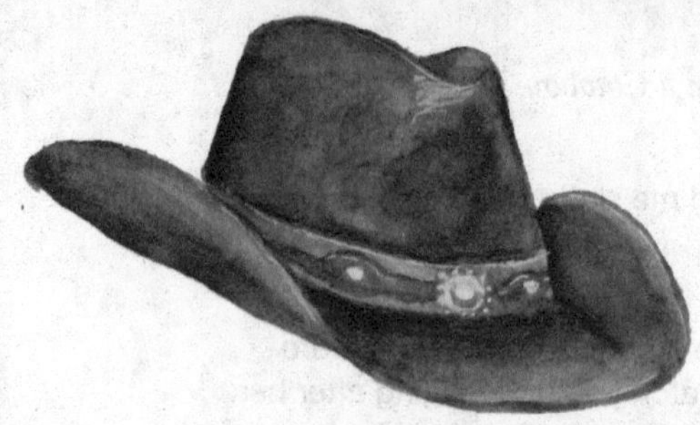

29

"Shouldn't I be the one pacing?" TJ asks as I complete another circuit of the large sectional couch in our living room.

My brothers, Austin, Deacon, and I are dressed in our gray suits, waiting for the wedding to commence. Violet, her mother, and her bridesmaids are all upstairs.

Yes, Sophie is with them.

No, I haven't heard from her....At. All.

All I know is that she returned last night.

Without even looking at TJ, I ask, "Why should you be pacing? In less than thirty minutes, you and Violet will be married. Your future will be beginning. Mine could be headed for the toilet."

"No, you're not melodramatic at all." Austin's tone holds a snicker to it, coated with a side order of dumbass.

"Hey, let's see how un-melodramatic you are when you one day fall in love," I grumble.

"Who says anything about falling in love? That's only for you two saps."

Noah holds his hand up to Austin and they high-five.

And it's official—they all know I'm in love with Sophie.

"Have any of you talked to her?" I ask, aiming for another lap of the couch.

"I'm guessing you mean Sophie," TJ says.

I nod.

Maui barks and scrambles after Deacon, who has his beloved teething rope. Deacon starts running and accidentally bumps into the side table by the couch. The vase full of flowers wobbles, contemplating if it should nose-dive onto the floor. I grab it, preventing it from fulfilling its mission.

I study the floral arrangement, remove a purple freesia, and head to the kitchen. Yes, it's one of Sophie's favorite flowers, which is why I know the name.

"Hey, where are you going?" TJ asks, calm as can be. He's been this way since he got up this morning.

"To write a note. I'll need to borrow Deacon so he can deliver it." Because there's no way Sophie will refuse a note from him. That little boy has her wrapped around his finger—like he does with most people.

"He can't go by himself," TJ says. "And Violet will be less than thrilled if I go upstairs and see her before the wedding."

"I can take it if you want," Austin tells me. "Then I can check on my sister. Maybe I can even get her to change her mind about marrying my best friend."

TJ laughs. "Good luck with that. You should know by now she doesn't pay attention to anything you say."

"That's because you corrupted her."

I leave them to their teasing and find a pen and notepad in the kitchen. I write a message, fold the paper in half, and tape it to the flower's stem.

Sophie,

I've missed you more than you can ever imagine.

Save a dance for me?

Jake

I return to the living room.

"Give this to your Auntie Sophie, okay?" I hand the purple flower to Deacon. He sniffs it, then he and Austin go upstairs.

And I resume pacing.

"Shit, man, you're making me nervous just watching you," TJ says.

"Why? We all know Violet isn't upstairs, escaping through the bedroom window."

Noah laughs. "Hopefully Sophie isn't either. Because the first step is a doozy."

I pause long enough to scowl at him. He laughs harder.

I pick up the speed of my pacing. "What's taking them so long?"

"You have to ask?" TJ says. "Right now they're all fussing over how adorable Deacon looks in his suit. It would have been quicker to just send Austin upstairs with the message."

Shit, why didn't I think of that?

I complete yet another circuit of the couch.

After what feels like ten lifetimes and at least thirty more laps—which has to be some sort of world record—Deacon and Austin return to the living room.

"How did it go? What did Auntie Sophie say?" The words race from me faster than a kid chasing an ice cream truck.

"He's only two and a half," TJ points out. "It's not like he was paying attention to what she was saying."

Just to prove his dad's right, Deacon giggles and resumes playing with Maui.

Well, if I'm not going to get what I want from Deacon...

"Did she read the note?" I ask Austin.

He flinches. The guy who used to serve with the Navy SEALs—who's faced life and death situations—goddamn flinches.

Which isn't good news for me.

I inhale a deep breath. "All right, lay it on me. What did she say?"

Austin opens his mouth to presumably answer.

"All right, gentlemen," Violet's father says from behind me. Austin's mouth snaps shut. "Time to take your places. I'm going upstairs to get the girls. So unless you wish to witness their wrath because you're still loitering here when they come down, you'll want to head outside now."

Before his future father-in-law carries Deacon upstairs, TJ gives his son a kiss and hustles us out the back door.

Violet's mother and my mother were busy this morning decorating the gazebo for the wedding. A colorful array of large flowers and greenery have been fastened to the top corners of the entrance to the rustic structure. The same flowers and greenery also sit in tall metal vases on either side of it.

The fifty or so guests are already seated on the wooden chairs that Noah and I set up this morning. Austin, my brothers, and I walk down the aisle to the front row, where our parents are sitting and waiting for us.

Once we get to the front, Mom and Dad stand. TJ, Noah, and I shake Dad's hand and kiss Mom on the cheek.

But that's not enough for her.

She hugs Noah and then me, saving the biggest hug for TJ.

She releases him, her eyes filling. "I'm so proud of you, son. You're going to make a wonderful husband and father."

She shifts her attention to Noah and me with an expression I recognize all too well. An expression that has future weddings and grandbabies written all over it. "And I know you will both one day also be great husbands and fathers. Once you've found the right women, you'll never look back."

Dad nods in agreement and wraps his arm around her waist. She turns to him and he gives her a brief kiss.

When we were much younger, my brothers and I used to make gagging noises whenever they did that. Now it just seems sweet. Something I can see myself doing with Sophie when we're much older.

That's if she ever forgives me.

Grandma Meg, who is sitting next to my parents' chairs, stands and pats TJ on the cheek like he's a five-year-old. A five-year-old who towers over her. "Your grandmother would be so proud of the man you've become, TJ. And I know she's watching from heaven and cheering you on." She gives him a big hug.

We hug Mom one more time, then take our places at the altar with Austin, TJ's best man.

The music begins. Sophie steps from the house and my heart comes to a skidding halt.

She's wearing a sleeveless navy dress covered in navy lace. The hem stops just above her knees, and on her feet are silver-colored cowboy boots. Her long blonde hair is pulled up in a loose bun with strands framing her face, and she's carrying a small bouquet of white flowers.

Christ, she's fucking beautiful.

I can only stare at her as she and Deacon walk up the aisle. Sophie's holding his hand. His other hand clutches a small stuffed dog, with the wedding rings attached to the collar.

He sees TJ and his face lights up. "Daddy!" He drops the dog and runs up the aisle to my brother. Soft laughter ripples through the audience.

Sophie crouches to pick up the toy dog, then resumes walking down the aisle, keeping pace with the music. She's wearing a soft smile as she keeps walking, but not once does she look in my direction.

My heart clenches into a tight knot—a knot suitable for a wedding gift.

Ouch.

TJ kneels next to his son, gives him a quick hug, and kisses the top of his head. He says something to him and points at Grandma Meg.

Deacon races over to his great-grandmother. Dad helps him up onto Grandma Meg's lap.

Sophie takes her spot opposite Noah.

And that's when she finally looks up at me.

Her expression doesn't change. The soft smile is still there —for the audience. She does, though, give me a slight nod. I'm just hoping it means what I want it to mean...that she'll save me at least one dance.

I have no idea what happens next. All I can do is stare at Sophie and hold back the urge to stride over to her and kiss her. Deeply.

But her gaze isn't on me. It's focused on the aisle.

Once the bridesmaids and Aubrey are in their assigned places, the music changes. Everyone stands and Violet starts walking down the aisle while holding on to her father's arm.

I tear my gaze away from Sophie to watch the woman I grew up with, the woman who stole my brother's heart, walk up the aisle. Her long brown hair, loose around her shoulders, glows in the late afternoon sun and is partially covered by a long veil. Thin straps hold up the top of Violet's dress, which shows off her cleavage...much to TJ's delight, I'm sure. The dress fits her slim waist, then becomes layers upon layers of cream-colored tulle.

My future sister-in-law is breathtaking...and judging from TJ's expression, he agrees with me one hundred percent.

The minister asks who is giving the bride away. My gaze

goes back to Sophie. She's beaming like the sun and watching Violet. Her eyes flicker over to me, but then hurriedly return to her friend.

The wedding goes without any problems. There are a few hiccupped sobs—some, no doubt, from Violet's mother and my own.

TJ and Violet exchange rings. The minister announces they are now husband and wife, and TJ may kiss his bride.

Which he does—to our cheers.

Once they've finished with the kissing portion of the event, the pair walk to Grandma Meg. TJ picks up his son from her lap. Deacon throws his arm around TJ's neck and declares, "My daddy!"

This is met by a chorus of *awww*s and an "Oh, that's so adorable."

Noah leans closer to me. "Let's switch places. You go with Sophie and I'll go with Bridget." Violet's cousin.

Sophie moves to the center of the aisle. Noah nudges me forward, not giving me a chance to reply. I do as he suggested and I offer her my arm. She hesitates for a second, then accepts it.

"You look beautiful," I tell her as we walk down the aisle.

"You look good, too. Kennedy certainly thinks so." There's no bitterness in her tone. Only sadness.

"She's not really my date. I mean she is, but she's here because you asked Ryan to be *your* date. I asked her only because I knew she wouldn't be hoping for a future with me just because I asked her out." Unlike some other women I might have asked. "The only person I want a future with is you, Soph. And I don't mean as *just* friends. I want something more. Something long-term."

She sighs, then says low enough so only I can hear her, "There's a word for that, Jake. It's called friends with benefits, fuck buddies, booty call."

I chuckle. "Those aren't exactly one-word names." Yes, I realize as soon as the words come out that they might be up there for the title of Idiot Move of the Century.

I don't get a chance to say anything else. The photographer whisks the wedding party away for photos.

"How's it going with Sophie?" TJ asks me at one point, while Violet and her bridesmaids are having their pictures taken.

I give him double thumbs up, even though double thumbs down would be more appropriate.

Fuck, how much longer before I get to talk to Sophie alone? Assuming she lets me talk to her alone.

<h1 style="text-align:center">30</h1>

I swear the wedding gods are conspiring against me. First, I don't get another chance to talk to Sophie after she and I walk down the aisle together. Second, she's now with Ryan, holding his arm like it's a life preserver.

Seeing her this way feels like someone is playing basketball with my heart—and bouncing it against the gym floor during the final seconds of a game. One person will come out the winner, and the other person will have to admit defeat.

There will be no second chances.

Bounce. Bounce. Bounce.

Guests are milling around the large open tent, talking, drinking, dancing, having a great time. The place really does look magical—just like TJ wanted for his new bride. The rustic, dark wooden tables are lined up from end to end, forming a giant horseshoe, with the dance floor in the center. A display of white roses, greenery, and short candles runs the entire length of the table. And the ceiling has been turned into a night sky. Hundreds of Christmas tree lights shine through the wide strips of cream-colored gauze, which has been draped from the outskirts of the tent to the center pole.

Kennedy approaches me, smiling, and looking as she always does...like she doesn't belong here.

Like she belongs in New York City.

"So, lover boy, how are things going?"

Before, I would have thought she was referring to me being *her* lover. But now I know better. She's referring to how I keep striking out with Sophie.

Yes, she does know some of the details.

The need-to-know details.

The rest she kind of figured out on her own.

I don't even bother to attempt a smile.

She mock-cringes. "That bad, huh? How can I help so that she finally admits to herself that she loves you?"

"Trust me, nothing you do will make things better, so don't even think about it. If anything, it will only make things worse."

"Well, from where I'm standing, she's definitely not into Ryan."

I frown. "How can you tell?"

"She has the look people get whenever they're mentally a million miles away. Pretty much the same expression you've had for the past thirty minutes."

A slow song comes on and Ryan says something to Sophie. She nods and they head to the dance floor.

Kennedy pats my arm. "C'mon, lover boy. Let's dance."

She doesn't give me a chance to say no. She grabs my arm and drags me along until we're standing next to the happy couple—and I'm not referring to the bride and groom.

Well, technically, *happy* is a little generous. Sophie's arms are around Ryan's shoulders and she's swaying from side-to-side. But Kennedy's right; Sophie does look like she's in another solar system.

"Do you mind if I cut in?" Kennedy asks Sophie.

Sophie blinks, and Ryan appears almost relieved at the request.

Her gaze slides to me and she nods; then she transfers her arms around my neck. My arms go around her waist and I gently pull her to me.

Back in my senior year of high school, I had been nominated for the state's highest science award available for that academic level. The kids who won it were destined to be future brilliant minds in the scientific community. It was a huge deal to even be nominated. And to win it put you at the top of the world—much like how Jack Dawson felt in *Titanic* while leaning out from the ship's bow, the wind rushing against his face.

My parents drove me to Helena for the ceremony. TJ and Noah and my grandparents came with us. The four other finalists and I stepped onto the stage and I'd never been more nervous in my entire life. But the moment they announced my name as the winner of the prestigious award in astronomy, with everyone giving me a standing ovation, I'd felt like Jack Dawson—tenfold.

That feeling...it was nothing compared to how I feel with Sophie in my arms.

Christ, I've missed this.

I can't help myself. I kiss the top of her head. "I really am sorry, Sophie," I say, my mouth close to her ear, my voice a low rumble over the music. "I never meant to hurt you. I was scared when I shouldn't have been. I trust you more than I trust even myself. And maybe that was the problem. I made a mistake two other times and trusted my judgment when it was faulty."

Sophie sways in my arms to the music, her gaze focused on the stars in the ceiling. "How can you be so sure it isn't faulty now?"

"Because I've known you for over six years, and you've been my best friend for the past two of them. I know you. I know you would never purposely hurt anyone. Hell, you won't even hurt a bug if you can avoid it."

I gently kiss her jaw and savor the feel of her soft skin against my lips. "But I also know you're scared of letting anyone get too close so they can hurt you like the asshole did. But you're forgetting something."

She finally turns her head and looks at me. "What's that?"

"You didn't know him very well. You were crushing on him from a distance, but you had no idea what kind of person he was. Guys like that are always assholes. You just never got to witness it until that night. And then I hurt you, and like what happened after that night, you ran."

She lifts her chin, stubborn through and through. "I didn't run. You were the one who walked away from me the day of the auction."

"That might be true, but you were the one who quit the ranch after telling me you loved working there." I brush my thumb lightly against her cheek. "I was planning to tell you that I love you, Sophie. I have for a while now, but I was afraid of losing you as a friend if things didn't work out between us."

I trace my thumb along her lower lip. "You know the company dating policy my brothers make fun of?"

She nods.

"We never needed it before you came along."

"That's because you never had a female employee before me."

I slowly shake my head. "That's true but it's not the full reason."

"All right, it was because you were afraid you'd never find another horse trainer like me."

"Okay, that's true, too. But it was also because I knew I couldn't breathe without you around. You were my oxygen, Sophie. You still are. And I'll do anything to prove it to you."

She's quiet for a moment and I think I've lost her. No matter what I do, it'll never be enough.

"You mean like how you rode through town in that ridiculous dress." There's definite amusement in her eyes. I can work with that.

I laugh, the sound quiet and teasing and full of remorse. A triple-header. "Don't ever say that to Roxy. You don't even want to know what it cost me when I wrecked it riding to Scottsdale Ranch to find you."

I'm not just talking about it costing me my dignity when I showed up at the ranch.

The corners of her mouth twitch. "I did hear something about you showing up in the dress."

"I did it because I couldn't wait another second to tell you how much I love you. I had no idea you weren't there."

The song ends—much to my annoyance. I haven't finished telling her everything I need to say.

Kennedy and Ryan leave the dance floor. I will the DJ to play another slow song.

He doesn't listen.

"All right, ladies and gentlemen. It's time for the bride to throw the bouquet. Now all you eligible young ladies—"

This is met with protests from Grandma Meg and her cohorts.

"Sorry, my mistake," the DJ says, appearing properly shamed. "*All* eligible ladies please gather on the dance floor."

I move out of the way before I'm trampled to death.

"Oh, no you don't, young lady," I hear Tilly say behind me.

I turn in time to see Tilly and Gertrude dragging Sophie back onto the dance floor. Their arms are interlaced with hers, neither woman giving her a chance to escape.

"We have every intention of marrying you off as soon as you find Mr. Right." Gertrude glances over her shoulder and gives me a meaningful wave.

In the past I would have groaned. This time I laugh and mouth *Good luck* to Sophie.

Good luck dealing with those two.

Good luck catching the bouquet.

Because once she gives me a chance to prove how much I love her, I have every intention of making her my wife.

The women find their spots on the dance floor. Sophie's in the middle of the pack. Violet turns around so her back is to the women—which includes Roxy.

Who, if you ask me, has an unfair advantage with her long legs and arms.

"You ready?" Violet calls out.

"Yes!" the women reply.

"All right. One. Two. Three..." Violet tosses the bouquet in an arch that would impress any basketball coach. Especially since she threw it behind her.

It flies up, up, up, and then down, down, down...to land in Gertrude's outstretched hands. She couldn't look more surprised than if a shooting star had landed in them.

"Andrew has to marry you now," Grandma Meg says with a laugh. All eyes turn to Andrew. He's standing to the side of the dance floor, grinning.

He shuffles to where Gertrude is standing. "I'd bend down on one knee, but I might not get up again if I try."

Gertrude continues staring at him, her expression even more stunned now than when she caught the bouquet. Her friends are grinning as much as he is.

"I've been in love with you for a while now, Gertrude," he says. "And it would be my honor to make an honest woman out of you. Will you marry me?"

Still stunned, she nods—and everyone breaks out in applause, congratulating the happy pair.

I return to Sophie's side and thread my fingers with hers. "Come with me." I don't wait for her to respond. I lead her away from the celebration, and down the path toward the stable. Sophie doesn't protest.

Nor does she say anything.

It's still light out, the sun an hour away from setting, and we find a quiet spot near the stable.

I look down into her eyes, searching for any clue as to how she feels about me. "Please tell me I can kiss you." My voice is low and rough.

"I was wondering when we would get to that." Her voice is equally low and rough, with a dose of vulnerability tossed into the mix...and my heart swells, my pulse sings, and my body hums with all kinds of emotions. Good emotions. The best emotions.

I lean toward her, but she puts her hand on my chest, stopping me.

"But first I need to say something, Jake. I'm sorry for not telling you sooner how I felt about you. I should have been honest with you when I realized I was falling in love with you. But I was scared if I told you, it would destroy our friendship, and I couldn't stand the thought of that.

"When I confessed how I felt about you at the picnic, you said you thought I knew you enough to know not to play games with you...like the other women in your life had. I did, and I'm not like those other women. I was afraid and I made a mistake. And I'm so sorry."

"I shouldn't have said that, Soph—"

She plants her fingers against my lips, preventing the rest of my sentence. "You were right to say it, Jake, because it was true. If I had pulled up my big girl panties and told you the truth sooner, things wouldn't have gotten so messed up. And I know I handled things wrong by leaving without saying a word to you. I thought my stupid actions had ruined everything between us. I went to my parents' cottage by the lake to lick my wounds and come up with a plan."

"A plan?"

"On how to win you back—as a friend, hopefully as something more. Although I must admit my plan wasn't anywhere near as dramatic as you in Roxy's ball gown. Apparently, I need to up my game." She grins and my heart swells some more.

"How about we just kiss—you and me? Us. The way it should have been before all the fairy-godfather nonsense. And then we can call it even."

"I'm all for that."

I study her face for the briefest of moments, unable to believe this is real. That she is real. Then I lower my mouth to hers and tenderly kiss her, my lips moving against hers for a heartbeat.

I start to pull away, needing to see her face, needing to see her reaction.

She doesn't give me a chance.

She lets out a whimper and knots her fingers in my hair, bringing my mouth back to hers. This time the kiss isn't slow and tender.

This time it's hungry and passionate.

Passionate like the woman I fell in love with.

Our tongues glide, taste, get reacquainted. I pull her closer, craving the feel of her against me. Sophie moans, and I deepen the kiss, needing her to fill every part of me, needing her to fill my soul.

We keep kissing. The gentle neighing of the horses can be heard from behind the stable doors next to us.

My mouth shifts to her jaw, her earlobe, her neck. Her strawberries-and-cream scent almost does me in. I never want to be without it again.

We eventually pull apart, breaths ragged.

"I want to make love to you," Sophie says, her voice barely more than a whisper. "Just like I wanted to make love to you when I pretended it was for research. I've been in love with you for as long as I can remember, Jake. I just never expected you to feel the same way about me. I kept telling myself I needed to move on, to find someone else to fall in love with. But I couldn't. There was only you. Will always only be you."

I smile while every cell inside my body does a happy dance. "I feel the same way about you. And I'm all for making love to you." I caress her jaw. "And even though I'm looking forward to bending you over a bale of straw and pounding into you from behind"—my cock hardens at the image I've just planted in my head, and I silently curse myself—"I plan to take my time once we return to the house. I want to make love to you in my bed. And in the shower. And anywhere else you might wish to do it. The evening's still young." I wink at her.

She giggles, her eyes dark with raw desire. "As much as I want to slip away and spend the evening with you and only you, we should go back and help Violet and TJ celebrate their big day."

"And then can I make love to you?"

"I don't expect anything less."

"Does this mean you're officially my girlfriend now?"

She smiles and nods. "I'm officially your girlfriend."

"Good, because only *I* get to dance with you for the rest of the night. Ryan will have to get over it."

She laughs softly. "I don't think he'll be too disappointed."

31

Sophie and I return to the wedding.

We left holding hands.

We walk back with my arm around her waist—where it's staying for the rest of the evening until she's in bed with me.

The next hour is spent talking to friends and other wedding guests. As Sophie predicted, Ryan doesn't appear beaten up over losing her to me.

I catch Grandma Meg and Tilly and Gertrude standing at the end of the horseshoe-shaped table, exchanging money like Vegas bookies. Judging from Gertrude's smug grin, she won the bet. She waves at us, the gesture as smug as her smile.

"They bet on us again, didn't they?" Sophie says as we dance to a slow song.

"That would be my guess." I dip her back, appreciating the fine view of her breasts jutting up, and earning applause from those watching us.

The whistle? I'm assuming it was Kennedy. It's hard to say based on where my eyes are focused: Sophie's beautiful, laughing face.

I guide her back up, her body pressing against mine, and continue swaying, with Sophie in my arms.

The final bars of the music fade away, and my patience disappears with it. The next time we slow dance will be in a few minutes, but this time clothes won't be permitted.

I kiss her neck, working my way up to her ear. "My bedroom. Now. Dirty talk optional."

Sophie beams at me. "I wouldn't have it any other way."

I take her hand and we weave our way through the guests. A few try to stop us, eager to ask Sophie questions about her new horse training services.

"By the way," I tell her after the second person brings it up, "I've rejected your resignation. You're still an employee...during the daytime. In the evening, you're the boss...of me. I mean, unless you don't want to work for us anymore." Hopefully that isn't true, because not seeing Sophie whenever I want sits in my gut about as well as sour milk.

"Consider your rejection of my resignation accepted. I miss the ranch and I miss working for you, even if you are a tyrant of a boss." She grins at me.

We eventually escape the tent and head back to the house without any more interruptions. Our fingers are still entwined when we climb up the staircase to my room.

My bedroom is dark when we enter, other than the light coming from the full moon low on the horizon. It glows softly on Sophie, turning her into a gorgeous moon maiden. I stand next to the window, longing to touch her, to taste her, but at the same time, more than happy to just drink her in.

Christ, how did I ever get to be so lucky?

"Before I show you how much I love you," I say, "I've got something to give you." I walk the short distance to my dresser and pick up the piece of leather I've been working on since my one-person parade down Main Street.

I hand her the carved picture of a horse looking to the side at another horse, who is returning the gaze. The design is nothing more than simple curved lines, showing the horses from behind. With a heart floating in the space between their heads.

"Did you make this?" she asks, her voice little more than an awed whisper.

"I know it's not much—"

Her arms go around my neck and her mouth smashes against mine, preventing me from finishing the sentence.

The kiss isn't particularly long, but I'm breathless all the same by the time she pulls away.

"It's everything, Jake. It's so beautiful and so sweet. I love it."

As I silently thank Andrew and everyone else who made this moment possible, I remove the picture from her hands and return it to the dresser. Then I trace alone the low neckline of her dress with my finger. "Love the dress—but I'll love it even more with you out of it."

With my finger still touching her, I slowly move behind her, caressing the skin along her neckline until I reach the zipper. Once there, I take my time slowly unzipping the fabric, relishing the feel of her and the curve of her back. She's a gift I plan to savor—a gift I want to keep touching.

I peel the fabric from her body...until she's standing in nothing but her lacy black underwear and bra.

I kiss her bare shoulder as my hands move around her and cover her lush breasts. A whimper tumbles from her mouth, and her head falls back against my shoulder, gifting me her neck to worship.

Her back arches, pressing her sweet ass against my hard cock. Apparently her actions aren't torture enough. She shimmies her body, making me even harder.

Two can play that game. I lightly pinch her nipples through the lace as I gently nip the skin on her shoulder.

"Oh God, Jake," she moans.

"Like that, huh?"

She makes a cute sound that's a cross between a whimper and a squeak, which I translate to mean yes. I release her breasts, quickly remove her bra, and trail my hand down her stomach. I keep moving past the waistband of her panties until my fingers rest between her legs.

I slip my fingers under the elastic. "Just as I suspected." Her pussy is slick with need. "The wedding cake was delicious, but I know you'll taste even better."

She releases a soft, needy gasp, and her breathing picks up a notch. "I'm all for that...but there's one thing you have to do first." The last part comes out a greedy but quiet moan.

"What's that?"

She attempts to turn around. Reluctantly, I remove my fingers from her panties and let her.

"I'm naked, but you still have your clothes on. That's highly unacceptable."

I lift an eyebrow. "You still have your panties on."

"All right, here's the deal." She undoes the top button of my shirt. My jacket is still on my chair back in the tent. "I get to remove all your clothes, and then you get to remove my panties. How's that for a deal?"

"I think you make one hell of a negotiator."

With her gaze locked on mine, she unbuttons my shirt as if she has all the time in the world plus a couple of extra centuries to spare. Her fingers lightly glide across my skin each time she unhooks a button, further tormenting me.

She finishes with the final button and slips her hands between the front of my shirt, tugging it away from my body. Like an explorer discovering land for the first time, she maps out the terrain with her fingers.

She brushes her lips against my skin and flicks her tongue against my nipple. I groan and tangle my fingers in the soft strands of her hair.

She continues worshiping the tightening peak as her fingers explore my body. They travel down, down, down.

She stops at the belt buckle and unfastens it. Her hands shift from the role of tormentor and become impatient. She unbuttons the waistband and yanks down the zipper.

Her fingers slide into the opening of the pants and she rubs my length.

She then drops to her knees and peels my pants and boxer briefs down and off my legs. I reach out and stroke her silky blonde hair.

She licks her lip, her gaze on my stiff cock.

And...my dick just got stiffer.

"Hmmm. Wonder if you taste as good as the cake," she says. Before I have a chance to say anything, her tongue runs across the head, then traces along the most sensitive part just under it. My body jerks forward in response.

Still with the devilish grin on her face, she slips my cock into her hot, greedy mouth—and I almost come right there.

Which is *not* going to happen.

Not now. Not tonight.

She moves her lips along my thick length. What she can't fit in, her hand makes up for, pumping in time with her mouth. She might have only done this once before—during our other marathon sex session—but she's definitely a pro.

"Sweetheart, I have every intention of coming inside you this time," I ground out. "So you'd better stop now."

She looks at me with defiant dark eyes.

"I promise you'll have plenty of opportunities for that. I'm not going anywhere." With my finger crooked, I beckon her to stand.

She slowly releases my cock from her mouth, giving it one final suck.

As soon as she's on her feet, my lips are on hers again, consuming her. Loving her. I begin reversing toward the bed, vaguely aware of its location. We keep going until the mattress hits the back of my thighs.

She giggles for a second, then goes back to kissing me as I lower her onto my bed.

Semi-reluctantly, my lips leave hers and travel to the part of her I've been waiting to taste for the past hour. That I've been waiting to taste again since the last time.

I kiss a trail as I move down her body. At the apex of her legs, I remove her panties, gently spread her legs wide, and kneel in front of her. I run my tongue along her pussy, tasting her. "I was right. You do taste better than the cake."

She chuckles. "And that was one damn good cake."

"It was."

I continue tasting her, teasing her, pushing her closer to the edge.

Closer.

Closer.

Until she screams out my name and comes hard against my face. I grin at her reaction and kiss the inside of her thighs. First one leg and then the other. "And that's only the appetizer."

As I wait for her to return to earth, I lean over and grab a foil package from my bedside drawer. I rip it open and roll the condom down my length.

Sophie gazes up at me, her eyes glazed over with satisfaction. I smile and gently kiss her.

"God, you're so beautiful. Like the night sky." I give her one more kiss, less gentle this time, and position myself against her entrance and thrust inside her.

Her heat welcomes me, hugs me, lets me know that this is where I belong.

With Sophie.

I move inside of her again. Filling her. Claiming her. Loving her. It isn't long before she tightens around me and calls out my name...bringing me along for the ride.

My balls tighten. I groan out my release and enjoy the rest of the ride as Sophie's body milks every last bit of me.

Once we're both physically spent, I remove myself, dispose of the condom, and return to bed. I pull her against me. She rests her head above my heart, which is thanking me for finally coming to my senses.

It took time, but like the best things in life, it was worth it.

I loosen her bun; it's barely hanging on as it is. "Thank you for giving me a second chance," I tell her.

She smiles at me. "Thank you for not giving up on me. And thank you for falling in love with me like I fell in love with you."

I smile back. "You're welcome. And now that I have you back in my life, I've got a lot of lost time to make up for. With you. Which reminds me. I seem to remember I owe you a prize."

"A prize? For what?"

"From the contest we had at the barbecue a few weeks ago. You earned the number of points you needed to win. You said you would eventually tell me what prize you wanted. So spill it."

She reaches up and lightly kisses me. "You've already given me the prize."

"I have? What was it?"

"*You*. All I wanted was for you to fall in love with me."

I chuckle. "Then you definitely got your prize."

This time her smile is brighter than a nebula. "Yes. I did."

EPILOGUE

Six Months Later

"So what did you think?" Sophie asks, laughing at my, no doubt, pained expression. A family pushing a stroller moves around us, eager to join the line for the Disneyland ride we just got off. Unlike back home where it's snowing, it's warm here. But they're able to move as fast through the crowds as they would be pushing the stroller through a snow bank.

"Please *never* make me go on that ride again." But it could have been worse from what I've heard. At least they weren't playing *It's a Small World* in a never-ending loop. One perk of coming here at Christmas.

She gasps a mock-horrified sound. "How can you even say that? The ride was absolutely adorable. With those cute little dolls singing the same Christmas carols again and again and again."

Cute? Try demented-looking.

I lean down so no one else is privy to what I'm about to tell her. "How about this...if you don't make me go on that ride again, tonight we'll do whatever positions you want—for as many times as you want."

Her eyes sparkle in reply. "You've got yourself a deal." She threads her fingers with mine. "Okay, where to now? We have thirty minutes before our Indiana Jones Fast Pass."

I make a show of looking around, pretending to deliberate where to go next. "We could see if Cinderella is still signing autographs and get one for Noah."

Sophie laughs. "Maybe you could ask her when her fairy godmother will be available for autographs. And then you can compare notes on which one of you is the fairest of them all."

"Wasn't that Snow White's wicked stepmother who was trying to be the fairest of them all?"

Sophie looks at me. Blinks once. And again. "A few months ago, your knowledge of the fairy godmother's job description was pretty lacking. How do you even know about Snow White's stepmother?"

"Deacon. He loves the seven dwarfs. He cracks up every time he sees them." It's his favorite movie. Unfortunately for me. He keeps making me watch it with him.

Maybe one day there'll be a vaccination to immunize me against his hopeful expressions. He puts Maui's puppy-dog eyes to shame.

"Let's check out the castle," I say, since we have to go through it to get to our next ride.

We walk to the stores at the bottom of the iconic castle and meander through a shop selling princess dresses that would make Roxy drool...if they came in her size.

My gaze falls upon the item I'm looking for. The adult-sized tiaras. Sophie releases my hand and walks to the rack of dresses, searching for one in particular. Not for Sophie, but for the daughter of someone we know. The four-year-old's career goal? To be a kickass princess one day. Or maybe it was a princess who kicks asses.

Either way works for me.

It just means Sophie will be distracted for a few minutes while she texts her friend pictures of the dresses.

I select a simple tiara from the display and pay for it. Sophie's still busy, unaware of what I'm doing.

A moment later, she turns to me. "I'm finished here. She just needs to get back to me and I'll pick up the dress on our last day here."

She throws me a pitying look, as though I've got some long-suffering expression on my face. "Sorry about that." She points to the merchandise in the store in a sweeping gesture. "I know this isn't your scene."

"Don't worry. I'm sure you'll find a way to make it up to me tonight." I wink at her and she laughs.

"I'm sure I will." Her gaze drops to the bag in my hand and confused wrinkles appear on her forehead. "Did you buy something here?" She scans the store, searching for what I could've possibly bought.

I smile at her, a sudden unexpected nervousness moving through my belly like a dancing drunk spider. "You'll find out soon enough."

I take her hand again and lead her from the store and through the passageway to the other side of the castle.

We continue walking, but as she turns right to head for Adventureland, I turn left, tugging on her arm. The place I want to go to is currently free of crowds. Cinderella was there earlier, signing autograph books, but she has since bailed.

Sophie glances at me, the previous quizzical expression back on her face.

"I thought we could get away from the crowds for a few minutes." I nod toward the path on the other side of the small moat. "Maybe sneak in a kiss or two." Because Christ knows, my lips miss hers. I haven't had a chance to kiss her since this morning…when I was demonstrating with my body just how much I love her.

"That sounds good to me."

Sophie hates crowds as much as I do. That's the advantage of living in Copper Creek and working on the ranch…crowds are not commonplace. Other than at Joe's.

We head for the short stone statues of the Seven Dwarfs, who are hanging out on the grass across from the moat. My heart bangs against my ribs like a caged bird hyped up on too much candy. A few people wander past, heedless as to what I'm about to do.

I remove the tiara from the plastic bag. The salesclerk already removed the price tag for me. I place it on Sophie's head.

She grins at me. "Does this mean I'm a princess now?"

"You've always been a princess to me, sweetheart. And I hope you consider me your prince." I grin back.

Her smile widens and just like that my nervousness vanishes in a puff of smoke. "Absolutely. At least I didn't have to kiss any frogs to find you."

"Good thing. I'm not sure I'd be happy kissing you after you made out with a bunch of amphibians." I gently nudge her shoulder with mine, letting her know that I'm kidding. I would have kissed her regardless.

I reach into my shorts pocket and fist the ring I put there this morning before we left for the park.

Then I drop to my knee.

Sophie blinks, her perfect lips slightly parted. I'm vaguely aware of hushed whispers.

"When I first took on the role of your fairy godfather, I never expected that *I* would be the lucky man who would win your heart. I never expected to be the man who would want to settle down and make lots of beautiful babies with my beautiful wife. But now I can't imagine a life without you."

Sophie sniffs. As does someone behind me.

I don't turn around to see who it is. I continue drinking Sophie in, and the way her eyes now glisten. "Sophie, will you marry me?"

She nods slowly, still in shock. "Yes." The word comes out slightly cracked, but definitely recognizable, and I stand. "I would love to marry you, Jake."

I slip the ring onto her finger but don't give her a chance to say anything else. My lips catch hers in a firework-inducing kiss.

The small audience applauds, and I mentally curse them, in the friendliest possible way. It's tougher making out with your future wife with people watching.

Not that it's stopping me.

Laughing softly, Sophie pulls away slightly, foiling my plan to keep tasting her. "Whoever said this is the happiest place in the world got that right." She kisses me again. "But any place you are, Jake, is the happiest place on the planet as far as I'm concerned." She leans into me, her breath warm against my ear. "Including our hotel room. So how about we make our next ride the last one for today?" She kisses my jaw. "I'm all for practicing for our honeymoon."

"You're right," I murmur back on a chuckle. "I think we'll need lots and lots of practice."

"I think I agree with you there," she says and returns her lips to mine.

**TURN THE PAGE FOR AN EXCERPT
FROM THE HOT AND HILARIOUS FIX
ME UP COWBOY**

CHAPTER 1

KATE

"Toto, looks like we aren't in Kansas anymore," I say to Charlie, my Cavalier King Charles spaniel, as I drive the rental Cadillac through downtown Copper Creek. On Main Street, quaint brick buildings with ground-level stores catch my eye.

It looks like something straight out of a postcard.

Truth? I've never been to Kansas. Or even a small town.

Unless a five-star resort counts as one.

Charlie barks from the passenger seat, accompanied by ABBA's "Dancing Queen" piping through the car speakers. I've been singing and bopping along to the movie soundtrack ever since we left Billings Airport.

"What do you think?" I ask him. "It's not quite Beverly Hills, is it?" No expensive boutiques, no posh spas, no restaurants boasting world-renowned chefs.

No dance clubs with exclusive guest lists.

From what I've seen so far, the closest thing the town has to a dance club is a building with a neon sign proclaiming that it's Joe's Bar.

It looks like something straight out of a movie.

My phone rings and I accept the call.

Drew's voice streams through the car's speaker. "Kate, what's this craziness about you going to Montana?"

That would be brother #1: Andrew. And no, you aren't allowed to call him Drew.

"Hi to you too, Drew," I say, and I swear Charlie chuckles.

Even though I can't see him, I can guarantee my brother is rolling his eyes. He does that a lot around me.

"Why on earth would you go to Montana?"

"The real question is, why wouldn't I come here? The air is clean and the mountains are majestic." Yes, I read that in a brochure about the area.

I haven't been out of the car yet to judge if the part about the air quality is true, but the brochure got it right about the mountains.

"You shouldn't be there on your own."

"I'm not on my own. Right, Charlie?"

Charlie barks in reply.

"That dog won't be able to keep an eye on you and help you when you get yourself into trouble."

"Yes, because I'm such a rebel, always getting into trouble," I say with a laugh. "News flash, Drew—I'm a big girl now."

"You're a woman with a permanent limp."

"What does that have to do with anything?" It's the same argument I've had to deal with from my family since the accident eleven months ago. They seem to think I'm no longer capable of doing anything on my own.

When the limp strategy doesn't work to get me on the plane back to LA, my brother tries Plan B. "You should be here, attending charity events with Lucinda." Our stepmother. "It's a golden opportunity to find the man who will one day take care of you."

"Oh, I'm sorry, I have to let you go, Drew. I have an incoming call from Chauvinists Unite. They want to interview me about your membership application."

"I'm serious, Kate."

"Me, too." Plus, I've long since realized that men aren't interested in me, because of my limp. It's a dark mark against me: I'm flawed. Broken. No longer perfect.

Oh, well. What's a girl to do?

Other than hang up on her brother—which is what I do after saying a quick "Good-bye."

A minute has barely passed before the phone rings again. I quickly glance at the screen, accept the call, and turn off Main Street. "Hi, Tiffany." My best friend.

"Please tell me it's not true?" Her tone drips with feigned horror.

"What's not true?"

"That you're in a hick town somewhere in Montana, packing up your crazy great-aunt's house."

"Yep, that pretty much sums it up—except my great-aunt wasn't crazy." Charlotte is my *deceased* great-aunt from my mother's side of the family. "She just didn't share our families' sentiments about living in Beverly Hills."

Story has it that she moved here in her twenties because she craved adventure.

That, and because she wasn't interested in marrying the man her parents had picked out for her.

Have I met her?

Once, when I was nine years old. She visited us but hadn't been back since. And Copper Creek isn't exactly on the family-approved list of vacation spots.

Not even close.

"But why do *you* have to do it?" Tiffany asks. "Couldn't you just hire someone?"

That's a definite no. My family can't afford to risk a stranger stumbling across some buried family secret that we'd rather remain buried.

And who knows what I'll find in Charlotte's house.

But I'm not admitting this to Tiffany.

A man's voice can be heard in the background on Tiffany's end. At the familiar low rumble of his voice, the equally familiar sensation of porcupine quills prickles deep in my chest and my gut.

Tiffany replies to whatever he asked her, but this time her voice is muffled.

She's your best friend. She couldn't help who she fell in love with. The words keep repeating themselves in my head, with the enthusiasm of a cheerleader hyped up on too much sugar and caffeine.

Granted, it would have been better if Mathew had at least been honest with me and ended our relationship first...and if Tiffany had waited until *after* he and I broke up before having sex with him.

You know what else would have been a fantastic idea? If I had listened to his housekeeper when she warned me he was too busy to talk to me. Instead, I raced upstairs, eager to share my good news with him, found him in bed with Tiffany, and then fled like a criminal caught at a candy-store crime scene.

And while we're adding to the list of great ideas, grief-stricken me shouldn't have hightailed it out of Beverly Hills in my cute Mustang convertible, so I could lick my wounds in private. Then I wouldn't have been in the wrong place at the wrong time when the delivery truck lost control on the highway. It wouldn't have totaled my poor baby, and my leg wouldn't be badly damaged.

Yes, in retrospect, I should have listened to my great-aunt Margie that morning when she warned me that, according to my horoscope, my luck was about to change.

She might have had a point there.

"Darling," Tiffany says, her voice like maple syrup on grilled salmon. "I have to go now. Mathew and I have one of those horribly boring charity events tonight. We promised his mother that we would attend. She's going to introduce me to some important people in the art world." Tiffany fake air-kisses me through the phone and hangs up.

The charity event she's talking about? It's the Reach for the Stars Fundraiser to help kids in low-income families achieve their full potential. I was involved with the planning, but since it was a romantic couples-only event and I had no one to go with, I opted for an early departure to Copper Creek.

"Hey, don't look at me that way," I say to Charlie. "She and I have been friends forever. She made a mistake, which is why I chose to take the high road and forgive her."

Twenty minutes later, I travel along the neglected driveway leading to my great-aunt's house. It's not so much the road that's neglected as the grass. It's at least thigh-high.

My gaze moves from the overgrown grass to the house that appears just as ill-kept—and my stomach free-falls. "It looks haunted."

Charlie barks in agreement.

"I wonder how easy it is to sell a haunted house. Do you think there's a big demand for them?"

Do you think the ghost will have a problem with me living here for the next few days?

ACKNOWLEDGMENTS

First, I want to say a big thank you to everyone who has eagerly been awaiting Sophie and Jake's story. Your enthusiasm for them to get their happily-ever-after is so sweet. You guys are the best!

As always, Hang Le did a wonderful job designing the cover. She's great to work with and seems to be able to read my mind as to what I want. I was thrilled when I saw the color of the font for Once Upon a Cowboy. It's perfect for a Cinderella-trope romance.

I also want to thank my editor Bev Rosenbaum, as well as Hope and Jessica from Flat Earth Editing for the copyediting and proofreading. All three individuals helped make this book sparkle. Working with Bev is a delight. She always has good suggestions on how to make the story stronger. I especially owe Jessica a huge amount of gratitude. While my experience with horses goes back to when I took weekly riding lessons as a kid in England, English-style riding is very different to western. The equipment is different, too. Jessica is the one who makes sure I get the horse-related terminology correct for western-style riding.

Naturally, I can't forget Brenda St. John Brown who shared her own brilliant wisdom when it came to this book. She's also a super talented writer. If you haven't already checked out her books, please do. They are so good! And hugs and kisses to my wonderful publicist Nina Bocci. I don't know what I would do without her. She's always there when I need her.

A huge thank you goes out to all my readers and fans of my books. I love each and every one of you. I couldn't imagine doing any other job. But what makes it especially wonderful is all the sweet and support comments you guys send me, whether it's on social media or via email.

Who fell in love with the adorable puppy Maui? I have Alex Taz Lozada from my Facebook group (Stina's Sweetheart) to thank for the name. While I was writing the book, I ask the members to suggest names for the black lab. Maui is the name of one of Alex's dogs. When she told me it, I knew it was perfect, especially with the Disney Princess theme I had going in the story. For those of you who don't know, Maui is the mischievous demi-god from the movie *Moana*.

And finally, I would like to thank my cheerleaders who have been there for me while writing this book. My husband Ralph, my kids, and even our cat, Callie. Although I'll admit that her support seems to involve jumping on my desk in the morning and demanding I pay attention to her and not my hero and heroine.

ABOUT THE AUTHOR

Born in Brighton England, Stina Lindenblatt has lived in a number of countries, including England, the U.S, Finland, and Canada. This would explain her mixed up accent. She has a MSc in exercise physiology, specializing in energy metabolism in sports. In addition to writing fiction, she loves photography, especially the close-up variety, and currently lives in Calgary, Canada, with her husband, three kids, and their cat.

Website: stinalindenblattauthor.com